MARRIAGE IS MURDER

An absolutely gripping cozy murder mystery full of twists

JEAN G. GOODHIND

A Honey Driver Murder Mystery Book 11

Joffe Books, London
www.joffebooks.com

First German edition published in Germany
by Aufbau Taschenbuch
as *Mord in Weiß* in 2014
First English edition published in Great Britain
by Joffe Books in 2023

Cover art by Dee Dee Book Covers

ISBN: 978-1-80405-657-8

PROLOGUE

The bride wore gold-rimmed spectacles over flashing dark eyes. Her shining black hair hung to her waist and her shocking pink outfit was teamed with blue suede shoes and a handbag big enough to hold a loaf of bread, a bag of potatoes and a pound of butter.

She wore her hat at a jaunty angle so that the wide brim covered her face. At first glance it appeared merely a fashion statement. If anyone cared to lift the brim and look, they would see a large mole, roughly the shape of a banana running down the side of her cheek.

The bridegroom was very tall and thin, his skin as glossy as a conker. He wore grey trousers with a dark blazer, the shoulders sprinkled with dandruff. His trouser legs barely reached his ankles and the colour didn't match his shoes. He looked everything a nervous bridegroom should be, shuffling from one foot to another, his face glistening with sweat and his black hair gleaming and thickly plastered to his head. Anyone in the least bit discerning would know they were far from a match made in heaven.

The registrar was a bespectacled woman wearing the sort of blouse Margaret Thatcher used to wear, even of the same blue; big bow tied at the throat.

Couples of all shapes and sizes had come before her to make their vows. It never failed to amaze her how oddly matched some were. These two for instance; she had her doubts as to whether they were a genuine couple, but it wasn't her job to ask questions. They'd followed the correct procedure and filled out the right forms. None of her business.

She intoned the words of the marriage service as required by law in a slow monotone, her gaze flickering between the confident bride and the nervous groom.

'Now repeat after me,' she said, her stern gaze unblinking, her voice carefully articulating each word as though they were children on their first day at school.

Despite her perfect articulation, the bridegroom had trouble repeating the words. She guessed it was because English was not his first language. The bride hugged his arm closer as though it might help aid his courage or at least prevent him from changing his mind and running away. He certainly looked nervous enough.

'Come on, sweetheart. You can do it,' she urged giving him a nudge with her elbow, her tight smile a mixture of warmth and warning, her voice as sticky as treacle.

He seemed to take courage from her words, looking down into her face, though it seemed more the look of fear than the look of love.

'I do.'

'I do.'

'You may kiss the bride.'

The kiss was fleeting. The bridegroom looked relieved that both the ceremony — and perhaps even the kiss — was over and done with.

Finally the register was signed by both them and the two witnesses in attendance; a fat woman wearing a bright red coat that looked too warm for the pleasant weather they were having, and a thin black man wearing a bomber jacket and torn jeans. The woman clutched a black handbag against her belly. The man looked thoroughly bored with the whole proceedings, continually looking over his shoulder towards the door as though expecting somebody else to come in.

Once outside, the bridegroom jerked his head and said something to a scrawny looking girl of about thirteen with big eyes, her head covered with a black scarf. She looked pleadingly at the two women and said something they didn't understand. The 'bridegroom' shook her. His tone was menacing, but whatever he said to her was lost on the two women through whom he had secured a British passport.

If they'd noticed or cared, they would have seen the fear on the girl's face as both the foreign bridegroom and his 'bride' followed the fat woman to a pub on the corner, the girl trailing behind. The man told her to stay outside whilst they went in.

'I'll have a brandy and Babycham,' said the woman without preamble. The bride made her way to the bar where she purchased the drink for the woman and a white wine for herself.

Meanwhile the bridegroom took out his wallet and counted out five hundred pounds, the final payment for his wedding and the right to a British passport.

The male witness had already left once he'd been paid his fee for merely attending and signing the register as required. He'd done it dozens of times.

Once the money was handed over, counted and found to be correct, the bridegroom left without a backwards glance at his 'bride' or a thank you to the woman who had arranged everything.

'So,' said the bride, once the drinks were set down in front of her and the woman in the red coat along with two packets of salted peanuts. 'Who's next?'

The woman in the red coat downed the drink in one, licking the excess liquid from her generous lips with a long, pink tongue. She left the peanuts untouched.

'There is no next. I'm retiring from the business, though I've no objection if you want to take over the running of it.'

'What are you saying? I *am* the business.' The younger woman splayed her hand across her chest as though to keep

3

her heart in place. Her eyes were radiant, and the mole on the side of her face seemed to pulsate.

The woman in the red coat pulled in her chin and looked down her nose at the woman. 'Says who? You?'

'I'm the bride,' came the indignant reply.

'Yeah, but you ain't the brains.'

The bride was not amused. 'Just you watch me. I've got the looks and I've got plans of my own. I reckon I can do better than what I've been doing, getting wed without the bed and without the brass. There's other ways.'

The fat woman raised her painted eyebrows. 'You thinking of getting married for real?'

'I'm thinking of carving out my own business in the marriage game.'

She shrugged. 'I'm not going to ask how. That's your business, but if you want my scene I'm not about to stop you. It's time I spoilt my grandchildren — that should annoy my daughter's partner — not that I care. He's a shit. So, are you dead set on this?'

'Dead set.'

'Then I wish you luck. Now I have to be off. I've got a train to catch.'

The woman in the red coat bought her accomplice another drink before leaving and said she was welcome to both packets of peanuts.

'How about my bonus, you know, my share of the profits? You said you'd give me twenty-five per cent of the take at the end of the year plus my share of the nest egg. We still have the nest egg, don't we?'

'Don't you trust me?'

'I hope I can. I told you I wasn't good where money was concerned. I'm looking forward to spending it — and not on a bloody wedding dress! I've had enough of them.'

'The money is safe and you'll get what's coming to you,' said the woman in red, pushing herself up against the table so she could better get to her feet. 'I'll just pop into the ladies before we go to the bank. It's all safely salted away. All we have to do is make a withdrawal. It couldn't be simpler.'

The bride sighed with pleasure, opened both packets of peanuts, and began shoving them into her mouth between sips of white wine.

Fifteen minutes later, there was still no sign of her 'business' partner. A feeling of unease began to churn around in her stomach.

Her eyes flickered towards the far end of the bar area and the sign saying toilets.

There was also a green exit sign next to the one for toilets.

Suddenly realising she'd been shafted, the woman who had played at being a bride about twenty times leapt to her feet and scurried to where the woman in red had vanished.

The ladies' cloakroom, a place of scented air and piped music from the bar, was empty. All the cubicle doors were open. Nowhere to hide.

The woman with the mole banged her head against a door post, an action of sheer despair. She only knew the woman as Mrs Fitz. They'd always been careful to cover their tracks, and Mrs Fitz, she now realised, had been particularly good at it. She had a mobile number for her, but even before she rang it, she knew it would be switched off.

She had been paid for today, but she knew now that she would never see the thousands she was owed. The agreement had been that when they gave up the game, the money in the bank would be divided. The bonus was gone.

'I'll bloody kill her,' she vowed. 'I'll bloody kill her!'

CHAPTER ONE

Humming a tune that only a trained ear might recognise as the Wedding March, Detective Inspector Steve Doherty sat down at his desk and shrugged off his coat so that it fell inside out over the back of his chair without him having to handle it. So he was getting married again. His bride- to-be was Honey Driver, real name Hannah, though nobody called her that except for her mother and her bank manager and both were mutually exasperating.

As was his habit, he perused his emails before turning his attention to paperwork. Not too much of it. Not like there used to be. His chest heaved with thanks for email which had certainly put a dent in the paper that actually landed on his desk nowadays. What was even better about email was that he could lie about it not arriving and nobody could argue with it.

In amongst the standard stuff were three envelopes. One was confirmation of an email supposedly sent and delivered via the internal post; someone was taking no chances with excuses about lost emails. His eyes swivelled upwards through the glass partitioning to the general office which was in full work mode, heads bobbing around at desks, uniformed fig- ures moving between desks, making for the coffee machine and back again.

He spotted the culprit behind the communication. Mackenzie was at one with her computer, head bowed over it, the flickering screen playing over her sallow complexion. A clever constable, she was determined to show that she was a few notches above her male colleagues and not afraid to stir the mud if it meant she got to the top.

'Heaven help us,' he muttered. She'd have the whole police force electronically tagged if she had her way.

The second envelope he opened was from some woman complaining about porn pictures being sent through the post to her. She had already complained by email.

'I WANT ACTION!'

He noted the capitals. He knew what that meant in the world of electronic mail: she was shouting at him.

The other was marked private and confidential. It was a proper note, placed inside an envelope posted via Royal Mail and delivered in the old-fashioned way.

He noticed the paper had a rough edge at the top. No big deal. Just a standard sheet torn from a writing pad, the kind purchased in any stationers. The handwriting was elegant, all scrolls and flamboyant tails. The message was not.

Marry that middle-aged trollop and you die!

It was unsigned of course.

'Who the bloody hell . . . ?'

He rubbed a finger over one frowning eyebrow. Getting threatening letters was all part of the job; nobody loved a copper except perhaps a long-suffering wife or a dog. Dogs gave their undying loyalty. Wives, well, he'd seen plenty of marriages fall by the wayside, including his own. But he'd been young then. The plan to marry Honey Driver was founded on a firm foundation; he was older now. They both were.

So somebody didn't want him to marry Honey? It wasn't widely known that they were kind of engaged. They'd had a long chat and decided to look into the idea together quite seriously. Seriously meant discussing where the ceremony would take place and the probability of going on honeymoon.

So why would somebody object to their marriage? His ex-wife wouldn't; their parting had been acrimonious but improved drastically once they were properly divorced and miles away from each other. He didn't see much of his daughter either. She was doing her own thing, needed her own space. Sometimes she sent him a text, usually for his birthday, Father's Day or Christmas.

Seeing as Honey's ex-husband was dead there were no objections from that direction and her daughter was all in favour of them getting spliced. Her mother was a different matter. Gloria Cross didn't think much of him. Being a policeman was bad enough, though she might have wavered if he'd been Chief Constable. Not maintaining a secret bank account in Switzerland was another black mark against his suitability, that and the fact that he didn't like shaving. Designer stubble just didn't do it for her. Honey, on the other hand, loved it.

Hearing the rasp of whiskers as he passed his hand over his chin made him smile. And to think he'd been against meeting her when the Chief Constable had suggested he should be Honey's police contact when she'd first taken on the job of Crime Liaison Officer on behalf of Bath Hotels Association. He was slick, hard and as good looking without his clothes on as he was in them. He dressed casually even when on the day job: jeans (expensive), black T-shirt; shoes with soft soles, the sort suitable for swift movement when running down a felon; and didn't go anywhere without his favourite leather jacket, years' old but it suited both his physique and his streetwise manner.

His eyes were cobalt blue and tended to turn a darker shade when involved in serious business. They also darkened when Honey was in his thoughts; secret thoughts that when voiced out loud were for her ears only. And she liked running her fingers through his hair especially around the nape of his neck.

Initially he'd been opposed to the idea of liaising with any member of the Hotels Association, picturing some mincing hotel manager with a politically correct agenda. He needn't have worried.

Instead of that he'd got Honey Driver; middle-aged, traditional figure, i.e. well covered hour-glass, and a sense of humour.

Before they'd met, he'd shaken his head and scratched his stubble. He'd told the Chief Constable exactly how he felt.

'I don't dig middle-aged amateurs,' he'd stated. That was some time before he'd asked her to marry him. Once he'd got to know her, his attitude changed.

She was sexy in a comfortable way, had an agile mind and was average on the fitness front. She looked good in clothes and, like him, good out of them.

She wasn't one to wear tiny 'g' strings or live on lettuce sandwiches and he knew she sometimes wore undergarments that sculptured the figure, though only when wearing something tight. And she looked good in something tight.

He'd got to know her, then like her, and then sleep with her. Now they were considering marriage.

He'd never considered there would be a problem — until now.

Annoyed rather than intrigued, he refolded the piece of paper and thought about it. As he thought he flicked it against his fingers.

'Sticky fingers, Gov?'

The speaker was nicknamed the Wizard. His real name was Harold Potter and up until J K Rowling had done her stuff, everyone had called him Harry or Potter. Since the Boy Wizard had hit the bookstands and the cinema, he'd become the Wizard.

The Wizard was suggesting the paper was stuck to his fingers, though in reality he was prying, tentatively suggesting that Doherty might wish to share the contents of the letter — purely as a friendly gesture.

Doherty did not wish to share it. This was personal.

'Is there a cup of tea going?' he asked brightly.

Of course there was. The Wizard always had a kettle on the go alongside a tin of chocolate digestive biscuits.

'Still not taking sugar?' asked the Wizard.

'I've got my figure to think of.'

The Wizard accepted the terse response with a smile.

'Can't think what you're saving yourself for,' he added as he slid sideways out of the door with no more than six inches to spare.

Alone again, Doherty studied the envelope the letter had arrived in. He could just about make out the postmark. Edinburgh. He pursed his lips. Edinburgh was not a city he had ever visited and he couldn't recall knowing anyone from there. Still, old friends moved on to pastures new and somebody might have moved up there. Old friends not contacted become strangers over the years.

The plain brown envelope was totally nondescript and cheap, addressed directly to him and concerned him alone — and Honey of course. He would not enter its arrival in the incident book. He'd tell no one.

The envelope followed the letter into his pocket before the Wizard came back with the tea.

Doherty thanked him for the tea and the two chocolate digestives sitting on a yellow spotted saucer. It used to be four chocolate digestives, but the Wizard was putting his own needs before anyone else's. His appetite had increased with his girth, or perhaps his girth had increased with his appetite.

Doherty eyed the note while waiting for his tea to cool. Its presence taunted him.

Someone had gone out of their way to send it. He could do a DNA swab on the envelope, but something told him it would be inconclusive. Unless they'd been living on an uncharted desert island for years, everyone knew that DNA could be traced. And anyway, it was probably just a crank with a grudge . . .

But what if it wasn't? The sender could be watching, waiting for a chance to get close and carry out his or her threat.

He hadn't been aware of somebody following him and Honey hadn't mentioned stalkers popping in and out of shop doorways behind her.

So, now what? He sat there with his fingers intertwined thinking it through. The thing was he couldn't bring himself to show her the note. For a start she wouldn't take kindly to being referred to as a middle-aged trollop. Then there was the scare factor; he didn't want her to feel scared. He wanted her to be fun, like she usually was. And sexy of course. Always sexy.

Put it aside for another day, he decided, unless something happens to make you do otherwise.

CHAPTER TWO

'Trevor Templeton's the name. I'm here for my granddaughter's wedding.'

The man's curly hair was cut close to the skull and greying in places. The soft grey of his morning suit was teamed with a yellow waistcoat and a burgundy cravat. A tiny pin in the shape of a 'T' winked diamonds from amongst the silky folds of the cravat. A grey top hat was tucked beneath his arm.

Honey tried to think of where she'd seen him before.

Or had she *heard* him somewhere before? His voice was as memorable as his appearance. He spoke in a hushed baritone. As though his mouth is close to my ear, she thought.

Steady, girl. You're spoken for, remember?

Her thoughts translated into words without giving her chance to think about what she was saying.

'You're very . . .'

'Tall? Dark? Handsome?'

His smile was incredibly titillating and although Honey had a marriage proposal under her belt, she firmly believed in the old adage that even if you were on a diet, you could still study the menu. And Trevor Templeton was a dish to be savoured.

Honey put on her professional persona as easily as she did her clothes. This morning she was wearing a dark blue dress, dark tights and a pair of Italian court shoes. They were black suede, had three-inch heels, a small platform and a silk bow over the toe.

It wasn't her habit to wear such glamorous shoes during the working day. Three-inch heels were best confined to those seductive little moments before discarding them and everything else. But for these shoes she had made an exception and was glad that she had. So far, they were as comfortable as slippers.

Hidden behind the reception desk, she stretched one calf then the other. Her legs were fit to go on display.

She smiled sweetly at Trevor Templeton.

'I'm sorry. It's just that I can't help thinking that I've seen you somewhere before. Are you famous?'

He shrugged. 'I try not to be.'

She knew he was teasing her and almost blushed, but checked herself, pretending to be engrossed as she checked the reservation on the computer screen.

'A single room. Is that right?'

He nodded. 'There's no Mrs Templeton — well — not any longer.' His smile was sad. 'She's passed on.'

'Oh. I'm sorry to hear that,' said Honey.

'Don't be. She's passed on to a younger man with a speedboat and a large engine. The boat has the large engine. I'm not sure about the man!'

Honey chuckled, coloured up a bit, and booked him in.

The Templeton/Fox wedding was a 200-guest affair. The young couple had declared they only wanted a small reception. Two hundred in Honey's estimation wasn't that small and luckily the number was just about on the limit for the Green River Hotel.

The bride, Soraya Templeton, was a B list celebrity. She'd appeared on a reality TV show and was a model, seen mostly modelling lingerie, and now she was aiming for the dizzy heights of international stardom. The same assets that did it for the brassiere market would probably take her all the way.

Her hair was long and glossy, and her legs looked as though they went all the way up to her shoulders, so long that when she sat down her body seemed to unfold bit by delectably gorgeous bit.

She'd had work done; Honey was sure of it. Lindsey, her daughter, had confirmed it.

'Bullet boobs. Nipples like doorknobs.'

Honey raised her eyelids high enough to scrutinise the bride's twin assets. It would need a suspension bridge to hold a pair of big boobs that high. As if that wasn't enough, the bride's dress emphasised the enhanced appendages. She'd gone for empire line, notably popular in the Regency period. Jane Austen would have loved it. The neckline plunged and the skirt started just below the breasts, slinky over the hips and ankle length.

The bridesmaids' dresses echoed the same style although in a pale shade of green.

The bride wore a veil and carried a bouquet of white flowers interspersed with trailing strands of variegated ivy. The bridesmaids wore bonnets and carried bouquets of purple and yellow. No ivy.

Vintage cars had been laid on for the bride, her father and the bridesmaids; modern cars for the main guests. The cost of the whole lot would have kept a starving nation in rice for at least a week.

The bridegroom, who wore silk britches and a tailcoat, plus a dark pink cravat, was Adrian Fox, a TV comedian of dubious reputation and, in Honey's opinion, very little talent.

'Sarcasm is the lowest form of wit,' she'd said to Lindsey her daughter who, for some obscure reason, thought he was funny.

The guests' arrival back from the Abbey was preceded by Honey's mother. Gloria Cross came breezing in looking a picture in turquoise chiffon, two triangular portions of it streaming out behind her. She'd gone to the Abbey to watch and had got caught up with the guests. Judging by her outfit alone, she certainly looked compatible with the plethora of designer labels and dental implants.

Honey whispered to Lindsey. 'Your grandmother looks like an angelfish — or is it just me?'

'Grandma looks like an angelfish,' Lindsey whispered back.

'I've decided it takes two to tango,' she declared, raising her voice in order to be heard above the clamour of wedding guests' laughter, taut conversations and ribald remarks.

Honey didn't have time to listen to her mother's gossip or catch up on her latest money-making scheme so she failed to catch all that was being said. If she had, she might have been prepared for what happened later.

Honey shouted an apology unsure whether it was heard or not.

'Sorry, Mother. I can't stop. The reception's under way and I need to make sure the kitchen is coping.'

As it turned out, she needn't have worried. If there was one thing Gloria Cross adored, it was a wedding at Bath Abbey, preferably of people with money who knew how to put on a good show.

Guest after guest greeted her like a long-lost relative without needing to know her name. The greeting was generic and accepted worldwide.

'Darling! How are you?'

Her mother was in her element, though she did briefly bend Mary Jane's ear to confide that her daughter was going to be sorry that she hadn't spared the time to listen to what she had to say. 'You wait. I'm not too old to spring shocking surprises!'

'Are you Great Aunt Periwinkle?' asked a passing guest. 'Yes, of course, you must be. Cynthia told me to look out for you. Come this way dear.'

Honey's mother smiled sweetly and didn't bother to explain that she was nothing to do with the gathering. Though being labelled a great aunt grated a bit.

Anyway, the man in the navy-blue suit with the shiny head wasn't listening. It was a case of mistaken identity, and Gloria Cross did not resist as she was propelled into the heart of things.

Honey checked and counted all the extras the lucky couple had ordered.

Crystal wine glasses, white table linen, white napkins — none of the two-ply paper stuff that disintegrates halfway through the meal. There were also silver streamers and table decorations, and vast floral displays hanging from silver chains and posies in the middle of the table.

Click, click, click went the keys on Honey's calculator. It was bulky and old, the numbers big and bold, just like the final tally for the Templeton/Fox wedding.

'There,' she said, almost licking her lips as she surveyed the deliciously exorbitant total.

It was important to make sure everything went smoothly, and to that end, Honey flitted in and out of the dining room and kitchen.

It wasn't until the speeches were being made, coffee served and miniscule pieces of wedding cake handed out, that she had time to relax. The guests were replete with food and drink and dulled into semi-consciousness by dreary speeches and jokes that fell dead in the water. The break between the afternoon reception and the evening disco was the chance for staff and management to take a break.

'Popping over the back,' she said to the head waiter.

Her feet were now killing her. Nothing to do with the shoes, she told herself. They were Italian. Everyone knows that if you want a good hairdo or pair of shoes, go Italian.

Secluded in her private living quarters, she kicked off her shoes, took off her tights, made a cup of tea and plunged her feet into a vibrating footbath. She had until eight o'clock and she was sure as hell going to enjoy herself. Soaking her feet was first priority.

Lindsey also took advantage of the break, pouring a cup of tea and swigging it down before flopping onto her bed plugged into her iPad.

Whilst Honey shut her eyes and chilled out with three marzipan petit fours she'd lifted from a tray in the kitchen, Lindsey grooved to something medieval being played on a lute. Both were at peace with the world. Hassle, in the form of the wedding disco and drinking session, restarted at eight that evening.

* * *

Feeling ready for action — wedding discos rarely finished before midnight — Honey and Lindsey came back to the sound of music; the wedding party proper had begun. A buffet replaced the set tables, displayed around a silver punch bowl. The guests were happy. The bride and groom were happy. Best of all, the bride's father, the chap who was footing the bill, was happiest of all. Not one single person looked grumpy or annoyed to be there — with the exception of the kids who hadn't been relegated to an early night with grandparents. Seemed OK.

The first inkling that something was wrong was the music.

A combo named the Corsham Cupcakes had been hired, quite a formal, professional outfit that had been used by other wedding parties before.

They were usually excellent. However, the tune they were presently playing was missing more chords than it hit. The tune was barely recognisable.

On top of that, the song, 'We're Having a Gang Bang' had never, until now, formed part of their repertoire. It just wasn't normal wedding party music . . . but then she did recall there were a number of rugby players amongst the guests. They often had their own agenda.

Honey stopped picking at the piece of wedding cake secreted out of sight behind the reception desk and voiced her thoughts to Lindsey.

'Does that sound a bit out of tune to you?'

Lindsey looked up from the computer screen, hands poised above the keyboard. Her surprised expression mirrored that of her mother.

'Never mind out of tune, it sounds out of character for the Cupcakes. Just a question, but what did you put in that punch?'

Honey shrugged. 'Just the usual suspects. Whatever ancient liqueurs that never sold mixed with fruit juice and a bottle of cheap sherry.'

'Heady stuff by the sound of it. I wonder what's happening.'

Honey frowned. She'd never had a wedding that had got out of hand, and she didn't want one now.

'I'll take a look.'

Lindsey turned back to the computer, changing screens once her mother was out of the way to something that might be a kind of career change, a step into the past perhaps? The page was headed, '*So you want to become a nun?*'

On opening the door to the dining room, that today was doing service as a function room, Honey's jaw dropped. Patrick Swayze in *Dirty Dancing* had nothing on this lot.

Correction, a full Greek Bacchanalian orgy had nothing on this lot. The dance floor was a mass of barely-dressed couples; legs and writhing bodies were just visible from beneath some of the tables.

The bride was down to garter belt, stockings, underwear, and four-inch heels; and the groom was without his trousers. The lucky couple were dancing what looked like the tango though it was the most erotic tango she'd ever seen.

The Corsham Cupcakes seemed to have resorted to their earlier years at the close of the punk era, shouting the words of the song with gusto though falling off more notes than they were hitting. On reflection that was fine because it suited the music. But the music didn't suit the event.

Trevor Templeton, the bride's grandfather, who Honey had considered quite a dish, was heading in her direction chasing a giggling woman. Honey gulped. She'd know that goldfish style dress anywhere.

Honey grabbed her as she attempted to sprint and giggle past.

'Mother! What are you doing?'

There was a glazed look in her mother's eyes. Her cheeks were flushed and her smile a silly slit.

'I was dancing, but this fellow wanted me to go outside with him.' Her mother leaned closer. 'I said he had to catch me first. I was giving him a run for his money. Is he married, do you know?'

Honey closed her eyes and opened them again. No. The nightmare was still going strong.

Trevor Templeton's expression was as way out as her mother's. The guests, the combo, even the waiting staff, looked to be off their heads.

'You're coming with me,' Honey growled.

Her mother was in no state to protest and, anyway, Trevor Templeton was now propositioning a tall blonde.

After propping her mother with Lindsey, Honey headed for the kitchen. Never before had throwing obsolete liqueurs into a punch bowl and adding fruit juice produced results like this. Somebody had added something . . . but who?

She stormed in, took root in the middle of the kitchen, pushed the door open hard so it smashed against the wall, folded her arms and prepared herself for a fight.

'Right! Who did it?'

The kitchen staff exchanged puzzled looks. Smudger Smith, her head chef frowned and asked her what the bloody hell did she mean, barging into his kitchen and demanding who had done it.

'You know what! Out there!' She pointed in the general direction of the mayhem erupting from the wedding party. 'Whoever added whatever they did to that punch is for the high jump. Now. Who did it?'

Smudger Smith frowned. 'Did what?'

'There's an orgy going on out there,' she hissed. 'People are taking their clothes off.'

There was a flurry of action. A huddle of chefs clustered around the door, faces pressed against the glass top half, their combined weight opening the bottom half, ever so slightly.

In came the sound of mayhem, giggles, singing and that terrible din from the Cupcakes.

'Stop right there.'

It was useless. The whole entourage crept stealthily along to the end door that opened directly into the dining room.

'Wow! Look at the tits on that!'

Honey ordered them back to their workstations.

'Haven't any of you ever seen a pair of tits before?' she demanded, riled at the way discipline could so easily fall apart at the mere mention of something sexual.

There were grins and mutterings about joining in before Smudger suggested they draw straws — cheese straws — to see who was going in to retrieve the bowl of punch.

Kurt, the kitchen porter, drew the short straw which in this case meant he'd won.

'Without sneaking a taste,' Smudger said to him.

Kurt promised he would not indulge.

Honey stayed where she was, fists on hips, one toe tapping impatiently. When that foot got tired, she changed sides and tapped the other.

Howls of protest preceded Kurt's reappearance and the setting down of the punch bowl down on a stainless-steel surface in the kitchen.

The kitchen porter was breathless. 'They were none too pleased about me taking it. I thought they were going to lynch me.'

'More likely debag you,' suggested Smudger.

Honey, Smudger, and rest of the kitchen staff huddled around the table gazing down into what was left at the bottom of the bowl.

'It looks OK,' said Honey. She dipped in her finger and sucked. 'Tastes OK.'

Smudger pursed his lips. 'To you it might. To me it might. I'm thinking something's been added here. We need somebody who'd recognise the taste in a moment.'

'I'm your man.' The offer came from the washing up area.

Rodney Eastwood's nickname was Clint; that was where his resemblance to the Hollywood star ended. He was broad shouldered, thick necked and his head was tattooed with spiders and webs. Clint was their regular casual washer-upper, cash only. He also knew an illegal substance when he tasted one. Rumour had it he'd tasted quite a few in his time. He hadn't gone for a look at the guests because he was avoiding Anna, one of the hotel's receptionists. Honey wasn't sure whether their relationship was off or on.

'Be my guest,' she said to him.

'Allow me.' He dipped his finger into the brew and sucked, staring into space as he rolled the taste around his tongue.

Everyone looked at him for his verdict.

'Not sure. One more.' Again he dipped in his finger and sucked. 'Yep,' he said nodding. 'Yep. This is good stuff. Top of the range.'

Honey tried not to be aggrieved that she might have tipped in something really good by mistake.

'Don't tell me that dusty bottle of sherry was a Château Lafite worth zillions!' she said, gripped with the fear that she might have poured away something akin to a lottery win.

Clint shook his head. 'No. A bit extra's been added, but it ain't booze.'

Honey noticed that Clint and Smudger, big buddies on the sly, were exchanging wide grins.

'What? What aren't you telling me?' she asked, puzzled at their smug faces.

'Top rate stuff. Cannabis. Lethal mixed with booze.'

Honey searched the grinning faces around her for a hint of guilt.

'If one of you added . . .'

Everyone denied it.

Smudger asked her the pertinent question. 'Who made it? Who took it in?'

Honey was speechless. She made it. She was the one who had taken it into the dining room.

'It wasn't me! And if it wasn't me and it wasn't one of you lot, it has to be . . .' She paused. 'Somebody else.'

CHAPTER THREE

Separating the wedding guests from their drink hadn't been easy, but the party had gone with a swing. The last guest had been carried up to bed at around three in the morning.

The following day saw them pretty subdued as they checked out. Most of them had breakfasted on toast and black coffee. Nobody was in the right frame of mind for a full English.

The bride and groom had left for their honeymoon both wearing Ray- Bans to hide their bleary-eyed looks.

'Thank goodness that's over,' said Honey, comfortably installed in her office, her hands cradling a cup of strong, black coffee.

Lindsey agreed with her. Today was Sunday, their day of rest, as far as it was possible to have a day of rest when you owned a hotel in Bath, a world heritage site which was pretty busy at all times of year.

Alexi, a blonde Lithuanian with cool features and a firm butt, was holding down the fort in reception. The under-chef was handling Sunday lunch. Smudger, the head chef, had gone to a cricket match.

Honey's mother, Lindsey's grandmother, had been poured into a taxi the day before. So far the telephone was silent. Mother was obviously still sleeping it off.

Honey sighed, wriggled her toes and commented on how happy they looked. Sunday was a day of rest and her toes, and indeed her feet, were certainly in need of a rest.

Lindsey made no comment. She was sitting with her head back and her eyes closed. Honey instinctively knew she wasn't resting. Her daughter was thinking hard about something, running it through in her mind with the speed and accuracy of the computers she was so good with.

A whizz with modern technology, she also had a penchant for history, especially of the medieval kind.

Honey assumed it was because of a man. 'So who is he?'

'What?'

'A new man in your life?'

'Not exactly. No one in fact.'

Honey wasn't fooled. There was something in her tone that suggested she was hiding something. Honey reflected on her daughter's behaviour over the past week, searching for clues.

She'd worked Monday through to Saturday covering the breakfast shift through to late evening because Alexi had been on holiday. Anna, now part time on account of family responsibilities, was unable to come in because one of the kids had chicken pox.

'You do not wish for spots?' she'd asked in her roundabout way.

'I never wish for spots,' Honey had replied. The prospect of guests and diners breaking out in spots was not welcome.

Only on Friday had Lindsey been totally absent. When asked, she'd declared she'd gone to confession to ask for forgiveness.

Honey had laughed out loud. They were Anglicans of the modern variety, only attending church for christenings, wedding and funerals. As far as she knew there had been none in the offing last Saturday.

'Was it Clint?' Lindsey asked suddenly.

Honey knew what she was referring to, though sensed her daughter's remark was an effort to change the subject — which made her all the more suspicious.

'No. It was Clint who identified what had been put in the punch, but swears it wasn't down to him.'

'So who was it?'

Honey shrugged. 'I've no idea, though I'm presuming it was one of the guests.'

'Difficult,' said Lindsey and closed her eyes again.

Honey considered her daughter's profile, thinking how much she looked like her father.

Carl had perished on a transatlantic sailing trip along with his all-girl crew. No bodies had ever been found. Sometimes she wondered whether he'd just done a sleight of hand thing, disappearing along with all evidence, renaming the boat and setting off for some Pacific island with his nubile crew; his idea of heaven.

As regards the doctored punch, Lindsey was quite right. Nothing could be gained from interrogating the wedding guests except a bad reputation. They might even lose their four-crown rating if it got to the ears of the English Tourist Board. Reputation mattered.

The Green River Hotel wasn't exactly the Ritz or even the Royal Crescent and their chef was named Smudger Smith, not Escoffier.

'It might have been an outside job,' suggested Lindsey.

'Possibly. The most likely answer is that one of the wedding guests thought they would have a spot of fun.'

After finishing her coffee, she went across to the coach house away from the hotel for a couple of hours at least.

Off came the shoes and the tights, out came the footbath. She turned the knob to vibrate. A froth of water was accompanied by a low-level buzz.

If she was to marry Doherty, she had to look her best and that included her feet.

They'd tossed around a few ideas about where and when to get married. Church had to be considered. Honey was a widow. There were no barriers as such. Doherty was divorced, but the church wasn't so straightlaced as it had been in the past.

To this end, tomorrow they were visiting the church they favoured most; St Michael and All Angels in the village of Lower Wainscote, just outside of Bath.

Everyone knew the church and the village commenting how pretty it was. Only Caspar, chairman of the Hotels Association, voiced an objection.

'What does a village church have that Bath does not?' He'd sounded quite insulted.

'Peace and quiet. No traffic. No members of the public walking across between the wedding party and the photographer . . .'

'And no mayhem or murder, I suppose,' Caspar stated loftily.

Honey hoped he was right.

CHAPTER FOUR

The Reverend Constance Paxton, vicar of St Michael and All Angels parish church in the village of Lower Wainscote, declined another piece of fruit cake made by Mrs Flynn, head of the flower arranging committee. She also declined another schooner of sweet sherry.

Mrs Flynn lived in a four-storey cottage on a side road just behind the Angel Inn, the oldest and best eating establishment in a village that dated back to Anglo Saxon times. Suffering from arthritis, she only used the lower floors of the cottage, the upper levels remaining unused for years.

The village had an upper and lower level, the upper consisting mostly of detached houses from the inter-war years, square solid lumps now dissected from Lower Wainscote by the main road connecting Bath to the M4. Connection between Upper and Lower Wainscote was by way of a tunnel beneath the main A46.

Lower Wainscote had glorious views across open farmland. The houses were all quaintly historic ranging in size from terraced two-bedroom cottages to magnificent, detached edifices with mullioned windows and stone or slate roofs.

There were no shops in the village and the school was some way distant, a modern conurbation that although very functional was nowhere near as pretty as the old school which on closure had been purchased and turned into a private dwelling by a family from Birmingham.

The church was picturesque as well as historical and stood apart at one end of the village. Rumour had it that a lady-in-waiting to Anne of Cleeves was buried there.

Trees, songbirds and the smell of flowers and warm grass prevailed in the churchyard where a drystone wall separated it from the High Street. It also had an air of continuity, a number of names on some of the ancient tombstones still appearing in the local telephone directory.

The churchyard's ancient lychgate of old oak and stone tiles had formed a backdrop on wedding photos for many happy couples. The fact was, St Michael's was picturesque, in an up-market village not far from Bath, and thus very popular for weddings.

Mrs Flynn had three cats, all black with orange eyes, and a direct way of looking at people. Centuries ago ignorant folk might have thought even one black cat a sign that she brewed up more than porridge in her tiny cottage but those days had gone.

She also had a budgie named Philip that was so quiet, Constance wondered if he was stuffed. Out back, a few chickens seemed to have the run of the garden and occasionally strayed into the house.

The house smelled of musty feathers; Constance put it down to the chickens, though the budgie couldn't be entirely without blame.

Mrs Flynn was recounting weddings past and present in a long, drawn-out way. It was clear she did not approve of outside contractors coming in to provide floral decorations for the many weddings that took place so regularly.

'Of course you didn't get these outsiders coming in and taking over when the old vicar was here. He wouldn't have any of that nonsense,' she pronounced, her false teeth clicking at least three times throughout the sentence. 'It was the responsibility of the church to provide floral decorations back then. The bride's and bridesmaid's bouquets and the buttonholes were provided by outside contractors of course, but decorating the church was always in-house, if you know what I mean.'

The Reverend Paxton nodded sympathetically whilst wishing she were somewhere else. Mrs Flynn was the most obnoxious woman she had ever met.

'Well, we have to give people what they want, Mrs Flynn. It's the march of progress. We live in the modern world and have to accept that things change over time.'

'That may be,' Mrs Flynn said slowly. She eyed the female vicar somewhat accusingly, as though she too were a part of that change — which to some extent, of course, she was. Female vicars had not even been envisaged in Mrs Flynn's youth.

'Still. I think we could have done just as good a job if they'd let us.'

'No doubt.' Constance swigged back the last of her tea and dusted the crumbs from her chest as she got to her feet. 'Now I really have to be going. I've a sermon to write.'

'Of course, Vicar. And whilst you're there, you might take a look at the coffer? I'm sure somebody has spilt water on it. Now that won't do, will it. Not blemishing something as old as that.'

The coffer had been dug up around two hundred years ago, but an expert had put its age at over a thousand.

'Saxon rather than Norman, so here before the church was built, which means there was a Saxon church before this one,' he had pronounced whilst peering at her through spectacles that looked too big for his face.

Constance promised Mrs Flynn that she would take a look.

'No need to see me out,' she added pleasantly whilst trying not to appear too hasty to leave. 'I'll shut the door firmly behind me.'

Mrs Flynn nodded gratefully. She was on the waiting list for a knee replacement and her pain was obvious. She preferred to sit.

As she closed the door behind her, the Reverend Constance Paxton breathed a sigh of relief. Mrs Flynn was the dragon of the flower arranging committee, the woman who breathed fire if anyone dared to question either her opinion or her flower arrangements. At eighty-four years of age, it was her one remaining reason for living and she clung to it tenaciously.

Even now Constance could feel her ears burning as though they'd been soundly boxed. She promised herself she'd check them for redness in the bathroom mirror when she got back to the vicarage.

The sun was setting behind St Michael's Norman tower, and the air was fresh. Constance took a few more breaths to clear Mrs Flynn from her head and begged the Lord's forgiveness for lying about having a sermon to write. The truth was that she had two people coming to see her about the possibility of a church wedding, but daren't let Mrs Flynn know that. Despite her bad knees, the old girl would no doubt do a high-speed shuffle to the church, determined to berate them about having the flower committee decorate the church, and not some outsider who didn't know the old place like she did.

She shivered at the thought. Being faced with Mrs Flynn's demands was enough to put the couple off marrying in church, or at least in St Michael and All Angels.

As for writing sermons, well if there was one thing she was good at, it was that. It was one of the reasons she'd been allocated this parish, though hardly the only reason. On the death of her husband, also a vicar, the powers that be who were responsible for allocating the plum parishes, had taken pity on her. 'Praise the Lord,' she often muttered whilst surveying the handsome old houses and feeling — actually feeling — the sense of everlasting that comes with a church in the region of eight hundred years old.

Donald's death wasn't the only reason for securing this position of course, but she didn't dwell on the other things that had swung it for her — family connections and all that. She was grateful she was here and that was all there was to it.

Before heading for the vicarage, she took the lane leading to the church. The lane ran between the walls of the village hall on one side and an ancient tithe barn on the other.

Neither the narrow approach nor the bumpy turning space for the wedding cars outside the church was ideal. When it rained the muddy surface smeared wedding dresses and stuck to shoes, leading to muddy footprints all the way up the aisle, and wedding cars only just squeezed through the gap finally spilling out into an expanse of space in front of the lychgate.

She'd been badgering for the car park to be properly surfaced, but there were issues with one of the neighbours.

Harold Clinker lived in a red-brick detached house behind red-brick walls and his red-brick gate posts were topped with round stone balls.

The house had been built in the reign of Queen Anne on land that in medieval times had belonged to the church but sold during Henry VIII's rein to a Bertrand Hicks, for services rendered. No one knew for certain what those favours had been, though opinion veered between the two main suspects, sex and money, the end product being murder. Powerful people did like loose ends neatly tied up.

Nothing regarding ownership had been recorded amongst church documentation except for the sudden conveyance of the land to the owner of Belvedere House — one Thomas Fortune — a fortuitous name, for the sum of ten guineas, cheap even back then. It was Thomas who'd knocked down the medieval dwelling and built a more fashionable one of brick.

The church and the house had stood side by side in uneasy harmony for a few hundred years — until now.

Harold Clinker had seemed an ideal neighbour for the first six months until he proclaimed that the land outside the church belonged to Belvedere House; his house.

He'd cornered her one morning after the mothers and baby group in the village hall.

'It's written down. Here, in the deeds,' he'd shouted, waving an official looking title deed in one hand whilst slapping it with the other. 'I've taken a day away from the office to make this plain to you. No more wedding cars are to come down that lane. It's too tight and I'll hold you responsible if my front wall gets damaged.'

Constance had asked him if he didn't think that a little unfair. 'What about the brides? Their dresses will be ruined.'

For all his wealth and fine clothes, Mr Clinker had an uncouth manner and a North London accent — a man trying to be a gentleman but not quite making it.

He'd found her comment amusing. 'They can walk. It ain't far. Or wear shorter dresses, show their legs a bit more.' His lascivious leer had made her feel sick.

The matter had been passed to lawyers, a costly firm in Bath acting for him and the London-based firm who customarily acted for the Church Commissioners in all things secular. Although hailing from London, Clinker was distantly related to the family that had owned the house for generations.

Despite all she stood for, the Reverend Constance Paxton threw a spiteful look in the direction of the high wall, the handsome wrought iron gates and the glimmer of light coming from the porch light.

At first Constance had ignored the matter, hoping it would go away or some compromise would be hammered out between lawyers. Then a faded plan had been attached to the lychgate outlining the boundary in red.

Constance hated confrontation, but Clinker brought out the worst in her. Not that it did any good whatsoever. No number of arguments and calls for understanding had got through to him. He wanted the whole area covered in tarmac in order to minimise wear and tear on his top of the range Mercedes and his wife, Marietta's Range Rover. He didn't want any other cars using it except for his.

In the end, he finally compromised. Wedding cars would be the exception, but he did have the right to tidy it up a bit.

The parish council, led by the redoubtable Mrs Gertrude Acton, and seconded by the equally redoubtable Mrs Anne Flynn, supported by the vicar, had agreed in principle with the exception of the material to be used. The tarmac, they argued, would spoil the look of the church. Gravel they would accept, though they would prefer cobblestones. Harold Clinker declared cobblestones to be too expensive, besides which his horse box would be bounced around all over the place.

He told them he didn't give a rat's arse what they thought because the land was his anyway, and he was in his rights to claim it lock, stock and barrel. It was only down to his good-hearted neighbourliness that he wasn't fencing it off.

'And I could,' he'd shouted at full volume. 'If I bloody well wanted to, I could.'

As a last-ditch attempt, Constance had suggested that the deed he'd produced might have been countered some years later in a written agreement between the owners of Belvedere House and St Michael's.

'Prove it,' he'd said, his jaw set and his eyes gleaming with triumph.

He'd even suggested the work being done over a period of eleven days, covering two weekends.

Constance was appalled.

'You can't do that! I have weddings booked. Think of all those disappointed couples about to enter into holy matrimony.'

He'd sneered. 'Tell them to live in sin. It makes more sense nowadays. Saves them bothering to get divorced! Think of the money they'd save.'

She'd been appalled and then more determined to get the matter sorted, at least giving the church more say in the disputed land.

The fact was neither she nor the church lawyers could prove it. The archives had been searched, but there wasn't a shred of evidence that either party in the dispute owned the property. Somehow the deeds had been lost.

Constance shoved her hands in the pockets of her sleeveless gilet and trudged on, not exactly cursing him under her breath, but not far from it.

It wasn't just a question of what the ground should be covered with, it was the threat of Clinker taking it over entirely;

she had visions of him carrying out his threat and building a fence around it, leaving only enough room for pedestrians to pass through. Wedding cars, the joy of St Michael's existence, would have to park at the far end of the lane. And what about funerals? Imagine manhandling a coffin along the lane and over the rough ground before even entering church precincts.

'Like something from a horror movie,' she muttered.

As if to confirm her statement, a bat flew out from beneath the lychgate. Constance stopped, her eyes following its flight up to the tower. There were a whole colony of them up there. Had been for years.

Constance quite liked bats and had no objection to them living in the belfry. She entertained the vague hope that one of them might be a vampire bat, would bite Clinker and he would fall dead. 'Lord forgive me,' she muttered to herself.

Just lately she'd taken to locking the church door. In times past it had been left unlocked, but a single break-in at the beginning of her tenure had made her more cautious, at least until the culprit had been caught — if ever.

Not that anything had been taken, not even the collection box, a rough looking thing sitting on the table close to the entrance and surrounded by free pamphlets detailing St Michael's history. The idea was that people might donate a small coin in lieu of the free pamphlets. The highest denomination of coin she'd ever found in there had been a twenty pence piece.

The big iron key turned in the lock and she entered the church. For a moment she stood still and silent, savouring the atmosphere of ancient sanctity.

The church was a place of shadows except where the last rays of the setting sun fell like orange torchlight through the west facing window.

Constance did her obligations at the altar and instantly felt a great sense of relief. She couldn't help muttering a little prayer of thanks.

'Thank you for giving me the strength to face Mrs Flynn, her fruit cake and her sherry. I promise, Lord, I only had one. Honest!'

33

In her mind she fancied God smiling and being pleased that she'd survived the ordeal without hitting the woman on the head. Mrs Flynn wasn't an easy person by any means. A village old-timer, she'd attended the church for years, wheedling her way onto every committee, having a say in every lay decision, and also attempting to influence the clergy. The vicar who'd retired before her had undergone the same ordeals.

'She got quite cross with me when I wanted to clean up the older graves down in the southeast corner,' he'd told her. 'Threatened to write to the bishop if I dared disturb them.'

Mrs Flynn liked everything to stay the same, especially who organised the decoration for weddings.

'A good marriage should be for life. That's why it should be in church. People aren't so likely to break their vows if they're married in the sight of God.'

Whether the deceased Mr Flynn had thought the same, Constance wasn't sure. He was never mentioned. Neither were children though she had heard there was a daughter. When she'd asked about her, Mrs Flynn had glared at her as though she'd suggested having an orgy in the vestry.

'My daughter is dead to me,' she'd snapped.

As the orange of sunset diminished, Constance remembered the latest task Mrs Flynn had set her. *Check that the old coffer had not been damaged by water.*

She very much doubted any damage had actually been done, but was obliged to check.

Weathered through hundreds of summers before it was even cut down, the oak from which the coffer was made had no shine, no carvings, no decorations of any kind. It was just a very old chest, about six feet long, by three feet deep, by three feet high.

It was actually big enough to have served as a coffin, but there was no record of a body ever having been interred inside. More likely it had once been used to store surpluses and other vestments, but there was a cupboard for that now.

Constance could see no evidence of water damage. Nothing at all.

'Another of Mrs Flynn's fantasies,' she muttered as she headed for the door leading to the belfry. Mrs Flynn liked to keep people busy and that very much included the vicar.

There were three bells up in the tower and a number of ardent campanologists in the village. The electricity supply only went as far as the main nave of the church, not to the tower, though the light switches were on the belfry side of the door. This meant that Constance had to go in there every time she wanted to switch a light on for somewhere else in the church. What the electricians back in the fifties had been thinking of was anyone's guess, though it was rumoured they frequented the Angel Inn for their lunch.

Constance was just about to open the door, when something caught her eye. It was a chisel, sticking up from the floor, as though someone had used it to lever up a flagstone.

She bent down for a closer inspection. A sudden scuffling made her jump, though being of stout figure and brave heart, she held her ground.

'Hello? Anyone there?' Her voice bounced back off the bare stone walls.

Daft thing to say, she thought. If anyone was there who shouldn't be, they were hardly likely to answer. Intruders might have evil intent, but they weren't stupid.

If only she'd turned the lights on earlier. It was getting dark. Shadows were getting longer. The sun had set and the air had turned suddenly cold.

Nervous now, she took backward steps in the direction of the door to the belfry, her eyes darting in and out of shadows thrown by the pillars lining the nave. There were no gargoyles inside the church to leer at her, but the sombre engravings of the rood screen made her feel nervous.

'I'm not alone,' she shouted out.

The watcher in the shadows stayed absolutely still. The vicar was backing away from the light and into the darkness. Closer and closer and . . .

The Reverend Constance Paxton didn't see the blow coming, and even if she had the result would have been exactly the same.

CHAPTER FIVE

Steve Doherty held the church door open for Honey. 'Hey it's pretty dark in here. Don't they have lights? I thought churches had lights nowadays. Creepy old place, don't you think?'

Honey grimaced. A church wedding wasn't necessarily what they'd go for, but no stone was being left unturned.

'Are you sure about this? You sound nervous,' Honey said to him.

His restless eyes darted from side to side, flagstones to rafters.

'Churches make me nervous. I've only ever had one ceremony in here before that I was obliged to attend. Had no choice in the matter in fact.'

'Your first marriage?'

'No. I told you before that I got married in a registry office. I meant when I was christened in a church. I only ever expected to come here again for my funeral.'

'Now there's a jolly thought!'

He caught the sarcastic tone. He hadn't meant to sound offhand about a church wedding so went out of his way to make amends.

'It's OK. I'll do whatever you want to do. I don't mind getting married in a church. I don't mind getting dressed up all fancy for the occasion.'

'No worries.' She grinned. 'I'll be the one in the dress.'

'Suits me.'

It had been a joint decision to evaluate the options before actually tying the knot. They'd both wanted to see how they would feel about it, whether it be a white wedding in a church, or perhaps just the two of them on a Caribbean island, or an elopement to Gretna Green — although of course Gretna Green no longer carried out instant weddings; notice now had to be given.

The fact was that they both wanted to know which appealed the most, seeing as they had both been married before.

Doherty took a couple of steps forward so he stood level with her in the aisle.

'So where's the vicar?'

Honey looked around. Doherty did the same, though more professionally, eyes peeled, nose held high as though he were sniffing for trouble.

'Are you sure we've got the right time?' he asked her.

Honey slowed so she could scrutinise the pews. Who knows, maybe the vicar might like practical jokes and was presently playing hide and seek. A few more steps and she might leap from hiding and shout 'boo!'

Honey wasn't the greatest for jotting notes in a diary, even special birthdays or events and Doherty had sown a doubt. She frowned as she did a quick rummage of her hand-bag; a big pink one that had only recently replaced a big brown one. Think travelling office.

'Hold on. I'll double check with my diary. I wrote it down.'

Juggling bag and diary, she finally managed to open it. Not that it proved of any value. She couldn't see a thing.

'It's tonight. I'm sure of it. Perhaps the vicar forgot.'

37

She looked up. Where had Doherty gone? There was no sign of him.

'Steve?'

'The vicar is here,' she heard him shout.

She ran down the aisle. Doherty was bent down beside a black robed figure lying flat out on the floor. Her straight black bob hid her face. Honey prepared herself for the worst.

'Oh my God! Is she dead?'

'No. But she has had a nasty knock on the head. Phone an ambulance.'

The hair fell away from the vicar's face as she moved, blinked and opened her eyes.

'No! No! I'm all right. I fainted. That's all. Please. Help me to my feet, will you?'

The vicar raised herself onto her elbows before Honey and Doherty took hold of her arms and helped her to her feet.

Doherty asked her where the light switch was.

'Through there,' she said, pointing to the door behind her which was very slightly ajar.

Once the vicar was sitting down, Doherty went to turn on the light switch.

'Are you sure you don't want a doctor?' Honey asked Constance. 'You look quite flushed.'

She shook her head. 'No. I'm fine thank you. Just a funny turn. Must be getting old.'

She gave a little nervous laugh that Honey didn't like the sound of. Not so much nervous, she decided, more as if she was frightened.

Once she'd composed herself, she looked at them as though nothing whatsoever had happened.

'You must be Doherty and Driver come to discuss the possibility of holding your wedding here.'

'That was the idea,' said Honey, exchanging a quick glance with Doherty. 'We wanted to take a look round and ask about the possibilities — seeing as we've both been married before.'

'Both divorced?'

Honey shook her head. 'No. I'm a widow.'

'I'm sorry.'

'I'm not. He was doing what he wanted to do with a crew of lithesome ladies.'

'More than one indiscretion?' said the vicar, obviously warming to the event and looking overly keen to hear more.

'They were crew on his racing yacht, though I suspect that he had stretched the meaning of the term 'first mate'.

'Ah. I see.' The effort of nodding was a bit too much. The vicar's head rolled back as though she were about to faint again.

'I think we should leave this for another time,' suggested Honey.

'Oh no. I won't hear of it. Not after you made this journey especially.'

'It's no problem. We can make an appointment for another time when you feel better.'

'What's the pub like here?' asked Doherty.

Honey shot him a scathing look before turning back to the vicar.

'I think the best thing you can do is have a hot drink and an early night. Let's get you home.'

'That's very kind of you,' said Constance, getting to her feet. 'But I can find my own way . . .'

She stopped suddenly as though something important had suddenly occurred to her.

'Someone hit me.'

Doherty's attention was instantly captured. He moved in closer. 'Someone hit you?'

'Yes.'

'Did you see who it was?'

She shook her head, then tottered a little. 'No. He . . . I presume it was a man, came up behind me.' She raised a hand and rubbed the back of her head. 'Ouch. I think I've got a pigeon's egg.'

'Then I think you need to see a doctor.' Honey was adamant.

The Reverend Paxton refused to go to hospital, but agreed for the local doctor to call.

'I can't go to hospital. I've got too much to do. We've got a wedding tomorrow. It should be lovely.' She smiled at them bravely as Honey and Doherty supported her between them.

'Do come along if you can. It will give you some idea of what your wedding could be like.'

The vicarage was built of stone and shared its garden with the car park and shrubbery surrounding the village hall.

Before they had made the front door, three people of disproportionate size, all looking in a state of flap, came rushing out to meet them.

'The parish council,' the vicar explained. 'Well, three of them anyway.'

The first to face them was a man who seemed as broad as he was high. He looked like an old-fashioned bank manager.

'What's all this?' he demanded, looking straight at Doherty who promptly explained what had happened. All three members of Wainscote Parish Council followed them to the vicarage door and into the house.

Threadbare rugs covered the flagstones — shabby chic rather than fit for throwing out. A small dog came rushing out to meet them, yapping in ear-splitting staccato whilst wagging its tail fit to fall off.

Still holding her head, the vicar told the beloved pet to be quiet whilst one of the villagers helped her into a chair.

'You poor thing,' the woman cooed. 'We were wondering where you were. It wasn't that dreadful Mr Clinker, was it? He did pop into the meeting to warn us only to use the land for weddings, but didn't stop long. It wasn't him that did it, was it Constance? He is something of a gangster, not at all the type we want in this village.'

Honey was all ears. She also couldn't help noticing that the leader of the parish council, who had introduced himself as Mr Masters, deftly moved the dog out of the way with the side of his shoe. Honey wondered whether his action might have been more forceful if they hadn't been there.

'Someone get the vicar a cup of tea,' barked Mr Masters.

One of the two female members of the parish council scurried off to the kitchen to put the kettle on. Mr Masters straightened and looked towards the door.

'Is Mrs Flynn not with us? Can someone go outside and see where she's got to?'

'He used to be in the army,' the vicar whispered to Honey. 'Sometimes he still thinks he is.'

'Who's this Mr Clinker?' Honey asked.

'An ignorant man who came here from London and wants to change everything,' said Mr Masters huffily. 'Now do as I say, will you, and see where Mrs Flynn has got to.'

Even though she didn't have the slightest clue what Mrs Flynn looked like, Honey knew she'd been volunteered.

'A fine night this is turning out to be,' she muttered as she peered around the garden and towards the village hall.

There wasn't a soul in sight, but she did hear the sound of a car driving off — just before the doctor arrived.

The doctor told everyone to give the vicar some air, to go home, and that everything was being done that could be done. The vicar was quite all right.

Honey and Doherty left gladly, Doherty yet again mentioning the pub.

'Just to see if their beer stands up to scrutiny.'

The sky outside was crowded with stars and the moon was full and bright. It would have been quite romantic if it hadn't been for the yaw yaw of a police siren.

Doherty stepped through the lychgate, Honey bringing up the rear.

'I didn't know anyone called them,' remarked Honey.

'Even if they did, it wouldn't warrant a screaming siren,' muttered Doherty with a frown.

The police car careened over the uneven surface, finally stopping with its nose into the double gates of Belvedere House.

The driver recognised Doherty.

'Sir? I thought we were going to be the first ones here. We were only a couple of miles away. Your car must be a bit of a goer.'

'Teleported,' said Doherty without the trace of a grin. 'It's the Flying Squad's new secret weapon. We're trying it out for a time.'

For a moment it seemed as though the driver had swallowed it. His partner looked more sceptic but wasn't going to ruin either the joke or his chances of promotion. In his opinion, it paid to keep in with one's superiors; that included falling in with their wind-ups.

The electronic gates chose that moment to open.

'Better get to it,' said the driver.

'So what were you told?' asked Doherty, unwilling to admit that he didn't have a clue what was going on.

'Domestic. A complaint from a Miss Marietta Hopkins against her partner, Mr Harold Clinker.'

Honey recognised the name Clinker as mentioned by Mr Masters, the leader of the parish council. She also recognised that of Marietta Hopkins.

'Better get to it then,' said Doherty.

'Do you want to . . .'

Doherty shook his head. 'No. I'll be at the pub if you need me.'

Honey nudged him. 'That Mr Masters, the leader of the parish council mentioned a man named Clinker.'

'What's he done?'

'I've no idea, but I did get the impression there's some kind of dispute going on.'

'Hmm.'

It wasn't much of a response, so Honey gave him another dig. 'I used to know a girl called Marietta Hopkins. She was called Mary then but sometimes took on airs and graces and called herself Marietta.'

Again that non-committal sound.

'Shouldn't you make the effort, you know, seeing as there's already been one incident tonight — get a bit of background information?'

Doherty looked as though he was chewing a thistle. He had that look in his eyes, like a greyhound about to spring from the trap. His gaze wandered to the main street and the wooden sign swinging outside the pub.

A pint of beer beckoned, but Honey had waved the duty flag. There was still a chance of a pint seeing as closing time was some way off.

'Mary Hopkins used to talk about changing her name to something like Marianna or Marietta,' Honey continued. 'She was very glamorous and had high hopes of a modelling or film career. Loved Hollywood, right down to the style of those old white telephones and polar bear rugs; I did mention to her that it just wouldn't suit the semi-detached she'd probably end up with.'

'Did she take much notice?'

'Don't know.' Honey shrugged. 'We lost touch.'

CHAPTER SIX

From the outside, Belvedere House looked your run-of-the-mill historic place with a hefty price tag. The moment they were shown inside, Honey knew that Mary Hopkins had become Marietta.

The maid who answered the door asked them to take off their shoes. Her request was denied when Doherty flashed his ID card.

The room was very white: white walls, white carpet, white furnishings. If Belvedere House had ever had any colour, it didn't have any now. All its period features that might once have made the house look interesting had been obliterated. History had been whitewashed in favour of recessed lighting and penthouse décor. It was like having a near-death experience, the white light all around instead of at the end of the tunnel.

Miss Marietta Hopkins was sporting a black eye and there was blood streaming from her nose. She was accompanied by another woman was administering a piece of lint and a bag of peas.

The two uniformed policemen had been told to wait outside.

Marietta pushed away the bag of peas. 'I want him arrested,' she shouted, then frowned on spotting Honey.

'Sorry, but I feel that I should know you. I've got a lousy memory. Remind me . . .'

'Yes. I knew you when you were Mary.'

As if her bruised face wasn't enough, Marietta scowled. 'Please don't call me that. Marietta. My name is now *Marietta*.'

She was dressed in animal print leggings and a black thigh length top. Her hair was blonde and shoulder length and she wore lots of gold studded with flashing jewels. Honey doubted they were real — she knew that Christian Dior did a good range of costume jewellery.

'Your husband did this?' asked Doherty.

'That's what I just said,' lisped Marietta through a nostril of bloody mucous.

'So where is he now?'

'Off to cause aggro elsewhere, I'm sure. He's had it this time.'

'What time did this happen?'

'An hour ago.'

Each response was snapped whilst she held her head back and the other woman, who so far had not been introduced, dabbed on the lint and the frozen peas.

'Were there any witnesses to this attack on your person?'

'I was upstairs getting dressed,' said the woman with the peas.

'You live here?' asked Doherty.

'No. I was visiting.'

It occurred to Honey that an odd expression had passed between her and Marietta. She wasn't sure Doherty had noticed.

'And your name?' he asked, making notes as he did so.

'Carolina Sherise.'

'How do you spell that?'

She spelled it out for him.

'It's an unusual name.'

'It's my professional name.'

Doherty nodded. 'And your profession?'

'Exotic dancer. I'm employed by Mr Clinker.'

45

'Oh, so you know him well.'

'Perhaps a bit better than some and not as well as others,' she responded with a smirk.

'So you saw Mr Clinker hit Miss Hopkins.'

'Yes. It was immediately after she hit him. We both came down the stairs when we heard her come home.'

Doherty stopped writing. Like Honey, he'd assumed it was common assault; i.e. an argument between common-law spouses that had got out of hand. 'Both?'

'Mr Clinker and me. We'd been gettin' it together up in the bedroom, then Marietta here came waltzing in all unexpected-like.'

'Are you from Liverpool?' he asked, recognising her accent.

'I was once. But not now.'

'She was screwing Harold,' said Marietta between sniffs and swallows. 'And before you say anything, Harold and I have an open marriage.'

'You're still married?'

'I retained my maiden name.'

Honey tried not to look surprised but her face simply refused to do impassive.

Marietta glowered at her with the eye that wasn't sporting the frozen vegetables.

'Research shows that marriage is always a compromise. That's why some fail and some survive. Mine survived because both of us were willing to compromise,' she said defiantly. She sounded as though she'd learned the statement by rote.

'So you do compromise and confrontation, or was this a one-off? I mean, have you come to blows before?'

Marietta pursed her lips. 'He hadn't brought a stranger into our bed before!'

Doherty's notepad was halfway to firmly shut. He wasn't getting this.

'You had a fight because he'd brought this young lady home.' He gave a brief nod to Carolina.

'He broke the agreement. He brought her into our bed. We'd agreed never to do that.'

'So you hit him.'

'I saw red. Besides . . .'

She stopped, swallowed whatever she'd been about to say.

'Have you been having other marital problems?'

'We all have them from time to time.'

And then some, thought Honey, although in her experience they never came to the weight of blows these two had exchanged.

It wasn't part of Honey's remit as liaison officer for Bath Hotels Association to get involved with domestic violence, but that was on a professional level. This scenario was getting juicier by the minute and definitely the stuff good gossip is made from.

Honey wondered what Harold Clinker was like. Given that Marietta was a glamour puss, he had to be a wealthy man, certainly wealthy enough to own Belvedere House. Was he old, young, ugly, handsome?

Her curiosity was roused. Given the circumstances, she could hardly ask Marietta and a sly glance around the room gave nothing away; there were no photographs in silver frames of a smiling couple on their wedding day or on holiday. One large painting depicting four interlinked circles of various shades of white hung on one wall. Three smaller pictures, all very much the same, hung in a row immediately opposite. So much for period décor!

'Do you wish to press charges?' Doherty asked, his attention fixed on his notes though he had noticed Marietta's plunging neckline.

Marietta shrugged. 'If you can find him.'

'We can give it a stab. Where does he usually go if you have a misunderstanding?'

'If he hasn't taken the car, he's probably gone for a walk.'

'Not to the pub, by any chance?' said Doherty hopefully. His throat was getting dry from all these questions.

'He doesn't drink in pubs. He doesn't usually go for a walk either, but if he hasn't taken the car, he can't do much else but walk, can he!'

'OK,' said Doherty, notepad tucked away, hands tucked in his pockets. 'I'll register the complaint, though I will still have to formally charge your husband. We'll take a look outside, but if you see him before I do, let me know. He can come by the station.

'That's all we can do,' said Doherty once they were outside and squeezing past the police car.

'All done?' the driver asked.

'Sorted,' said Doherty. He slapped the roof and told them to go home. 'And go easy on the siren. You're not starring in *Miami Vice*!'

The car left, siren now silent.

It was so typically male; policemen loved the sound of their sirens, thought Honey. It was a bit like the Charge of the Light Brigade; shout to the sky to let everyone know you're coming.

'Under the circumstances, I don't think *they* had a church wedding,' said Doherty once they were outside.

'Of course they did! Mary — or Marietta as she calls herself now, always did love being the centre of attention.'

'So I guess she had a white gown, eight bridesmaids and a four-tier cake. A cathedral though rather than a village church.' Doherty smirked.

Up ahead of them in the heart of the village, squares of amber light fell from the windows of the Angel Inn. Half a dozen cars lined the forecourt out front. The sound of a car door and two people laughing drifted on the night air.

Doherty eyed the pub mournfully. 'Shame our Mr Clinker doesn't drink.'

The pub door opened and closed as he said it. A figure came out, head hunched into shoulders, walking towards them quickly.

By the time he drew level with them, they could see his intense expression and the fact that his bald pate gleamed in the glow of a solitary street lamp.

'You anything to do with the coppers?'

Doherty explained that he was.

'What a terrible thing to happen. But there, nobody's safe nowadays are they.' He made a sucking sound through his teeth.

'People should be safe enough in their own home,' Doherty responded.

The man frowned and said, 'Well she don't exactly live there, do she. I mean, it's God's house really, innit?' He sucked again and his smile edged on a leer.

A question relating to the whereabouts of Harold Clinker was on her lips, but Doherty got there first.

'Are you Mr Harold Clinker?'

The bald-headed man, who looked to be in late middle age, looked affronted.

'Not bloody likely. I'm Alan Price.'

'Where do you live?'

He pointed to a narrow opening between two buildings, barely the width of a car. 'Down that alleyway. Third cottage on the left.'

'You don't happen to have seen Mr Clinker pass this way?'

'Clinker? Out on his own in this village? I should cocoa!'

His tone was the other side of friendly.

Honey jumped in. 'Not one of your favourite neighbours I take it?'

'He's nobody's favourite neighbour, especially the vicar. Take my word for it the woman's a saint to put up with him. I wouldn't want to deal with him that's for sure.'

'Do you know his wife?'

'Only in passing.'

'Not to speak to? I find that hard to believe.' said Doherty.

'What you trying to say?'

No sucking this time, just a jarred look.

Doherty shrugged. 'I asked a perfectly reasonable question, sir. I asked if you knew his wife and pointed out that it was no crime in speaking to her.'

Mr Price considered and nodded his head. 'Nice looking woman and friendlier than that git. I'm telling you now, he'd never win the popularity stakes in this village. Most people who move to the country make the effort to adjust, but not 'im. He expected the village to change to suit him.'

Once Mr Price had moved along, Honey and Doherty stood silently looking at each other.

Doherty screwed up his face. 'How do you feel about an open marriage?'

She knew what he was *really* asking; is Marietta Hopkins for real?

'Look, if you don't want the cost of a white wedding, you only have to say.'

His grin was only a teeny bit nervous. He shook his head. 'That isn't exactly what I meant.'

'I haven't met this Mr Clinker, but I already dislike him. Live together if you must, but what's the point of getting married if you're not going to follow the rules . . . especially the one about *keeping only unto her or he, for as long as you both shall live.*'

'And she kept her maiden name.'

Honey frowned. 'Yes. I know women do, especially professional women.'

'Will you keep yours?'

They stopped walking and turned towards each other.

Honey pulled a so-so kind of face. 'It was the name I took when I got married. I could go back to my maiden name, but Doherty has a certain ring about it.'

'Thanks. I like it too.'

'Then that's settled. Back to the case in hand.'

'Sounds as though the village didn't like him much either. What say you to getting the lowdown on Mr Clinker?' said Doherty sounding brighter than he had all evening. 'Ask around a bit. Get the lowdown from the locals. Any comments?'

'Yes. It's your round. I'll have a vodka and tonic.'

CHAPTER SEVEN

A covering of plates, platters and old paintings helped hide the rough walls at the Angel Inn. Pewter tankards hung from dark beams and enamel signs advertising everything from Sunlight Soap to Coleman's Mustard filled the gaps the plates and platters failed to cover.

By the looks of it, somebody had a passion for collecting old furniture. Jacobean style chairs with barley twist legs and raffia seats jostled with Victorian balloon backs, rounded Bentwoods and lyre backed Chippendale styled with cabriole legs.

The same could be said for the tables; some refectory style, the smaller ones round and stout.

Diners were digging into whatever food was on offer. Typically, the locals took up the bar stools, and those without bar stools crowded around the bar. Beer mugs hanging from overhead racks barely skimmed the top of their heads.

Conversation died once the strangers were spotted. Heads turned, eyes scrutinised. It was like a host of flashbulbs going off. Honey had an urge to strike a pose.

'Good evening.' Doherty met their hard stares full on as he nudged the locals aside to make room for himself and Honey at the bar.

The man behind the bar was at least six feet four with dark hair and small eyes. He stooped, hands resting on the countertop, and even then his head only barely missed the hanging mugs.

The pub was built at a time when people were not very tall. The publican would only look comfortable if he were twelve inches shorter. He'd landed behind the wrong bar and, in Honey's opinion, he would have better suited a Regency or Victorian hostelry where the ceilings were higher and half his head wouldn't have been hidden behind a rafter.

His smile was plastic. 'Staying in the village, are you?'

'Seems a sleepy little place,' said Doherty without answering the question. He took a sip of Ruddles County and found it to his liking. Honey noticed there was no lemon in her drink. No ice either. Like the beer, it was warm.

'It is usually,' one of the customers was swaying slightly on his feet. 'Sleepy. Mostly it is.'

He was referring to the village and the question that had been asked.

'Is that so?' Honey took in the grey hair, the flaccid jowl and the colourless eyes.

Even without a glance at the amber-coloured liquid in his glass, his ruby red conk was a dead giveaway for a cider drinker. 'All happening tonight though!' he exclaimed before taking a sip from his glass.

She gave him an encouraging smile while noticing the look of warning on the face of the barman.

'Did you see anything yourself?' she asked him.

The barman intervened. 'I think it's time you were going home, Abe. You've had enough.'

The drunk — it was pretty obvious he was two sheets to the wind — threw the barman a surly look. The barman counteracted, towering forward on clenched fists, his nostrils flattened and flaring; all in all a pretty good imitation of King Kong, thought Honey.

'Well if I'm not going to get any more . . .' said the man, slamming down his glass hard enough to break it.

'You're not!'

The barman grabbed the glass.

The drunk wobbled.

'Right. Then I'll just hang around and talk to these nice people. Visiting 'ere are you?'

'On business,' said Doherty.

The drunk leered at Honey, his gaze fixed on her bosom.

'Are you the business then?'

'Would you like to pull your eyes out of my cleavage?' she snapped.

'Eh!' He looked up at her face. 'So what kind of business are you in? That was all I was asking. What kind of business are you in.'

She knew what was going to happen next — and it did.

Doherty got out his ID.

'The vicar was attacked in the church tonight. Did anyone see anything?'

A posse of heads turned to look and listen. The question was repeated, murmured from one customer to the next.

'We did hear word,' said the barman, his words slowly measured. He shook his head. 'I saw the vicar walking past, but that's all.'

'What time was that?'

'About nine.'

'She'd been to see Mrs Flynn. I saw her coming out of her place,' said somebody else.

Someone laughed. 'Wonder she didn't come in here for a drink. Everybody needs a drink after spending time with Mrs Flynn!'

'Indeedy,' said another bar-seated local. 'The old bat is enough to drive a saint to drink!'

Doherty listened politely. He hadn't felt it right to mention the domestic argument. He knew what villages were like. The fight between the couple living at Belvedere House was the stuff that fuelled gossip. Still, a crime had been committed. Marietta Hopkins was sporting a black eye and a bloody nose though the latter didn't look as if it were broken, not this time.

'I'm also looking for Mr Harold Clinker. Has anyone seen him this evening?'

'Clinker!'

The name brought forth a volley of exclamations and angry mutterings.

Doherty eyed them all coolly. He wasn't going to be drawn into local politics, but he was going to listen.

Honey also remained silent, but her eyes were everywhere, seeking something suspicious, or at least some reaction.

She noticed three people — a couple who had been dining and just finished their coffee, and another leaning at the far end of the bar — get up and walk out.

It occurred to her that the couple might not have paid their bill. The other person, a red-haired woman dressed as though she were going dog walking, had tensed at the mention of Harold Clinker.

Seeing as they'd been quite happy to listen and observe until Clinker was mentioned, it seemed a good idea to follow them out. It wouldn't hurt to ask them a few questions.

The three people who had left the bar disappeared around the side of the building. Honey recalled seeing a path leading to a pub garden where a few dissolute fairy lights had been slung between trees.

Nothing could be more suspicious, she thought, than bunching together in a pub garden when the sun wasn't shining. It was a place used in daylight, not late at night — not even for summer dining. After all, this was England. Fifty per cent of the time, rain stopped play, as they said in cricket.

Almost on tiptoe, but not quite, she kept close to the wall, feeling her way along. She was on her own; Doherty would think she'd gone to the little girls' room. That is, until he realised that she hadn't drunk enough to pay a visit there just yet.

Bright lights fell onto the path from the frosted windows of the kitchen. The familiar clattering of pans and crockery mingled with jolly conversation and loud laughter. The chef and his staff were feeling good — quite normal — they always perked up once the shift was over and they could grab a drink in the bar before making their way home to bed.

At first the threesome in the garden who would have been silhouettes if it hadn't been for the rainbow falling on them from the fairy lights, spoke in low voices. Gradually, as they warmed to their subject, their manner became more heated, their voices louder.

First she heard a male voice. 'It was never any of our business.'

Then a second male voice. 'Come on. We couldn't just sit back and do nothing.'

'You think below the waist. That's your trouble.'

Honey grunted; the third voice belonged to a woman.

'Someone had to stick up for her. Strikes me there's too much idle gossip going on in this village — and we all know where that comes from!'

Honey stepped from the shadows and into the light. 'Ahem! Excuse me for butting in, but I find this conversation very interesting. I would like to know more. Can I have your names?'

Three surprised faces turned her way. The notebook in which she'd intended recording first impressions regarding the church, the vicar and how she would feel marching down the aisle, came into its own. She had plenty of room to jot down their names.

They could ask her to show her ID in which case her plan would be scuppered. However, she had caught them on the hop, not giving them time to think straight.

The first man heaved a big sigh. Honey caught the smell of an expensive aftershave. He was dressed well too.

'I'm Nicholas Thompson. This is my wife, Hermione. We live at The Laurels. The big house with the brick chimneys? You probably saw it on your way in,' he said in the manner of somebody who frequently boasts about being better off than everybody else.

Honey thanked him and said that she'd seen a lot of chimneys on the way in, but couldn't say for sure that she'd noticed his.

The other woman, who looked as though she should be walking a dog rather than lingering in a pub, had a square chin and a dark scowl. A harder nut to crack, thought Honey, but now she'd started, she had to brave it out.

'And your name, madam?'

Deep wrinkles spread out like the rays of the sun from the woman's pursed lips. Honey knew a smokers' bow mouth when she saw it. Even a reformed smoker couldn't smooth out those wrinkles.

'Janet Glencannon.'

'Is that Mrs or Miss?'

'Mzzzzz!'

She sounded like a bumble bee.

'And where do you live?'

'Bobby's Bottom. And before you make a comment about the name, I run an animal sanctuary. It used to be called Brindley's Bottom. I altered it. Bobby was my dog. He's dead now. I thought it very apt to name my animal sanctuary after my dog.'

'Your place, your choice,' said Honey, still scribbling like crazy in her notebook.

'Why are you questioning us?' asked the man who had introduced himself as Nicholas Thompson and his wife as Hermione. He was frowning, a definite sign that he was likely to check her credentials. She could do without that, simply because she didn't have any.

'I haven't questioned you except to ask for your names and addresses,' she said. 'I'm only requesting that you assist with enquiries.'

Even to her own ears, she sounded pretty sure of herself. 'However, I couldn't help noticing that you left the bar pretty sharply when my colleague flashed his badge and mentioned Mr Clinker. Do you know where Mr Clinker is?'

Hermione Thompson pushed forward. 'Dead, I hope!' She almost spat the words up into Honey's face.

'Would you like to explain yourself?'

Taking a deep breath, Hermione Thompson's head seemed to rise a few inches up from the collar of her crisp white shirt.

'When Harold Clinker first came to this village, he was all charm and sunshine. He insisted on getting involved with everything that went on here, including attending church, getting voted onto the parish council, joining the Horticultural Society. You name it, he did it. He was even chairman of the Carnival committee at first. Not now though. The veneer of respectability was that thin,' she said, a sliver of space between finger and thumb. 'After that, it was downhill all the way. He began to make fun of us, telling us how superficial we all were, how we didn't know how to make the best of either ourselves or the village. Called us a load of fools. The opportunities were there if only we cared to look. But we didn't, so he was the one doing all the looking, upsetting people, blackmailing, telling lies . . .'

'Is he capable of knocking the vicar on the head?'

'That man is capable of anything!' Mrs Thompson was trembling, her bottom lip quivering.

'Hermione . . .' Nicholas Thompson laid his hand gently on his wife's arm, the consequence of which was that she burst into tears.

'He tried to change everything,' said Ms Janet Glencannon. 'He made it his business to search out old deeds and lay claims to tracts of land that people had been using for years. That included the church. He had it in for them most of all. The Reverend was beside herself, especially when he had a writ served on her regarding the state of the road outside the church.'

'I take it, Ms Glencannon, that your animal sanctuary covers quite a lot of land. Did he try and claim that too?'

Janet grimaced. 'He tried to serve a writ on me. I set the dog on him. Not Bobby, who was a terrier. I let Gertrude at him. Gertrude is a Great Dane and she's very protective of her territory. Now, if you'll excuse me.'

Janet Glencannon bid a terse goodnight, her wellingtons making sucking sounds against her strong calves as she marched off.

'Us too,' said Nicholas Thompson.

'One more question. Mr Clinker and Miss Hopkins were married, but she hadn't adopted his name. Was it a good marriage do you think?'

'I wouldn't know,' snapped Mr Thompson, turning to go.

Honey followed for a few steps. 'There are rumours of an open marriage, would you . . .'

He spun round on her. It might have been the fairy lights, but his face looked red and angry.

'I've already told you. I do not make a habit of interfering in other peoples' business. Now. If you'll excuse me; come along Hermione.'

Nicholas Thompson wrapped an arm around his wife's shoulders. Mrs Thompson shrugged it off, her pale face abruptly facing straight ahead.

Honey slid her notebook into her copious bag. As it dropped to the bottom, she noticed the sound of rustling wrapping papers. Food! She remembered the toffee éclairs she'd slipped in as emergency rations — just in case they didn't get home for supper which now seemed very likely. Her searching fingers found what she was looking for. Once the wrapper was off, she popped it into her mouth.

Doherty's long dark shadow fell along the pathway before his lean form, clad in his usual black leather jacket and jeans came into sight.

She turned round to face him. Placing both hands on her shoulders, he pulled her close to him, then wrapping his arms around her, kissed her.

'You taste of toffee. What are you eating?'

'A toffee éclair.'

'I want one.'

'We'll have to share it.'

Seeing as she only had three, she hoped he wouldn't want one. She'd already swallowed the first and was chewing the second. Naughty but nice.

'Feed me,' he said.

Wrapper discarded, she held the toffee between her teeth and smelled the fresh, earthy smell of him as his nose touched hers, his lips wrapping around his half of the toffee.

She tingled when his hands slid down her back; yelped when he went further and squeezed her bottom.

The toffee was lost.

'That was unfair strategy!'

'All is fair in love and war. Go on,' he said once the toffee éclair was tumbling around his mouth. His hands remained clutching her bottom. 'Tell me what you found out.'

'What makes you think I found out anything?'

'Three people left the bar with wings on their heels. You followed them.'

'I didn't realise you noticed.'

'I miss nothing,' he said, giving her bottom another squeeze. 'You're not wearing pants.'

'I am. Kind of . . .'

She'd only lately taken to wearing thongs after Lindsey had informed her that such underwear made one's bottom look more pert.

'Promise me you'll wear one beneath your wedding dress.'

'Of course I will,' she said then clamped her lips to his as much for the toffee as for the kiss.

On their way back to the car she repeated what the Thompsons and Ms Glencannon had told her.

'Not the most popular man in the village, though I got the impression that Mr and Mrs Thompson have their off days.'

'Doesn't everyone? That's marriage for you.'

'He got angry when I asked whether he knew anything about the Clinkers' marriage. In fact I dared to mention they might have an open marriage. He didn't like that. He got very protective of his wife suddenly.'

'It's a village. Bath is close-knit, but that's nothing compared to a village. Villages are incestuous. I mean it.'

'I didn't ask the woman in wellies about Mr Clinker's marriage. She didn't seem the sort that would know — or care.'

'You can never know for sure.'

'First impressions count. Ms Glencannon is a more doughty type. She runs the local animal sanctuary. I get the impression that if Mr Clinker tried any funny business with her, she'd set the dogs on him.'

'We could do with dogs — if he's still around that is. He could be anywhere.'

Honey looked around. The village was pretty dark, which was only to be expected. There were few streetlights around a village green dividing the houses on one side of the road from the other.

She was just about to comment that they probably played cricket on the green, or danced around the maypole, when she spotted a blob of diaphanous whiteness moving through the centre of the green.

'That's not cricket,' she mumbled.

'Cricket?'

Doherty, who had been phoning Mr Clinker's details into HQ, lifted his gaze to see what she was looking at.

'No. It looks like a runaway bride. Did you ever see the film?'

'What?'

'Well the bride liked weddings but didn't like marriage. She liked the dressing up, but not the domestic bliss — or drudgery — depending on how you look at it.'

'That was only a film,' he replied, sounding sceptical.

Honey pursed her lips as she thought it through. 'Might be something special to this village, some kind of traditional thing — you know, like maypoles and Morris dancing.'

Doherty shook his head solemnly at the thought of men prancing about to the sound of bells, decorated with flowers and brandishing a sheep's bladder on the end of a stick.

'Well that's villages for you. Dig deep and they're all a bit strange.'

CHAPTER EIGHT

It should have been a perfectly ordinary day at the Green River Hotel. Breakfast had been served and the first of the guests were checking out.

A sweet little Chinese couple had just left. A red-faced Frenchman was approaching. One glance and Honey could tell she had trouble.

'There was a worm in my porridge.'

Seeing as she was in a pretty good mood, her initial reaction was to say that porridge was pure carb and proteins were extra. However, judging by the gnashing teeth and fiery-red complexion, she guessed he wouldn't find it funny.

Being able to adopt a look of apologetic surprise at a moment's notice was a prerequisite for surviving in the hospitality game. After a while it came naturally.

'I'm sorry? Could you repeat what you just said?'

This time he spoke slowly as though she was stupid or that English to her was a foreign language.

'A *worm*. It was swimming in my porridge.'

Refraining from asking whether it was doing a forward crawl or the breaststroke, her expression of apology morphed into one of outright shock.

'Are you absolutely sure?'

He looked affronted. The Gallic features she had initially thought quite handsome turned to Gothic stone.

'Of course I am sure. It wriggled. Worms wriggle, do they not?'

This was one of those moments she absolutely hated. She couldn't even argue because she hadn't seen the worm. She'd have to check it out with the waitress and whoever had cooked breakfast this morning.

'Monsieur, I am so, so sorry. Please stay here a moment and I will check what you have told me with a member of staff.'

She offered him coffee but he shuddered at the suggestion, almost as though she had suggested he drink slime.

Maria, a Spanish waitress who hadn't long been with them, confirmed that indeed there was something wriggling around in the porridge.

Dumpy Doris was cooking breakfast. She confirmed that the porridge was freshly made and was quite upset at the news.

'What with that and the frog in the bed,' she cried.

'Frog?'

'The Scottish gentleman said that he'd found a frog in 'is bed. Quite put out he was.'

Honey frowned. First a worm. Now a frog.

'Whatever's 'appening,' said Doris, her plump face taking on the look of a squashed pumpkin. 'Worms, frogs and stuff in the punch that shouldn't 'ave been in the punch . . . Somebody's put a curse on us, that's what I think. Everything goes in threes. Three unexplained occurrences. It ain't natural.'

With a jolt Honey realised she was right, not so much about being cursed, but the fact that they had indeed had three awkward occurrences. Not that all of those affected had been outraged; the magic mushrooms, or whatever had been in the punch, hadn't caused any complaints, just a number of requests for the recipe.

'I'm not sure about being cursed,' Honey said slowly, shaking her head.

'You don't s'pose somebody's got it in fer us?' Doris stood with her hands resting on her broad hips. Her fingers were as fat and pink as sausages.

Honey shook her head. 'I can't see it, Doris.'

'Well, I do. There's funny things afoot, you mark my words.'

Honey shook her head again, though more vehemently this time.

'No! That way lies paranoia, and anyway, isn't it true that everything goes in threes? Three bouts of unlucky coincidences have happened, so that should be it. Now I'd better deal with Monsieur Parmentier.'

Compensation hurt, but she had no choice.

'No charge,' she said to the red-faced Frenchman and smiled sweetly. He'd had a damned good deal having stayed for two days and no charge for what he'd eaten. Still, it couldn't be helped. The last thing she wanted was a visit from Environmental Health.

After grabbing his luggage, Monsieur left quickly muttering something about getting a flight from Bristol to Paris and hoping to get an upgrade in seating to make up for this shock to his system.

Mr McDonald, the amiable Scotsman who'd had a recent run in with a frog, was striding across from the bottom of the stairs, beaming from ear to ear.

Honey oozed humility. 'Mr McDonald, I am so sorry.'

'First time in a while I've shared my bed with anyone memorable,' he said, laughing as he placed the frog on the reception counter. 'There it was — he or she, whatever — sitting in the middle of my bed.'

'You didn't see anyone entering your room? Was anything else amiss?'

He shook his head. 'No. I didn't discover it until this morning. I was in no state you might say. You see, my wife and I had a big row early yesterday afternoon after I overindulged at lunchtime with some twelve-year-old malt at the bar. You've got a good selection you know.'

Honey agreed that indeed the Green River did maintain a very good selection of malt whiskies.

'Did your wife see the frog?'

'Oh, no. She stormed out after calling me a drunken sod and saying she'd be consulting a firm of solicitors regarding a quickie divorce. Not that I care. I reckon that she put the frog there or had somebody do it. Not that I minded that much. Quite frankly, the frog was livelier in bed than she ever was!'

Honey almost choked, her mind boggling at the thought of a ginger-haired Scotsman in bed with the frog.

Once someone else was able to take over reception duties, Honey escaped to her office accompanied by a croissant and a cup of black coffee. When the single croissant didn't give her the usual sugar fix, she ordered another.

Just as she was about to bite into this second helping of comfort food, relishing the thought of the mascarpone filling oozing into her mouth, the phone rang.

'Are you eating breakfast?'

It was Doherty. Honey almost choked.

'No! Of course not. You know I've been on a diet. I have to look my best for the big day.' Hastily hiding the unfinished croissant beneath a sheet of A4 helped the lie roll off her tongue.

'I'm at Lower Wainscote. We have a dead body. Can you make your way out here?'

Honey frowned. It wasn't Doherty's habit to openly invite her to a murder scene; and in the very village where they were considering holding their wedding. Seeing as the vicar hadn't been on top form after receiving the bump on the head, they'd made an appointment for about two weeks hence. Now this! What a turn up!

'I don't understand. Is this something to do with our wedding? Is it the vicar? Is it Mr Clinker?' The vicar was important to their arrangements. Mr Clinker was a lout. The fact that he wore Armani did not make him a gentleman.

'No. The vicar is still alive, kicking and available to do the business. It's a Mrs Flynn. The thing is, you may be a witness. She was found sitting in the front pew of the church wearing a wedding dress.'

In her eighties and wearing a wedding dress; now where had she heard — or rather read of that before?

'Was it new, the wedding dress? Was it new or was it faded and a bit tatty around the edges.'

There was a pause at the other end.

'What's that got to do with anything?'

'Was it new?' she repeated.

'No. It looked a bit grey and old-fashioned. Does that have some significance?'

'Like something out of Dickens.'

'Who?'

'Never mind. I'll explain when I get there.'

'By the way. We've found Harold Clinker. He was hiding in the long grass in the churchyard with a hood over his head and his hands tied behind his back.'

'Hiding?'

'I should have said found, but to my mind he was hiding. His ankles weren't tied. He could have escaped at any time. But he didn't. Reckoned he didn't hear the police sirens. Figured his attacker was still hanging around.'

Honey made disagreeable sounds. 'A suitable place to be found seeing as his wife described him as a bit of a snake in the grass. Didn't hear the sirens, my foot!'

'He did have a sack over his head, but even so I'm inclined to agree with you. It's very likely he had another reason for staying put.'

'Still,' said Honey thoughtfully, 'he was tied up and might very well have been scared.'

'Plus you would think he'd want rescuing.'

Honey murmured an agreement and added, 'So who tied him up?'

'His other half. So he reckons.'

'Marietta!' Honey exclaimed, her expression one of profound disbelief. 'I don't believe it. She's an airhead, not a contender for the World Wrestling Championships! You saw her yourself.'

'I saw her.'

'Well there you are.'

'Bloody hell. Bath has a few problems, but this village takes some beating!'

'Language,' Honey whispered. 'You're on holy ground and if we do decide to marry there, we should show some respect.'

CHAPTER NINE

Honey could hardly believe what had happened. And in June. Such a beautiful June, perfect for summer brides.

As she drove through the High Street to the church, she passed one police vehicle parked outside a red-brick cottage with green-framed windows; the victim's home. Keep it sealed. Keep out the gawpers or anyone who might disturb things.

Two more police vehicles plus a white van were squashed into the parking area outside the church. There was no sign of life from Belvedere House and certainly no sign of Mr Clinker.

The usual teams had set up their tape and tents and were pulling on their crystal white onesies.

Doherty waved her in from the other side of the lychgate.

Inside the church was cool and smelled of polish and dust, but also a heavy perfume. Flowers, she thought, on seeing the breathtaking displays placed in alcoves and on wrought iron stands to either side of the altar. Another large display was positioned on a long box — a blanket box, she thought — of roughly hewn wood that looked only fit for kindling.

Mrs Flynn was propped up in the fourth row, her back against the rood screen so that only the very top of her head was showing from behind.

Honey eyed the deathly white face of Mrs Flynn whilst giving Doherty a brief resume of *Great Expectations*; woman jilted at the altar wields her revenge through her beautiful young ward on the luckless Pip.

'If that is the reference, Mrs Flynn wouldn't have been married. Miss Haversham kept the dress she was supposed to get married in. In fact, if I remember rightly, she used to wear it every day after she was jilted at the altar. Even the wedding breakfast including a wedding cake was still spread out on the table. The food was rotten and crawling and everything covered in dust and cobwebs, including Miss Haversham herself.'

'Is that so?' Doherty filled in the basic facts. 'Apparently Mrs Flynn's wedding dress was a one-off. She dressed normally enough for a woman in her eighties the rest of the time.'

'Was she married?'

'We think so. According to the villagers, she did occasionally mention her husband dying years ago so we can presume she was, though I'll get it checked out.'

'Children?'

'We're waiting on that too.' He paused, wrinkling his nose in the direction of the dress. 'Did that Miss Haversham really wear that dress day in and day out?'

'Uh, huh.' Honey nodded. Staring at the woman's dead face was bad enough but staring at the dress was something else. Miss Haversham had come back to haunt her. The book had always been a nightmare. All those English literature lessons, ploughing through a book in a dusty classroom day after day after day; a story that had started out as a joy became, with familiarity, a contemptible nightmare.

The angst she'd felt as a child threatened to overwhelm her. 'I hated *Great Expectations*.'

Doherty wasn't sure of the relevance of all this but said he would bear it in mind. He had a questionable death on his hands. The procedure he might need to follow was like the disembodied voice of a satnav. Left to this juncture, right to this one, assess and evaluate then straight on till morning. If the death did turn out to be suspicious, it would indeed be straight on till morning. The first twenty-four hours following a death were crucial. After that the trail tended to go cold. If it is a murder, he reminded himself, but hoped it was not.

Placing his hands on his knees, Doherty leaned forward for a closer look.

'The dress doesn't look as though it's been lived in. It's a bit faded, but it doesn't smell dirty.'

Honey had to agree with him that it wasn't in bad condition for its age.

'So it is old? I'm no fashion expert, but I am right in thinking this dress is out of the ark, as my old mum used to say. Am I right?'

She pushed out her bottom lip when she nodded. 'Full marks for your fashion appreciation.'

The dress had a tight bodice, lacy full-length sleeves and a straight skirt. She jettisoned the 1950's idea, placing it more accurately at the end of the sixties, possibly early seventies. The veil was short and held pertly in place by a swan feather headdress.

At one time it must have been brilliant white as befitted a virgin bride. It was now veering towards yellow, the lace limp and tired and the feathers wilting and squashed as though a broody hen had been sitting on her head and had left the feathers behind as a kind of thank you.

'So what do you think?' Doherty asked.

Honey gritted her teeth. 'I have to ask myself whether the reason she's wearing this dress is for a similar reason to Miss Haversham. Was she jilted at the altar? On the other hand was she wearing it in remembrance of her dead husband? People do odd things through grief.'

'What about the bride you reckon you saw running over the village green when we were last here?'

Honey shook her head vehemently. 'It couldn't have been her! The bride I saw was running and the dress was different . . .'

'Was it?' His expression read that he wasn't convinced. 'How do you know one dress from another at that distance?'

Honey laughed. 'Believe me! A woman knows.'

Doherty knew better than to question a woman's ability to tell one dress from another. It certainly wasn't a skill he possessed.

'OK. So I'll take it the woman you saw was not Mrs Flynn.'

'Does she have any relatives?' Honey asked.

'Not sure. As I've already said, the records are being checked.' He looked at her sidelong then shook his head. 'I can't believe it. I thought you'd be more curious.'

'About what?'

'You haven't asked how she died.'

'Do I have to guess?'

'Only if you want to.'

'Is there a prize for getting it right?'

He grinned briefly. 'I'm a generous man. You'll get a prize if you get it right and a prize if you get it wrong.'

'Don't tell me. Win or lose, I get the same prize.'

'Aren't you the lucky one!'

He ran his hand gently down her back.

'OK.' She bit her lip and did her best to concentrate. It wasn't easy. Earthquakes leave an aftershock. Doherty's touch was like that — at least for her anyway.

'Let's see.' She studied the body. Mrs Flynn's head was held to one side. She had a surprised expression on her face.

Honey chewed her bottom lip as she chewed over her thoughts and leaned forward to get a closer look.

'Don't touch,' warned Doherty.

'Don't worry. I know better than to contaminate a crime scene.'

She managed to crane her head so she could peer around the back of Mrs Flynn's head.

'That's a whopper of a bump. Still, it doesn't mean she was murdered. She could have fallen down and hit her head. Old people are always doing that.'

'So are some young people come to that,' quipped Doherty. 'Have you seen the centre of town on a Friday night? Still, I do know what you're saying. It's up to the pathologist to tell us the cause.'

'Odd though.'

'Very odd.'

'I mean, this dress.' She frowned. 'Perhaps she got married when she was middle aged.'

'The dress tells you that?'

'Oh come on! She's in her eighties. Most young women of her generation married when they were in their twenties, even in their teens. It was no big deal back then. But that dress, if it was her wedding dress, is definitely late sixties, early seventies.'

'Perhaps she just liked dressing up.'

Honey sighed. 'Perhaps she did, poor thing.'

'Makes you wonder . . .' His voice trailed off.

'About . . . ?'

'About dressing up. I mean, at the end of the day a wedding is for a day, a marriage is supposed to be longer.'

'You could be right. Perhaps she liked reliving the event. Some of my closest friends were closet serial brides. They loved the dressing up bit, but the rest of it left them cold.'

'Really?' Doherty looked surprised then one side of his mouth lifted in a smile. 'I thought that was the best bit, taking off the clothes and getting down to what it was really about.'

Honey glared at him but couldn't hold it for long.

'Depends on what you find the most fun.' She grinned.

A look passed between them that confirmed that when it came to fun, they were pretty much in agreement.

'So we need to wait for the post-mortem to be carried out before we know for sure if it was murder. However, I must admit my nose tells me it was. I don't think that bruise on the back of her neck could have been caused by a fall, and yet . . .'

'You're not Hercule Poirot. Your nose and little grey cells carry no weight in a court of law. Though I know what you mean. How could somebody have crept up behind her and whacked her on the back of the head. That screen's in the way.'

'Noted.'

'It could have been an accident, as I said.'

'It was phoned in as a murder.'

She turned to look at him. He had a strong profile, dark against the coloured glass of the arched church window.

She'd admired that profile in a similar light, outlined by the window in her bedroom.

'Why did they think that?'

He shrugged. 'We don't know. We had no chance to ask questions. Whoever it was rang off without giving a name.'

'Man or woman?'

'The operator wasn't sure. Could have been either.'

Honey sighed. 'So that's one reason for thinking it's murder, the murderer themselves phoning it in?'

'Perhaps. I think all we can do is stand back and await developments.'

'How boring.'

'Excuse me,' said a forthright voice. 'Have you finished in here?'

They turned to see a female figure standing in the arched doorway.

The vicar's dark hair was cut so that it clung around her face like tulip petals. Her deep-set eyes flickered from one to the other.

'I hate to intrude,' she continued. 'I know you have a job to do.'

'I'm sorry to upset your schedule, vicar. Rest assured we'll be as quick as we can. I'll get one of our constables to let you know when we're finished.'

'That's very kind of you, Inspector . . . ?'

'Doherty. Detective Inspector Doherty.'

'Constance. Reverend Constance Paxton. Pleased to meet you.'

'And this is Honey Driver, Hannah is her real name, but Honey suits her better. You may recall we were here last night when you took the hit over the head. We were thinking of getting married here. Do you remember that?'

'Oh, of course, of course! Sorry. I'm still a little groggy. I've been up half the night.' As if to emphasise the point, the vicar gripped the bridge of her nose and closed her eyes. 'It was quite an experience, one I have no wish to repeat. I'm just not with it yet. Not with it at all.'

'We understand. Seeing as you're here, are you up to answering some questions, or do you prefer to wait until you feel better?'

'I sense you'd prefer me to ask me questions now. I know time is of the essence, at least that's what it always says on the TV crime shows.'

Doherty thanked her. 'Can you tell me when you last saw Mrs Flynn?'

'Yes.' The vicar clasped her hands in front of her as if in prayer, her whole body jerking forward in one confirming nod. 'Last night. I left her cottage at nine to come down and meet you as arranged. She'd summoned me to hear her out on the matter of outside florists decorating the church for weddings. She was quite convinced that it should be the prerogative of our own flower arranging committee and nobody else.'

'That was all you talked about?'

'Yes. I knew even before I went what I would hear. But that was Mrs Flynn for you. "Focused", I suppose, is the most polite word, though the less charitable might have called her overbearing.'

'Did she seem agitated at all?'

'No.'

'Worried about anything?'

The vicar smiled. 'No. Unless you could call the prospect of outside florists upsetting your routine worrying!'

'How bad were her legs and her balance, do you know?'

'She had good days and bad days. It was more a cartilage problem than a joint problem. Sometimes she was quite spry.'

On hearing this, Honey's thoughts went back to the vision she'd seen running across the village green. Could it have been Mrs Flynn?

'And Mrs Flynn was quite happy when she saw you out?'

'I let myself out.'

'Did Mrs Flynn ever speak about her family?'

'Not if she could help it. In fact she used to get quite angry if her daughter was mentioned.'

'Do you know why?'

The vicar cupped her right cheek as though it were suddenly aching. 'I heard that they had a falling out. I don't know what about.'

'And her husband is dead?'

She nodded. 'Years ago. I used to think he was buried here in the churchyard of St Michael's, but if he is his grave is well hidden, though she did take me to task when I suggested the wild patch of grass over by the east wall should be cut so the headstones were more easily seen.'

'When was the last time you came into the church today?'

'About four o'clock this morning. Because of what happened, I hadn't been in here all day. I'm still feeling groggy, but thought I should make the effort.'

Doherty thanked the vicar for her help and shook her hand.

Honey did the same.

'Once things have settled down, we'll be back to carry on where we left off. We've still got it in mind to get married here.'

'Ah yes. As soon as you're ready, do give me a ring.'

'I'll get somebody to let you know as soon as we've finished,' Doherty repeated.

The vicar threw him a quick flap of her hand as a parting wave, her trim figure exiting into the vestry where her robes were kept.

Just as the men in white suits arrived to take away the body, Doherty's phone rang.

'OK,' he said, hanging up. 'Mrs Flynn does have a daughter. Her name's Alice. We're trying to locate her. Back to business. We'll go to the deceased's cottage next,' he said, taking hold of her shoulder and turning her away. 'It's within walking distance. On the way there we can stop by the village green and perhaps you can take a look and think again on who or what you saw running over the green in a wedding dress.'

Honey paused beneath the canopy of the lychgate. 'A thought's just struck me.'

'Which is?'

'The vicar never asked who had been killed and whether it was murder. Strange, don't you think?'

'I did ask her when she'd last seen Mrs Flynn. Perhaps she just wasn't that curious.'

'Possibly. Odd though.'

CHAPTER TEN

On the way to inspect the interior of Mrs Flynn's cottage, they paused to take a look at the village green.

'Right. Let me think. I'll do the camera shutter thing.'

Honey shut her eyelids then opened them swiftly. The aim being for her brain to tie up a snapshot of the scene with her memories of the night before.

Nothing happened. Memory, she decided, was unreliable. There was nothing except the vision of someone wearing a wedding dress sprinting through the village.

The snapshot hadn't worked. She had to admit defeat.

'She was running across the grass late at night in a wedding dress. That's it.' She shrugged. 'Just running. Not like an old lady with dodgy knees would run. She was running fast like somebody younger. Just . . . running . . .'

She felt the intensity of Doherty's gaze, the penetrating eyes looking down at her as though she had indeed said something very important. He had that cool, authoritative look about him. God, he looked so hot when he did that.

'In what direction?'

She waved her hand. 'She was running in the direction of the church.'

'Who was she running from?'

She shrugged. 'I don't know. I didn't see anyone. Perhaps she was running towards someone?'

'Come on, Honey. That's hardly very likely. She was running towards the church.'

'Perhaps Mrs Flynn's legs weren't as bad as she made out.'

'Possibly. Or perhaps in a past life she'd been an Olympic athlete.'

'That's down to you searching the records.'

'It is, but my instinct . . .'

'The Hercule moment . . .'

'. . . tells me she is not and never has been an Olympic athlete. Anyway, we've already heard from those that knew her best that she did have dicky knees and was in fact waiting for a replacement knee operation — both knees if my memory serves me right.'

'OK. So she was more likely being chased than chasing.'

'You spotted her before I did.'

'She was hard to miss, running in a long white dress on a dark night.'

'And you didn't see anyone chasing her?'

No matter how intensely he looked at her, it didn't stir her own grey matter. A few other things responded, but personal feelings and libido had nothing to do with the mystery and had to be saved until they were alone together.

Try as she might, all she could recall was the white dress running and a backdrop of lights shining from cottage windows and various trees waving like a line of can-can skirts behind the running figure.

'I wasn't concentrating,' she said with a sigh. 'I was thinking of Marietta and that creep she married.'

Doherty shoved his hands deep into his pockets, obviously disappointed.

'Oh well. Onwards to Rockery Cottage. Let's see what we can learn from the old girl's homestead.'

Mrs Flynn's home lived up to its name. There was no front lawn, just rock plants with mean leaves growing amongst scattered stones of odd shapes and sizes.

Both the cottage and the garden had a neglected and old-fashioned feel, plants tangled together and the smell of lavender and dusty green leaves scented the air.

If the outside is like this, Honey thought, the inside is likely to be much the same.

Her suspicions were confirmed as she followed Doherty into a square room of china dogs, a pattern of brown leaves on pale beige wallpaper and a tiled fireplace which had probably been the pride of the Ideal Home Exhibition at the same time as Bill Haley and the Comets were Rocking Around the Clock.

A glossy radiogram — circa 1960 — sat on splayed black metal legs beneath a three-tier shelving system. The shelves were crammed with long playing albums, not a CD or iPod in sight. There was everything from Jim Reeves to fifties' crooners like Johnnie Rae, Harry Belafonte and Frank Sinatra.

Honey ran her fingers over the nearest row. These singers had been hot stuff when Mrs Flynn was young. Jim Reeves was the most modern album there and she knew it had been recorded some time before the advent of the wedding dress Mrs Flynn had been wearing.

Her thoughts kept going back to that dress. It definitely wasn't a fifties model, unless Mrs Flynn had planned to marry or had indeed married later than most women of her generation.

The chirping of Doherty's mobile phone disturbed her thoughts.

'You're a doll.' He disconnected. Honey wondered who the 'doll' was.

'You remember I said there was a daughter, Alice,' he said, 'perhaps her reason for calling herself "Mrs" rather than "Miss", but she dropped off the scene some time ago. There was some speculation the daughter got married, but nobody seems to know who to and where the wedding took place. There's also no word on how Mrs Flynn felt about it.'

'Oh, I expect there is,' said Honey. 'She might have confided in somebody. Another woman most likely. Women quite usually confide secrets to other women. I wonder if she belonged to the WI? I bet she did.'

They fell to silence as they thought through which woman she was most likely to confide in. They both reached the same conclusion.

* * *

The vicar was adamant. 'I can't believe you think that I was the most likely person Mrs Flynn would confide in.'

'Nobody else seemed to like her very much.'

'Neither did I — though a woman of my calling shouldn't really say that of course.'

'Is there a WI in the village?'

'There used to be, but what with the influx of people commuting to Bath and London, it faded away.'

'How sad,' remarked Honey.

The vicar shrugged sadly. 'Sign of the times.'

'How long has this been the vicarage?' Honey asked her.

'Quite a while now. It's serviceable and cheap to run, but certainly not palatial. The old vicarage had five bedrooms, attic rooms and even a nursery. Neither myself nor the vicar before me had need of such a large establishment hence the box we're in now. More tea?'

The vicar posed with the teapot at the ready. Honey and Doherty declined, though neither could resist helping themselves to a third macaroon whilst the vicar — call me Constance — regaled them with the history of the vicarage. The old vicarage was a Gothic affair dating from the nineteenth century, its twisted chimneys and timbered upper storey meant to mimic those of Tudor times. The solid grey stonework was a testament to the more robust Victorian age.

The box, as Constance Paxton referred to it, was a modern detached house dating from the eighties. Its expanse of sloping roof vaguely resembled a Swiss chalet and the garden surrounding it was of normal size.

'Up until it was closed down, the school used to hold their sports day in the garden,' the vicar said wistfully. 'Shame really, but there, that's progress as people never tire of reminding me.'

It was obvious that Constance would prefer to live in Gothic splendour, thought Honey as she returned her plate to the coffee table. Like the rest of the furniture, the coffee table was of period style, more suited to an old cottage than a modern house.

As Honey let her gaze wander around the room, Doherty finished asking the vicar general questions about how she was feeling and about Mr Clinker. She told him everything about the dispute regarding the land.

'He's such an obnoxious man,' she said in conclusion.

'What was your opinion of Mrs Flynn?' he asked.

The vicar's teacup clattered as she put it back in its saucer and she a deep breath as though trying to contain her frustration. 'She was hardly the easiest of my parishioners, especially where church flower arrangements were concerned.

'To hear her,' she continued, 'you would almost think she was in sole charge of the church, especially when it came to decorating the church for weddings. Some couples prefer to use an outside contractor and have the floral decorations matching the bride's bouquet or the bridesmaids' dresses. Quite understandable of course, though Mrs Flynn didn't see it that way.'

'How long had she been in the village?' Doherty asked.

'Not as long as she would have had everyone believe,' the vicar replied. A half smile curved her lips, the kind people adopt when they know a secret. 'She was born here but left when she was about ten. Her mother died and she was brought up by an aunt in the Forest of Dean. She only came back here about fifteen years ago, though to hear her talk she's been here forever. Her mother's buried in the churchyard.'

'And the daughter?'

'I know very little about her, though get the impression she was either put up for adoption or they were estranged. Either way she almost denied her existence. Sad really.

Disowning your own flesh and blood. I personally couldn't do it. But there, back then unmarried mothers were looked down on.'

'So she told everyone she was widowed before she actually came to the village — or came back,' said Doherty.

'Correct. There were rumours that she had never married despite the ring on her finger; after all, anyone can wear a gold band.'

Doherty rested his elbows on his knees and clasped his hands together. He threw the vicar one of his searching, desperately-need-to-know looks.

'Vicar . . .'

'Constance. Call me Constance.'

'Constance,' he said, smiling warmly as though everything in the world was lovely.

Honey felt her stomach muscles tighten. She knew that look for what it was.

'I'm intrigued. You never asked me how Mrs Flynn had died. In fact you never even asked me who had died. Can you explain that?'

Up until now the vicar's expression was best described as open, but suddenly everything changed. Her eyelids flickered and a pink flush came to her cheeks.

'I . . . I . . . haven't exactly . . .' She made a big effort to stop stammering, sucking in her breath before beginning again. 'The truth of the matter is, I was scared. I saw her there, you see. She was sitting in the front pew in the dark. It gave me quite a start when I did see her. I thought whoever had attacked me had attacked her too and killed her. That's what I thought. Her neck was floppy. I took a quick look.'

'So it was you who phoned it in as a murder?'

'Yes. I had my phone with me. I did it quickly and rushed out. You see I really believed whoever it was had come for me but got her instead. They'd lured me there, saying there was something going on in the churchyard. It was dark. I didn't see anyone outside and although I had a torch, I didn't relish the thought of walking around in the dark. It's what I'm supposed to do, keep an eye on things. I did phone Mr Jenkins, one of our deacons, to accompany me. He said he would be right there, but he is getting on a bit. I knew it would take him some time.'

'Did Mr Jenkins see Mrs Flynn?'

The vicar shrugged. 'I don't know. I don't think so. You see, he didn't get to the church. He tripped on a paving slab on his way down the garden path of his cottage. Shook himself up a bit. His wife came out and got him indoors, then she phoned me to tell me what had happened. I was back here by then.'

The vicar sucked in her lips and looked down at the floor, her fingers constantly moving backwards and forward on the chair arms.

'You should have told us earlier.'

She nodded. 'Of course I should. It was just . . . well . . . after last night . . . my nerves and my thinking aren't quite sorted out.'

Doherty got to his feet. Time to go.

'All the same. It would have been useful if you'd said something sooner,' said Doherty.

'Of course.' The bowed head. 'I'm sorry.'

'Thanks for the tea. The macaroons were lovely. Sorry I scoffed so many,' said Honey. 'They're my favourite.'

They weren't actually her number one favourite, mainly because she had a lot of favourites, but it didn't hurt to soothe the vicar's embarrassment.

'So! Where to now?' she asked, once they were walking back to Doherty's low-slung sports car.

'I'm off to check on cause of death. The paperwork should be on my desk by now. I'll drop you off at your place en route. OK?'

'OK. And then what?'

'I'll pick you up tomorrow at around four and we'll have a word with Clinker.'

'I can continue to be your sidekick? Even though I'm not a police officer?'

'You're a friend of his wife. You know her. Let's see what you make of him.'

His plan made sense. There was no confirmation for sure whether Mrs Flynn's death was natural or homicide. For the moment she was on the back burner. It was Harold Clinker who was up for a roasting.

CHAPTER ELEVEN

The atmosphere at the Green River Hotel was uncommonly calm. The moment Honey pushed through the doors separating reception from the foyer she couldn't help feeling that something was amiss. There was such a thing as being too quiet. She put it down to missing Doherty and being challenged by the outstanding questions on the current case.

She knew how the place usually felt when she arrived; firstly she felt a sense of pride. She'd bought and built this place up herself. Secondly, she enjoyed the people she employed there, she had friends who were characters, and characters were rife in her family.

Lindsey was sitting behind reception, her back to her mother and seemingly absorbed in whatever she was studying on the computer screen.

'Anyone at home?'

Lindsey bolted upright at the sound of her mother's voice. Honey couldn't be certain, but she was sure the computer screen had done something resembling a backwards somersault. Wherever Lindsey had been on the internet, she wasn't there now. The current job was revitalising the website and Lindsey was onto it.

GROOVE AT THE GREEN RIVER HOTEL, RIGHT
IN THE CENTRE OF BATH.

Groove wasn't the exact word Honey would have used,
but Lindsey was experimenting with a new home page and
her mother certainly knew how difficult that could be. The
right words had to be used.

'Not groove,' she said biting her bottom lip and relaying
her disquiet as best she could without upsetting her daughter.
'I don't think we groove here, do we? I think we are more . . .
sedate . . .'

'Old-fashioned.'

'Are we?'

It hurt being told the hotel was old-fashioned. She didn't
find it so . . . but was that the problem? She didn't find it
dated and old-fashioned because it suited her, in other words
she was just as old-fashioned as the hotel itself.

'We don't appeal to young couples coming down here
for a weekend of getting lathered and laid.'

'They're just having fun,' Lindsey replied.

'I don't want to appeal to youngsters coming here for that.'

'Of course you don't.' Lindsey gave her a very direct
look. 'You have to be in tune with whatever generation fre-
quents your establishment, and so does the building, right
down to what's on the walls and the availability of a wide
selection of sex and snogging channels.'

'Do you think so?' Honey raised her eyebrows.

'I do.'

'Do these channels instruct people how to do sex and
snogging?'

Lindsey lifted one side of her mouth in something that
could have been a smile or a grimace.

'You could say that.'

Honey took a nanosecond to think about it then shook
her head.

'I don't think I want that. My other guests wouldn't like
that. I mean, think of what Mary Jane would say . . .'

On cue, a door marked private opened, and there was Mary Jane, thin as a reed and as tall as the Eiffel Tower.

'So there you are! I've been waiting on you out back . . .'

Honey decided it wouldn't do any good to castigate Mary Jane for using the staff entrance at the rear of the building and the door marked private. She would take no notice anyway. After all, Mary Jane was part of the furniture, like a pot plant that you get used to having around and sometimes forget to water.

Professor of the paranormal and hailing from San Diego, California, Mary Jane was a long-time resident of the Green River Hotel, drove erratically around the city in a pink Cadillac coupé, was just a little over six feet tall and had been in her seventies for some time now.

She also had chilling blue eyes that sometimes seemed to look deep into your soul and other times seemed to be looking beyond you and the real world to something only the likes of her could comprehend.

Mary Jane adored colours; if it wasn't bright, she didn't wear it. Today her choice of outfit was a suede purple jacket with a zip fastener and epaulettes on the shoulders. The winged collar of a yellow shirt poked out at the neckline and a flirt of hemline — it was no more than two inches, thus only flirting to be seen.

Her jeans were navy with sequins down the sides and her shoes were red and matched her handbag. The red clashed vividly with the other colours, but that to Mary Jane was the whole point of colour; if it didn't clash, it didn't work.

Honey smiled and after complimenting her on her outfit, said, 'So, you've been waiting out back.'

'Sure I have. You said to bring my car round and wait out back in the lot, then you'd go with me to your car and you would follow me to Ahmed's place.'

'Oh, yes! Yes! Of course,' Honey exclaimed as she finally got her bearings. 'Your car is booked in for a service and I promised to follow you whilst you dropped off the car and then I'd bring you back.'

'That's it, Honey. Are you fit?'

Honey did a pretty good impression of somebody who is absolutely on the ball, knows where she is and where she's going.

The truth was that she'd completely forgotten her promise.

Lindsey gave her mother a casual wave and went back to whatever internet site she was cruising. Honey heaved a big sigh, made sure every department, including the kitchen, was working smoothly, and followed Mary Jane back through the door marked private to the parking lot.

Being a city built for the ease of access of a sedan chair, Bath had traffic problems. It didn't easily cope with buses, heavy transport or too many cars. The problem of heavy transport had only partly been addressed by the new bypass. Unfortunately it truncated on the east side of the city thanks to protests by interested — and wealthy — parties. Trucks still had to squeeze their way along the outer road. Cars were a different matter. Too many still wove their way through the centre, swarming like bees in front of traffic lights that never seemed to show anything but the red stop light. Blink and the green light had come and gone.

Today the traffic had swarmed big time for which Honey was extremely grateful. It meant Mary Jane had to keep her speed down which in turn meant she had to follow the car in front, which in turn meant she would keep to the right side of the road.

Honey relaxed once she'd got her own car and was following at a safe distance behind Mary Jane. It was two o'clock in the afternoon.

Ahmed Clifford came out of the single storey lock-up where he did his business, wiping his hands in an oily cloth. A green Beetle lurched slightly as Mary Jane pulled in behind it. Mary Jane's fender had kissed that of the Beetle's.

Ahmed winced at first, then breathed a sigh of relief once he'd checked that no damage had been done.

'Hi,' said Honey and waved as she got out of her car.

Ahmed waved back and although he smiled, it was closed mouth, no half laugh and flashing of ultra-white teeth. He certainly didn't seem his normal self but had a haunted look.

Mary Jane was in the process of handing Ahmed the keys when she paused and looked him straight in the face.

'Hey, Ahmed. Your spirits are not singing and dancing. I see them sat in a circle wailing and gnashing their teeth.'

Mary Jane, it had to be said, had a direct line to the spirit world, or, to put it another way in Mary Jane-speak, Ahmed was a bit pissed off.

He attempted his usual smile but it solidified on his face as though his lips refused to stretch any further.

'The perils of life,' he responded. 'And luck. If the luck is not with you . . .' He shrugged. 'The luck has run away.'

'Not another marriage?' Honey asked. Ahmed's mother was very keen on arranging a marriage for her favourite son. Ahmed was not keen on the idea at all, but he did like meeting all the potential brides. He had gone along with her plans for some time now, striking up relationships with the girls, but failing to go the full distance. He fully admitted that sex had a lot to do with it. Some of the girls had gone home carrying more than a suitcase.

'Some were dogs, and some were delicious,' he'd told Honey, his eyes shining. But on this occasion it wasn't that.

He shook his head. 'No. I told her straight that I wasn't ready to marry, and, when I was, I would do the choosing. After all, it's me that's got to live with the result, not her. Anyway,' he added his expression still pensive. 'I wanted a word with you, Mrs Driver. If you don't mind. It's about my car. My wedding car. It's been stolen.'

'A wedding car?'

He nodded. 'A white Rolls Royce. I bought it from a bloke in Keynsham two years ago and set myself up for weddings. It's been going pretty well.'

His face brightened at the memory before falling flat again.

Honey expressed some surprise. She hadn't realised he'd gone into the wedding car business.

'You should have told me. We could have done a wedding package, you know, car, wedding breakfast, luxury room at the Green River Hotel with champagne and four poster bed . . .'

'We could,' he said, his face brightening for a moment. 'But not now. Bloody shame it is. Bloody shame. I've had to cancel bookings.' He shook his head.

'You've reported it stolen?'

He nodded. 'Yeah. But you know how it is. It's just a car. How many cars go missing in this country every day?'

'Not many wedding cars, though, surely,' said Mary Jane who was all ears to what he was saying.

He shrugged. 'I suppose not.' He turned to Honey. 'That's what I wanted to talk to you about. Do you think you could try and find it?'

The thought of adding the finding of a white Rolls Royce to her already busy schedule, was daunting and quite frankly, she wasn't hopeful about the results. However, Ahmed was a sweetie; he was also lovely to look at, an ideal dashing driver behind the wheel of a Rolls Royce.

'Is it vintage?'

'From the sixties, so vintage enough.'

Against her better judgement, she found herself agreeing to do what she could even though she hadn't a clue where to start or a slot in her busy schedule to fit the task in.

'I'll do my best. When did you last see it?'

'Last Saturday. I'd just done a wedding over in Larkhall and was washing the car down before putting it away. I keep it in a lock-up in Keynsham. Unfortunately when I came to opening the garage to lock it up for the night, I found I'd left the key . . . at home . . .'

'With a girlfriend?'

He grinned and Honey saw a flush erupt on his cheeks. 'Yeah. She's got a flat in Walcot Street.'

'Ah yes,' said Mary Jane, her eyes half closed like they sometimes did when she was going into a trance. 'She's blonde, with pert boobs and wears a skirt that barely covers her backside.'

He looked at her in amazement. 'Wow! I know you're into the supernatural and all that, but you're good. Really good. Can you see her now?'

Mary Jane's eyes flicked open. 'No. But I saw the two of you coming out of McDonalds the other day. You were hand in hand.'

'Oh!' Ahmed looked disappointed.

Honey continued. 'So, this car. It went missing overnight. You went back the following day with the keys and it was gone.'

Ahmed nodded. 'That's correct.'

'No immobiliser fitted?'

'It was old.'

Mary Jane added advice. 'No tracking device? You know, I hear they're real good. You get it fitted then follow it on your computer with some programme you buy online.'

Honey looked at her open-mouthed. 'I'm impressed, Mary Jane. I didn't know you knew about stuff like that.'

'I don't. Lindsey told me. She's kind of offloading technical stuff and jargon; reckons that she's entering a more spiritual period of her life.'

Honey was even more surprised. To her own shame, she couldn't say she'd noticed, and Lindsey hadn't confided as such to her.

'She didn't tell me that, and I'm her mother.'

Mary Jane pulled a so-so face. 'You know how it is. Sometimes mothers butt in where they aren't wanted.'

Honey thought of her own mother. Yes. That was exactly what she did, interfered when her input was not required.

She pulled her attention back from her daughter's new path in life to Ahmed and his missing car. There followed a serious nodding procedure, the kind that's meant to reassure. 'It has to be joy riders. That's my opinion.'

Mary Jane nodded in agreement. 'Young kids. Out to drive fast and furious.'

Ahmed didn't look convinced. 'It's a Rolls Royce. It isn't meant to be raced. It's a sedate ride for sedate people.'

'Sure,' said Mary Jane, her nodding echoing that of Honey's, though with a longer neck and thus a deeper up and down motion. 'But some of the kids round here have got aspirations, you know. They're from pretty well-heeled families and know quality when they see it.'

It was obvious from Ahmed's expression that he wasn't convinced. It was possible he was considering how the car might end up when the kids were finished with it; wrapped around a lamppost or burned out in a final act of luxurious vandalism.

'Look,' said Honey, making the effort to sound as positive as possible. 'You're right, Ahmed. A Rolls Royce isn't the sort of ride a kid would normally go for. Some vintage cars are collectors' items. Could be we can trace it through known dealers and known collectors. At least they value this type of car. I'll see what I can find out. OK?'

He nodded hesitantly.

'You give me a call when my car's ready,' said Mary Jane, laying an affectionate pat on his shoulder. 'You shouldn't find much wrong with it.'

'Brake pads. Linings. Clutch,' proclaimed Ahmed. 'Gearbox might need checking too.'

Honey hid the grin that crunched her lips. Mary Jane's driving was famous. Ahmed knew exactly what he had to deal with.

CHAPTER TWELVE

Harold Clinker was being patched up in a cubicle at the Accident and Emergency unit at Bath's Royal United Hospital.

Like most modern hospitals, the RUH, as it was more commonly called, sprawled over a large area on the eastern side of the city behind towering Edwardian villas and the upper road into Bristol.

The unit was of a decent size though smaller than might be found in the Royal Infirmary in nearby Bristol, but then Bristol was a bigger city and the infirmary was crammed into the heart of it. The RUH had a better location, set in a quiet suburban environment, its modern additions softened by mature beech, fir and elm trees.

Harold Clinker had a bluff face and small eyes which gave him the look of someone peering out from within a deep pudding basin.

Honey wondered what had possessed Marietta to go out with him let alone marry him. On reflection her old acquaintance had entertained more than a passing interest in fast cars, magnums of Bollinger and anything that was nine carat and sparkled. Harold Clinker was staunchly stout but wore Gucci and Armani so he'd probably suited her very well.

He didn't look particularly injured unless you counted his pride. His clothes were dishevelled and sported muddy smears; his face shone with sweat and his hair — ginger and gradually waving goodbye — stood up in small angry tufts.

Doherty stood at the end of his bed looking down at him. Honey stood slightly apart and told herself she was here for Marietta's sake.

Doherty began the questioning. 'Mr Clinker. Would you like to tell me what happened.'

'Are you in charge?' Clinker snapped. He fixed his beady eyes on Doherty as he might a weevil.

Used to pompous façades, Doherty was unfazed.

'I'm Detective Inspector Doherty. Would you like to tell me what happened?' he repeated.

Clinker looked him up and down.

'Detective Inspector. Are you as high as it goes?'

'In the circumstances, seeing as the Chief Inspector is currently sprawled on a beach with his wife on holiday in Tenerife, then yes, I'm it.'

Clinker grunted his acceptance of the situation. 'I was getting out of my car . . .'

'What time was this?'

'About ten o'clock at night.'

'Where had you been?'

'Just driving around. Me and the wife had a bit of a domestic . . . I thought I'd drive around until both of us had cooled down.'

'So you drove around and came back around ten o'clock. We noticed your car was parked in the lane behind the church. Was there any particular reason for it not being parked in your own drive?'

'I'd forgotten the security number for the gate. I change it every day on the unit inside the house. Both me and Marietta are informed of the new number by text. I did it at six last night, then what with the row I left my phone behind and couldn't remember for the life of me what number I'd programmed in.'

'Would you like to explain to me what the row was about?'

'No. I would not.'

Mr Clinker drew in his chin indignantly, glaring at Doherty who glared straight back until Mr Clinker's deep-set eyes flickered and his rigid chin receded into floppy jowls.

Honey thought of Marietta's injured face. Sauce for the goose is sauce for the gander; nobody could blame his wife if indeed she had punished him for what he'd done.

'OK. If you're not willing to give your side of the story, we'll have to accept your wife's version. She reported that you assaulted her after she caught you in bed with another woman and intends to press charges. Would you like to comment on that?'

Harold did a fair imitation of the Big Bad Wolf, huffing and puffing, though he wasn't about to blow anybody's house down. Out came the excuses.

'It was her own fault. Just a little misunderstanding.'

'Apparently regarding Miss Sherise and the conjugal bed. Your wife explained the agreement. None of my business, Mr Clinker, that you broke rules agreed between you and your wife but causing her bodily harm *is* our business. You committed a crime.'

'Well she's had her revenge hasn't she! Ripped some of my best clothes to shreds, and as for my nerves . . .' He held up one shaking hand. 'Look. It was frightening I tell you, damned frightening! If she doesn't press charges against me, then I won't press charges against her. There! Stuff that up your bloody pipe and smoke it!'

Up until now, Honey had kept her mouth shut after all she was Doherty's fiancée, not his work colleague — except in her capacity of Liaison Officer between the police and the Hotels Association — but this was not on.

'What makes you so sure it was her who tied you up and left you there?' she asked. 'She was in no fit state to attack anyone when we saw her.'

'I smelled her perfume. She came up behind me and hit me over the head. When I came round I was so disorientated what with that sack over my head. It took me a while before I realised my hands were tied.'

Narrowing her eyes helped Honey visualise how Marietta had looked when she'd last seen her. Devil dragged as her mother would say. Bruised, battered and more than a little bit shocked. No, she thought. I don't believe it. Judging by the look on his face neither did Doherty.

On the way out Doherty received a call that Marietta had withdrawn all charges.

Honey was livid. 'I wouldn't!'

'That depends.'

'On what?'

'Whether you'd already taken your revenge.'

She saw his lips twitch as though about to smile before being brought back under control. Something was going on here.

'OK. What am I missing? What is it you're not telling me?'

'Did you notice the clothes Mr Clinker was wearing?'

'They were good quality.'

'And?'

'They were dirty.'

'Right. That's because they were covered in dirt. They'd been scattered around all over the place.'

Honey stopped in her tracks. 'You're joking!'

'No. Mr Harold Clinker was left with a bag over his head, his hands tied behind his back.'

'Yes, I know all that,' said Honey, impatience rising.

'And,' Doherty carried on with a flourish, 'completely naked.'

Honey punched the air. 'Whoa! Atta girl, Marietta.'

There was a clunk of a well-oiled lock disengaging as Doherty opened the car door. He eyed her with amused apprehension before letting her in.

'Am I safe with you?'

She grinned. 'How safe do you want to be?'

'Leave out the bondage and being left naked in a churchyard.'

On the way back to the hotel, Honey told Doherty about the drugged punch, the frog and the worm.

'I'm hoping it's all over and that it was just a run of bad luck, but it could be that somebody is trying to ruin me. I keep asking myself why, but can't think of anyone or anything in particular.' She shrugged. 'If it is some kind of vendetta, then I wish they'd show their face, though quite frankly I didn't realise there was anyone who hated me that much.'

Doherty fell to silence as though concentrating on steering the car back into the traffic on the main A4 was more difficult than it usually was. He asked himself if he should now tell Honey about the first threatening letter. That morning he'd received a second saying much the same as the first. He'd promised himself that he would only tell her if he received a third. Just a prankster, he thought, someone he'd arrested who'd served his time and still bore a grudge.

Not today, he decided. I won't tell her today. For that reason he was glad to be busy, not stopping for coffee but promising to meet up with her that night as planned.

* * *

The Zodiac was buzzing. There was the usual smell of grilled steak and garlic prawns, the clink of glasses, tinkling laughter and rowdy rugby players telling jokes.

Doherty came in half an hour later than he said he would, but that was par for the course. He didn't look set for a night on the tiles; on the contrary he was wearing his serious look and she knew only too well what that would mean.

His Jack Daniels' double was waiting for him alongside the vodka she'd ordered for herself. He had soda water, she went for slimline tonic.

His expression was easy to read. 'She was murdered?' she asked.

He nodded whilst slugging back half the contents of his glass.

'Let me guess. It wasn't the blow on the back of the neck that killed her.'

He rubbed his thumb and index finger over a wrinkled brow.

'What brought you to that conclusion?'

'The rood screen was in the way, unless . . .'

She saw the amusement in his eyes and knew she was wrong.

'Go on. Tell me.'

'There's new blood in the pathology department, a keen young man named David Chan. He did a few tests and found a large amount of insulin in the body of the deceased. There were no needle marks, and no history of diabetes or any diseases linked to insulin. But he did have a theory. He knew that if insulin is injected under the tongue it's practically untraceable; the perfect crime if you like. But you only need to inject a little to get the desired result. Whoever did this injected too much and made it traceable. Even so at her age the death could easily have been put down to diabetes if it hadn't been for our very keen-eyed Mr Chan.'

Honey frowned. 'But why hit her on the head then follow it up with an injection of insulin?'

Doherty downed the last of his Jack Daniels. 'It didn't happen that way. It was the other way round.'

'She was already dead when she was bashed over the head?'

He nodded. 'Seems there were two people who wanted her dead, one who administered an injection and one who hit her with something hard. I'm presuming the actual murderer who administered the injection was also the one who left her sitting in that pew. Number two assailant must have jumped at the chance.'

'So Mrs Flynn had more than one enemy.'

'She did indeed. The person who administered that injection wanted it to look as natural a death as possible. I'm still working on the wedding dress bit. Still can't work that one out. I thought I'd leave it to you.'

'I can't stop thinking about the comparison with Miss Haversham jilted at the altar and wearing the wedding dress for the rest of her life.'

'You read too many books.'

'But why was she wearing that dress?' She thought about it. 'Unless . . . she didn't put the dress on. Perhaps the murderer dressed her in it.'

'Why?'

She shrugged. 'Not a clue.'

'So there she was wearing her wedding dress, flopped over the pew in front as if in prayer . . . in which case it would have been easy to bash her on the back of the head.'

Doherty was frowning. Without uttering another word he got out his phone and rang the Reverend Constance Paxton.

'Sorry to disturb you, Reverend Paxton, but could you tell me if the church is locked at night?'

Honey saw him nod.

'I see. It's always locked.'

He finished the call.

'It was locked.'

Honey shook her head. 'I don't think it was. It can't have been. That was the night the vicar was attacked. Someone must have been in there already and perhaps that someone has a key.'

Doherty agreed that she was right and ordered some more drinks.

She took a sip of hers and pulled a face. 'Gin. I don't drink gin.'

'Shit.'

'Don't worry. I'll swallow it this time.'

She smiled as she said it, thinking to herself that he wasn't usually so distracted. There was something about the way he avoided looking at her that was worrying. Tired out, she decided. Look at his eyes. Eyelids made of lead; dark grey crescents that weren't there yesterday.

'You need some TLC,' she said to him.

'I need something, that's for sure,' he muttered.

'Poor darling Doherty,' she crooned, using his surname whilst her nimble fingers massaged the tightness in the nape of his neck. 'Time for bed?'

He stretched his neck in response to the steadfast press of her fingers.

She was no masseuse, but even she knew that a neck massage helped relieve tension. It reached other parts too. She was counting on it.

He closed his eyes and heaved a heartfelt sigh as though submitting to whatever she wanted him to do. 'Yes,' he said. 'Let's do that.'

* * *

The lights of the city and a crescent moon were reflected on the river below Pulteney Bridge. The hooded figure, elbows resting on the sandstone parapet, face cradled in firm, square hands, watched the water tear the lights into segments. The life of that person wearing the hoodie was like that; torn into parts. She was supposed to be in Scotland, but didn't really feel at home anywhere.

She blamed her parents. It was them splitting up that had spoilt her life. Nothing to do with her. Childish as it might seem, she'd always hoped her parents would get back together even after they'd divorced, and now her father was getting married again. She'd been flabbergasted when her mother had told her. Her mother had been accepting but she had shot out the door and contrived to do something about it, as little as that might be. Honey Driver! Stupid name. Stupid woman – though of course she'd never met her. Things could have been perfect if it wasn't for that bloody woman. For goodness' sake, didn't the woman know she was too old to be a bride? Did she have no shame? Marrying a man at her age! Disgusting. But there, it would only be disgusting if the marriage actually happened. Maybe, if events continued as they were, the marriage would not happen.

CHAPTER THIRTEEN

Daylight filtered into Doherty's bedroom before six in the morning, partly due to the time of year and partly because Camden Crescent was perched high above the city. The first thing you saw from the window was sky, unimpeded by buildings which fell away from Lansdown Hill into the valley below.

Honey stretched and yawned. Even before opening her eyes, she sensed something had changed in the bed's general dimensions and knew Doherty was up and about.

Lazily she ran her hand over the warm dip where Doherty had been sleeping wanting to know she was truly alone before opening her eyes.

Accepting the inevitable fact that morning had broken, she checked her watch. Yep! Definitely six in the morning. She rolled into the spot Doherty had recently vacated. A few more minutes wouldn't hurt. Closing her eyes she breathed in the fragile scent he'd left behind on the sheet and pillow. The moment wouldn't last for long.

'Omelette or porridge?'

Her eyes flicked open. 'Porridge,' she said, raising her head. 'Unless you fancy something different.'

She twisted around so she was looking at him over her bare shoulder. It was a blatant invitation back to bed, though even as she did it, she knew there wasn't much chance of it happening. His movements were purposeful, his eyes seeing her but darker than usual as though he were using some kind of optical force field to keep temptation at bay.

'With sultanas and honey,' she shouted after him.

He'd already swung out of the doorway, but she did hear a muffled, 'Yep. Got that,' as he made his way to the kitchen.

She heard the 'ping' of the microwave halfway through dressing. By the time she got downstairs a bowl of hot porridge, brimming with extras including the sultanas and honey, was breathing steam on the table.

Doherty was shrugging himself into a black T-shirt at the same time as chewing toast and drinking coffee. It should have been quite a juggling feat, but he made it look easy.

'I'll drop you off first.'

'I don't mind walking.'

'You hate exercise.'

He was right. '*Gym-type* exercise. Or serious jogging on the balls of my feet. My balls are not made for jogging.'

'Neither are mine.' He grinned.

'But I like walking,' she responded keeping a straight face despite the implicit sexual innuendo.

'So you want to walk?'

'I'll take a lift.'

She watched as he put the dishes into the washer and got his stuff together. Last night had been great, but she still had the impression he was holding back on something.

'You haven't changed your mind, have you?' she asked. She said it nonchalantly at the same time as retrieving her bag and jacket from the back of the kitchen chair. The chair was of dark wood. So were the kitchen cupboards. The kitchen needed a makeover but it would keep, at least until they got married.

'About?'

'Getting married, and . . .'

'And?'

'Selling this place.'

'No. How about you?'

'It's not the right time for putting the hotel on the market. Next spring would show it off in a better light. I need to fulfil the summer bookings; a hotel looks dreary in winter so I might not get the price I would like. That's if I decide to sell it.'

'It's your decision.'

'It would give us an ongoing income in case you decided to take early retirement.'

'Like I said, it's your decision. I'm easy, though having more than one option makes sense.'

She prattled on as though she hadn't noticed something was off, though not the wedding by the sound of it.

'You're not having second thoughts about moving into the coach house in the short term, are you?'

The idea was they live in the coach house until they could buy a small house or apartment that was theirs and theirs alone. The coach house wasn't ideal, as Lindsey lived there too. It was OK for two, but three would be a little less private. Honey had offered to sell the hotel if they got married, but Doherty knew it would be something of a wrench. There were stumbling blocks. One of them was Mary Jane, for one. Honey felt protective about the weird woman with the piercing eyes and a belief that she shared her room with a long dead ancestor. She'd got used to her; it was like having an aged and slightly dotty aunt living in the attic — although Mary Jane didn't live in an attic of course. She had a very nice en suite room at the front of the hotel overlooking the street. Not only did she believe in sharing with the long dead ancestor, she also proclaimed that the old man lighting the gas lights outside at dusk, always gave her a little wave before melting away. The old gas mantles had been replaced back in the fifties by electric lights, but Honey knew where Mary Jane was coming from; she saw things other folk just didn't see.

'What will happen to Mary Jane if you sell the hotel?'

It was as if he'd been reading her thoughts.

'It does worry me.'

He wrapped his arms around her, hugged her close and kissed her on the head.

'Then don't do it. Commute. That shouldn't be too hard, should it? And just for the record, I'm too young to retire yet. OK?'

She had to admit it wouldn't be difficult to commute, not if they bought a flat within walking distance of the hotel.

'On the plus side,' said Doherty as they vacated his front door and headed to where he'd parked his car, 'if Mary Jane wasn't around, you wouldn't have to endure the white-knuckle rides in a pink car. Pink! Of all the colours.'

Talk of cars brought Ahmed Clifford to mind. 'That reminds me. Ahmed has mislaid a white Rolls Royce.'

Doherty looked at her wishing they could have stayed tucked up in bed. He just wasn't focused on the game this morning. Warm bed and her warm body were still in his mind. Even the early morning phone call hadn't quite got him up and running. A meeting. He'd been called early to tell him there was going to be a meeting.

He didn't like meetings. He didn't much like staying put in the station at all unless there was a bona fide reason for doing so — like putting together all the pieces in a murder case; like a jigsaw.

Mention of the Rolls Royce jerked him back to the here and now and the job in hand.

'What the devil is Ahmed doing with a white Rolls Royce?'

'It's a new venture he's started up. He's into the wedding car game, been doing it for about a year.' She paused. 'Perhaps we could hire him to do our wedding.'

CHAPTER FOURTEEN

First off, on arrival back at the Green River, Honey talked to Smudger the Chef, listened to Dumpy Doris ranting on about the huge roast dinner she was planning to eat at home that night, and also spoke to her daughter.

Just for once, Lindsey was away from the computer, taking time off with a romantic historical novel. She was laying full stretch on a settee in the conservatory. By virtue of the sun warming up the glass and the area within, she was wearing a dark blue linen tunic and leggings.

'What are you reading?'

The cover looked appealing. '*The Plague Ship.*'

'Medieval?'

'Yes. It concerns the Black Death being spread throughout the Mediterranean. Quite macabre. Quite enlightening too.'

She put the book down and eyed her mother with a knowing look.

'Rough night?'

Honey felt her face colouring up. 'No more than usual.'

'Oh well. Make the most of it whilst you can.'

'What's that supposed to mean?'

'Basically I'm telling you to slow down. Be less physical and more spiritual.'

Honey eyed her daughter warily. 'Have you been talking spirits and seraphim with Mary Jane again?'

Lindsey returned her look without a flutter of indignation. 'She talks. I listen. I talk. She listens.'

Honey felt a pang of hurt. 'Are you saying that I don't?'

Lindsey sighed. 'You lead a hectic life.'

'I know, but . . .'

'Listen! I don't mind that. You're a very different person to me. Just as you're very different than your mother. So in lieu of that, I have to have somebody to talk to who knows what I'm talking about. Mary Jane does. So we talk spirituality and religion. People in the Middle Ages practised religion every day. Did you know that?'

'Before my time.'

'Quite. They never failed to say a prayer or enter a church, take confession or whatever. I quite like the life of the clergy, you know. It's so peaceful. It gives you time to think.'

'Then I'm not a terrible mother?'

Lindsey laughed. 'Of course you're not. You're my mother and you're fun and funny. But you're not religious or spiritual. Mary Jane is.'

Lindsey's smile, her words and her sudden leaping to plant a kiss on her mother's cheek, was reassuring.

Honey breathed a sigh of relief. 'I'll go over the back for a shower and a coffee and look at my emails.'

'Right. Go. I'll carry on entering the price list for next year. After that I'll carry on my research into the life of monks and nuns. It seems a very peaceful existence.'

It wasn't until Honey was sitting down with a cup of coffee and the only letter addressed personally to her that morning that a worrying thought came to her.

She sat very still, both hands around her coffee mug. A nun? Her daughter? Surely not!

She might have brooded on it and eventually trotted back over to reception or demand they talk this through before Lindsey committed to something she might regret. Instead she opened the letter and extracted it from inside the envelope with the copperplate handwriting. Once read, everything else flew out of her head. She took a deep breath, then read it again. No, she thought, shaking her head. It had to be a joke. A nutcase. A relative who didn't want her to marry Doherty? Who? What relative? One relative above all others sprang to mind.

'*A policeman! You're going to marry a policeman?*'

Surely not! But if it wasn't a joke, if it was deadly serious . . . ?

Doherty answered on the first ring.

'Ah. My betrothed.'

'Your betrothed has received a threatening letter suggesting I should not be betrothed,' said Honey feeling a definite shakiness in her knees. Anger too. 'Suggesting in fact that I might be bumped off if I don't drop the idea. They also suggest that you're a bent cop and a liar.'

'Ah!'

He put a lot of meaning into that two-letter word.

Honey frowned. 'What does Ah mean?'

'That's the third. I mean, I've received two. You've received one.'

'These letters; when did you receive them?'

He ummed and ahhed a bit. 'Only in the last few days.'

'You didn't tell me.'

'I didn't want to scare you.'

'I don't scare easily.'

'Are you scared now?'

'What do you think?'

Holding the letter close to her eyes so she didn't have to find her glasses, Honey read it out, purposely emphasising the bit about him being a bent cop and a liar.

'*I think you should know that your policeman boyfriend is your typically bent copper and, not only that, but he's a liar. Are you so stupid that you haven't noticed?*

'*If you dare go ahead with this stupid idea of marrying a bent cop, I will personally make your life a misery, or perhaps end it.*'

'Signature?'

106

'It's unsigned.'

'So were the two I received.'

'Why didn't you tell me about them before?'

She heard a heavily exhaled breath on the other end of the phone; Doherty at his most exasperated.

'I promised myself I would tell you when a third letter was received.'

'Well, here it is. Third letter received.'

She said it with an air of finality, challenging him to come out with an excuse now for not taking the matter further.

'Have you checked where it was posted from?'

The question took her off balance. She paused, picked up the envelope and studied the franked place and time. It was a little smudged, but she could just about make out Edinburgh. Four days ago. She told Doherty.

There was silence at first, and finally, 'Leave it with me.'

* * *

It wasn't often that someone as exotic as Carolina Sherise came into the village shop. Heads turned the moment the old brass bell jangled. The two construction labourers involved in the restoration of a brick and beamed property at the other end of the street were waiting for the pasties they had bought to warm up. On seeing her, their jaws dropped, all thought of eating forgotten.

Mrs Jenkins, the woman behind the portion of counter reserved for post office matters, looked up from lowered eyes whilst tearing a strip of stamps off for Janet Glencannon who ran the animal sanctuary.

Carolina Sherise was perusing the magazine selection so didn't notice the alarm that entered Janet's eyes. Neither did she bother to look round when Janet told Mrs Jenkins that she'd suddenly remembered she'd left something in the oven and would be back later.

Hermione Thompson, who on Mrs Flynn's demise had immediately stepped into her shoes, was on her way to the church, a vast bouquet of flowers boldly nodding from a huge wicker basket.

'Janet,' she shouted out, and waved.

Janet ignored her, clambered into her Land Rover, banged the door shut behind her and was gone.

'Oh!'

Hermione, who had moved here from a big city, was of the opinion that everyone in the village should make the effort to be friendly. It seemed Janet had purposely ignored her and she so hated being ignored. She really did like things to be all sweetness and smiles. By the time she had finished the flowers and was on her way back to the chocolate-box cottage she shared with her husband, she was sniffing, trying to hold back tears.

'Anything wrong, sweetheart?'

Nicholas, her husband, was out walking their Labrador, Quincy who was straining at the leash and was awarded a slap across the back for his troubles.

She smiled a sickly sweet smile. 'Not really, sweetheart, except I was thinking how childish some people can be.'

'Oh. She's still bearing a grudge is she, darling?'

The Thompsons were in the habit of adding endearments to every sentence they spoke to each other.

'I believe so, my love. Janet considers herself the rightful inheritor of the flower arranging committee.'

'Don't let it upset you. Don't get angry, just get even. That's my motto, my sweet.'

'Hmm. Yes darling,' said his wife, as her smile diminished into a scowl, her eyes glittering at the diminishing presence of Janet Glencannon's vehicle.

CHAPTER FIFTEEN

The Green River Hotel was uncharacteristically quiet and it had nothing to do with business.

Honey couldn't remember a day when she hadn't had interruptions from two quarters in particular. Number one was Caspar who was like a praying mantis as far as crime was concerned, hassling her with regard to progress — as if the perpetrator was amongst a collection of suspects, all sitting in a circle, waiting to be pounced on thanks to simple deduction.

Unfortunately that sort of crime solving now only happened in books. Guesswork and clever deduction had been replaced by science, fingerprinting by DNA testing and ploughing through reams of paperwork had given way to scrolling through electronic records kept on a computer database.

Caspar's absence was no big secret. He'd gone on holiday with a group of friends on a thirty-metre-long catamaran sailing from Mauritius to Sri Lanka. They did have a satellite phone on board, but he obviously wasn't paying too close attention to it, the Wi-Fi only being used for the weather and navigation issues. It had also occurred to her that Caspar St John Gervais wouldn't be too uptight seeing as the murder of Gladys Flynn had taken place in a village on the outskirts of Bath and not in the city itself. Caspar would be pleased about that — as far as it was to be pleased about a murder.

Caspar was absent but she knew where he was. However, she was unaware of her mother's whereabouts.

Lindsey hadn't heard from her. No visit, no phone call and no email. Gloria Cross had splashed out on a very swish tablet and enlisted her granddaughter's help in using it. Lindsey had been happy to oblige. It had been five days since they'd had a word from her except for an email four days ago to say she was on cloud nine. Lindsey suggested she meant *the* Cloud, that metaphysical archive that existed to devour all the information in the world. Honey wasn't so sure and wondered what her mother was up to. Not being in touch for any length of time just wasn't her thing. There was something slightly worrying about her not being around and although Honey did not welcome her interfering in her life, it was unsettling not seeing her. It was like getting used to living with background music and then somebody switching it off.

She might have popped round to her mother's if it hadn't been for the letter. She wondered whether it was her mother, interfering, warning from a distance. But surely she wouldn't threaten violence?

She decided to quiz Doherty further about the letters when the time was right and when he wasn't so busy. Hopefully the murderer would be found.

* * *

The kids were dressed as pirates, all part of a birthday party for Luke Simpson, a little kid with red hair and horn-rimmed spectacles and the energy of an electric Jack in the Box.

Having eaten the party food and opened his presents, Luke and his guests, girls as well as boys, were running across the field, shrieking at the top of their voices.

They careered off down towards Badger's Bottom towards the abandoned waterworks. The brick-built buildings were boarded up, the reservoir, that had once sparkled with water, was now empty. Cost-cutting had closed it down turning what had been an attractive feature into an empty hole with mud at the bottom.

A steep incline dropped down from the disused lane for access for water company vehicles. The whole area was surrounded with a six-foot-high wire fence but the padlock that had once kept the gate firmly closed against outsiders, hung forlornly, one half of the gate partially open.

The land beyond the fence backed onto the rear of Belvedere House and the top of the church tower could be seen above the trees.

The band of pirates ran whooping down to the drained lake, perhaps in the hope of finding a sunken treasure ship. Alas there was none, but parked to the side of what had been a small but very nice lake, was a white Rolls Royce.

The kids hesitated in going any further. They'd already left their adult minders behind, and so far had ignored the warning shouts not to stray out of sight. They were now hesitating at their own volition — except for Luke that is.

'Come on,' he shouted, unfazed by what the consequences of his actions might be and wiping his snotty nose on the back of his sleeve. 'Let's rescue the beautiful princess. She's been captured and imprisoned in a big white castle.'

Okay, to adults the Rolls Royce bore little resemblance to a white castle, but this was a gang of five- and six-year-olds with vivid imaginations.

Luke ran on regardless, his little friends alternating between outright enthusiasm and a mild trot. One or two hung back.

Luke's mother was the first adult on the scene, her lightweight summer skirt flapping around her skinny shanks. She'd expected them still to be going strong, but found them gathered silently around a white car.

She frowned, paused to catch her breath before striding on, her arms swinging at her sides. Tall and slim, she had a commanding manner which had landed her the job of chairperson of the PTA and other posts relating to children, education and the protection of seals, lobsters and the greater spotted lemur.

Her high voice shrieked out at them. 'Now come away from there. All of you. Come away from there.'

Nobody moved. The fact that they were all stood there, staring at whoever was in the car, made her blood boil.

'Courting bloody couples! Can't they wait until it's bloody dark, for God's sake? Come on. All of you. Get out of the way and get back to the house . . .'

Spreading her arms wide, she shepherded them away from what she thought would be two people in semi or total undress, doing what two people do when they're in a quiet spot accompanied by nothing but bird song and a soaring libido.

Okay for them, she thought to herself, her expression flushed and angry. *They don't have kids. You soon get too tired for that once you've got kids.*

Once she was sure the kids were at a safe distance, Paulette Simpson turned purposefully back towards the car, determined to tear them off a strip for lewd behaviour in a public place.

The fluttering of a piece of white ribbon stretched along the bonnet slowed her stride. It was hitched around each wing mirror and onto the famous Rolls Royce lady; the spirit of ecstasy wasn't it?

A wedding car? A courting couple were having sex in broad daylight in a wedding car? Sacrilege! To her mind a wedding car was almost as sacred as the marriage service itself. She herself was married. She did not believe in living in sin.

'Right,' she said, rolling up her shirt sleeves as though preparing herself for a bout with Lennox Lewis. 'You are going to get a piece of my mind, my friends. Just you wait. How dare you . . .'

She leaned onto the car, one hand on the bonnet, the other on the roof. Devoid of any form of make-up, her long face turned pale. Her protruding eyes loomed large.

She had expected to see two people locked in lust. Instead there was only one. A bride. A dead bride.

For a moment she froze taking it all in. The bride's veil was scattered with seed pearls and her face was as white as the dress she was wearing. Through a gap in the seed pearls, she espied half closed eyelids, just as if the bride was half asleep. Only she wasn't. She was dead. Stone dead.

CHAPTER SIXTEEN

At the sound of the police sirens, those villagers who were at home craned their necks from cottage and mansion alike.

Heads bobbed together over garden fences to discuss what was going on. Those who had been in the village store or merely traversing the High Street, stopped in huddled groups.

News of what was going on was spread by two mothers with children attending Luke Simpson's birthday party.

'A woman dead in a car. A wedding car. And wearing a wedding dress! Well fancy that!'

The kids, who had seen everything, filled in the details in a matter-of-fact manner.

'It's a lady and she's dead.'

'A bride. She was a bride,' added one of the more precocious little girls.

'How do you know that?' A boy's question of course.

'She was wearing a bride's dress, stupid. And she had a veil.'

'Why?'

Already having a less than favourable opinion of men and small boys in particular, the little girl rolled her eyes. Only a boy would be stupid enough to ask why a woman

114

was wearing a wedding dress and sitting in a wedding car trimmed with a broad white ribbon.

'She was going to the church to get married, but I think she changed her mind.'

This reason for the bride's demise was accepted by the kids as though it were just an extra entertainment to a moderately entertaining birthday party. The adults were more worried, more curious to know every salacious detail.

Rumours were rife and centred around Paulette Simpson who was responsible for finding the body and phoning the police.

There were various guesses at to the identity of the victim. Paulette Simpson, who dared anyone to call her Marge, declared that she had not studied the dead woman in great detail. 'Besides, she was wearing a veil. A very nice one actually — well, as far as I could see. Nothing cheap.'

Doherty buttonholed one of the SOCOs at the scene, asking him who had found the body. Les Partridge, a seasoned officer, pointed in the direction of the athletic woman with mousy hair and a plain face. She stood a head taller than the other women around her, arms folded in what Doherty instantly interpreted as a defensive position.

'Mrs Simpson. It was a kid's birthday party, one of these where they all go off on a treasure hunt afterwards and let off steam.'

'And the parents can take a breather,' Doherty added as he surveyed the interest their arrival had generated up and down the High Street.

And to think we were considering getting married here, he thought to himself. He recalled driving out here for a drink at the pub previous to meeting the vicar and visiting the church. He and Honey had been quite taken with the place, how pretty it was, how peaceful too.

'Right,' he said, bracing himself up for the inevitable. 'First things first. Let's take a look at the victim.'

Getting to the scene involved walking down a lane running between the church and Mr Clinker's home, Belvedere

House. Doherty wondered if he was home yet and if he'd made it up with his wife. He reminded himself that she wasn't pressing charges, so they had probably returned to normal married life — *their* kind of normal married life.

On one side of the lane the branches of weeping willows dripped over the churchyard wall. The higher wall of Belvedere House loomed on his left. The ground underfoot was muddy, odd seeing as they'd had no rain for at least a week, and then only a dribble.

A slight rise of just a few feet led him up to the chain link fencing surrounding the disused water works. Once inside the terrain fell down towards the old reservoir.

The car was parked on the tarmac track, its nose facing upwards towards the fence. It looked familiar, like the kind Ahmed was supposed to own for his wedding business. The kids had come from the other direction where the fence had long disappeared and a clear track led into the woods. They would have seen its rear end first.

Doherty approached and looked in.

The bride was slumped against the back seat. He took in the angle of her head, the way her hands were folded on her lap around a pink and white bouquet. The kids hadn't seen anything too dreadful. No blood. No mutilations or the bloated tongue of strangulation.

It occurred to him that if she hadn't looked so much like a floppy rag doll, he could almost believe she really was off to her wedding.

'Cause of death?' His question was directed at nobody in particular. An answer came anyway.

'Same as the one in the church. Knocked on the back of the head. It's very likely the same person, but I need to do tests including checking whether insulin is present as in the first attack.'

Doherty nodded once in acknowledgement. 'Was this how she was found? Was everything exactly like this?'

'Yes, sir. The veil was over her face. We did disturb it slightly just to check the means of despatch, but put it back again.'

Doherty nodded at the comments at the same time jerking his chin at the body. 'Let's take a look at her face, shall we? You can do the honours.'

The SOCO leaned over and lifted the veil.

Doherty gazed at the woman, his thoughts were jumping through hoops. He was looking at Marietta Hopkins — Harold Clinker's wife.

'You look as though you know her, sir.'

'She lives in the village. In that house there as a matter of fact. I was called to a domestic.'

'Ah! Could be an open and shut case then, sir. It's usually the husband, isn't it?'

Doherty grunted something unintelligible. Harold Clinker was definitely in the frame, but was he responsible for the death of Mrs Flynn too? Doherty could think of a few motives he might have had for bumping off his wife, but where did Mrs Flynn fit into the scene?

The manner of Mrs Flynn's despatch had turned out not to be as straightforward as they'd thought. 'Get her checked for evidence of an injection under the tongue and a high incidence of insulin in her system.'

'Yes sir.'

'And get somebody over to that posh house next to the church. That's where she lived. Her husband's name is Mr Harold Clinker. Tell uniform to use kid gloves at first when we break the news, then politely ask him to come in for questioning.'

Doherty turned and made his way back to the High Street. He'd given instructions that Mrs Simpson be detained until he'd had chance to speak to her. He found her there pushing her arms into a denim jacket that seemed in odd contrast to the flimsy cotton dress she was wearing. A series of pins on her lapel raged indignantly against authority; state, monarchy, government and the USA.

'I really can't stay here for long,' she snapped impatiently, her protruding eyes flickering. She placed both hands beneath her hair, throwing it upwards so it fell back more neatly onto her collar.

'I've left Luke with Nick and Hermione, but they won't put up with him for long. He's hyperactive you know.'

Doherty sighed. He needed to confirm a few other things elsewhere. He explained this to Mrs Simpson adding that she could come in tomorrow sometime to make a statement.

'It will have to be in the morning,' she replied. 'I have to collect Luke just after lunch. We've only just moved into the area and he's only just started school and is in the reception class. He doesn't have to do a full day until he's been there two weeks.'

Detecting her hostility, Doherty agreed to her coming to the station in the morning. Dressed in flowing gypsy style dress and Doc Marten boots, Mrs Simpson said she'd be there. She had the air of a woman who had brushed with the law in the past. Something about her suggested that in her younger days, Mrs Simpson had taken part in protest marches. What about Doherty didn't know and didn't really care. All he wanted was for her to cooperate. Bugger her beef against the police and society. A woman was dead.

'I'll see you then,' he said and when he thanked her for her cooperation, she looked surprised.

On his way back to where he'd parked his car, one of his officers remarked on the presentation of the Rolls Royce.

'There was even a bunch of flowers along with that ribbon. It fell off. We found it on the ground. Nice car. There's a thing,' he said, shaking his head mournfully. 'Her last ride in a car was the one that should have taken her to her wedding.'

'It's not quite her last ride,' commented Doherty. 'That's going to be in something totally different.'

The two police officers — a man and a woman — who had called at Belvedere House came back and reported that Mr Harold Clinker was not at home.

'The cleaner said he's gone abroad, he left last night.'

'Where?'

'Spain.'

'Who with?'

'A friend.'

'Name?'

'The cleaner said it was a woman. That's all I know.'

Doherty nodded. 'She's sitting in the back.'

'Brides usually do.'

'So who was driving the car?'

CHAPTER SEVENTEEN

June, glorious June!

Honey hummed to herself as she drove Mary Jane through Bath pleased that the weather was good and the streets were packed with tourists.

Life was good if she didn't dwell on murders, her mother's absence, the threatening letter, and accusations that Doherty was a liar and perhaps had even been taking bribes.

No! Not Doherty. She would never believe it of him. He held a certain laconic disdain for those who did try to slip him a brown envelope filled with fifty-pound notes. Not that he'd had that many offered to him, and those that had were offered by criminals too close to being arrested for him to even chance such a thing. Not that he would of course, though he'd known those who had. He'd told her that for those guys, taking the money was one thing; living with the guilt was another.

'Why do you think so many turn to drink or gambling, or make a hash of their marriage?'

She hadn't reminded him that his marriage had hit the rocks years ago. He rarely spoke of it and when it did rear its ugly head was quickly dismissed that they'd both been too young. It had never had a chance.

The subject was avoided as was that of his daughter who was rarely in touch. The last missive was a card posted from Venice Beach, California. Sometimes he received a text from wherever she was on her wanderings, but not very often.

'Your mother says not to worry,' Mary Jane said suddenly, breaking into her thoughts.

'I beg your pardon?'

'She says not to worry. She's having a great time.'

Honey frowned. 'She didn't tell me she was going anywhere. How come she told you?'

'She didn't,' said Mary Jane, shrugging her bony shoulders. 'She came through last night when I was asleep.'

'You mean my mother's dead!'

Honey felt instant alarm. Mary Jane was a professor of the paranormal; she got more messages from dead people than Honey got from old school pals via Friends Reunited — not that it was that unusual. Those that had got in contact she'd purposely ignored. Too many of those old school *friends* were of the sporting variety, the girls who'd relished wearing navy-blue games skirts and wielding a hockey stick with lethal intentions, i.e. bashing her ankles when she was in goal. Overall they were definitely the ones she'd never really clicked with. Why was it they even regarded her as a valued school friend? She certainly hadn't noticed it at the time.

Mary Jane reassured her.

'Oh no. She hasn't crossed over from this life to the next. She sounded pretty damned excited I can tell you. Secretive too. Whatever she's been up to, she says it's a surprise. It's something she wanted to do and didn't want you talking her out of it. That's what she said.'

Honey risked a glance at Mary Jane's profile which was dominated by a slightly hooked nose and a pointed chin. Her cheekbones were high, her face thin, and her eyes a piercing blue. This week her hair was a fetching shade of violet. Next week it might be multi-coloured, like a bunch of sweet peas in full flower. Mary Jane had a typically Californian attitude; please yourself how you look and never be boring.

Mary Jane was looking straight ahead, her head held high, her eyes hidden behind an enormous pair of Ray-Bans. Not that there was really any need to search for sincerity in her eyes. If Mary Jane said her mother had been in touch on the psychic plain, then that was the way it was.

Honey sighed. 'It never rains but it pours.'

Although she had spoken very softly, Mary Jane had the ears of a fruit bat.

'What rain is that? D'you wanna talk about it? We can do a reading when we get back. How would that be?'

'The weather. On the TV. They said it was going to rain.'

She felt Mary Jane looking at her but didn't meet her eyes. Like her ears, they didn't miss much and at this moment in time she didn't want to talk about murder, marriage, or the threatening letter. Neither did she want to discuss Lindsey until she had a firmer handle on what was going on, though on second thoughts, Mary Jane might not be a bad place to start.

'Lindsey seems a bit intense on the business of spirituality and religion. I understand you've been having discussions. She's not going to run away and join one of those weird communes you read so much about, is she?'

'Lindsey? No. Too level-headed. Kind of traditional in her ways too, plus of course she is so into the medieval life. I shouldn't be at all surprised if she goes down the traditional route and becomes a nun. I think it would quite suit her.'

'A nun? My daughter, a nun!'

'Sure. Why not?'

It occurred to Honey that Lindsey had never been a shrinking violet on the boyfriend front. She didn't know for sure, but surely nuns had to be virgins; didn't they?

The question went unasked. She had enough on her plate. Asking Lindsey about her future could wait for a quiet moment.

After battling through the traffic, they arrived at Ahmed's garage and Honey was thinking what a joy it was that she'd only had to ferry Mary Jane in her car. Worst case scenario was enduring her dear friend's driving of the pale pink caddy with its left-hand wheel and driving on the right-hand side of the road.

Pulling in front of the garage apron, it was something of a surprise to look in her rear-view mirror and see Doherty pulling in behind them.

'Hi.' She raised her hand and smiled, fully expecting him to smile back. He did raise his hand, but that was all. She instantly knew he was here on serious business.

'Doherty looks dour,' Mary Jane remarked. Dour was currently her favourite word because it originated in Scotland. She was presently into all things Scottish. Honey was unsure why.

'I think he's here on police business,' Honey whispered.

'Oh hell! Do you think it's about my parking tickets?'

Keeping her eyes fixed on Doherty, Honey shook her head. 'No chance.'

She smiled at him again. 'Anything wrong?'

'Very.'

Doherty didn't do smart suits and didn't get his hair cut that often, but he had charisma. Movie stars playing streetwise, rough machismo detectives on screen would be well advised to meet up with Detective Inspector Steve Doherty. He was the real thing.

Lean and purposeful, he turned to Ahmed. 'I believe you're missing a wedding car.'

Ahmed put down the yellow spotted tea mug he'd been gulping from and nodded.

'You bet. Have you found it? Has it been smashed up? I'll be dead gutted if it has. Don't tell me. No! Tell me. I've invested good money in that car.'

Doherty played it cool. 'Can you confirm the registration number?'

Ahmed did just that. 'Where did you find it? You have found it, haven't you?'

Doherty nodded. Honey saw the sombreness in his face and knew he was here for more than just a stolen car.

'We found it at Lower Wainscote parked in the old waterworks pumping station. It's none the worse for wear.'

Ahmed's teeth flashed bright against his brown face. Honey was glad for him.

'Great! I can begin to take bookings again. I had somebody enquire for this weekend because some other bozo let them down. I'll give them a ring as soon as things are sorted with you. When can I collect it?'

Doherty held his sombre look. 'Hold it. Don't do that just yet. I'm afraid this is a bit more serious than a simple take and drive away crime. There's been a murder.'

Ahmed's smile disappeared. 'And my car had something to do with it?'

'A dead woman was found in the back of your car.'

'*A dead woman?*' Ahmed sounded and looked shocked. 'What was she doing there?'

'That's what we would like to know. We'll need to know where you were on the night your car was taken, and once we're sure of time of death, we'll need to know where you were then too.'

Ahmed looked as though he couldn't get past the fact that a dead woman had been found in his car. Knowing Ahmed and his habit of trying out potential brides purloined by his mother, it wouldn't have surprised Honey if he'd had more than one girl in the back of that car. The Rolls Royce had a big back seat. Ideal for sex and Ahmed liked girls. He also liked cars, but he was no murderer. Ahmed Clifford, son of an English plumber and a seamstress from the Punjab, was a hardworking and enterprising lad.

Although he knew Ahmed as well as Honey and Mary Jane, Doherty stuck to the formal approach.

'I'm afraid we'll need you to come along to the station to make a statement.'

'Right now?'

'No. Get rid of the oil slick first. Then come down.'

Whilst Mary Jane settled her bill, Doherty filled Honey in on the details.

Honey was stunned. 'Marietta! Have you arrested her husband?'

'We would have, but our Mr Harold Clinker has gone to Spain with our exotic dancer friend.'

'Carolina Sherise? The one Marietta caught him in bed with. Their bed. She was touchy about that.'

'That's the girl. Sounds as though you know more than me.'

'It's a girly thing. Instinctive. And it means he's guilty.'

Honey had never felt quite so angry with the occasion of a murder as she did now. She'd seen the bruising on Marietta's face. With hindsight, she wished she'd kept in closer touch with Marietta when her name was Mary and the world looked like being her oyster. Perhaps things might have been different.

'She was wearing a wedding dress,' Doherty reminded her. 'We're presuming it's hers.'

Honey guessed where this was going. 'You think it might not be hers.'

He shrugged. 'As I said before, I'm no fashion expert.' A sudden grin lit his face. 'So don't ask for my opinion when you're choosing yours.'

'I'm not going to. It's bad luck for the bridegroom to see the dress before the wedding day.'

'Ah yes. Of course,' he said nodding sagely, relieved to be let off from a shopping trip. 'Carole thinks the dress dates from at least ten years ago. There's no proof it belonged to our friend Marietta.'

'Who's Carole?'

'New kid on the block. Straight from Hendon. She did a degree in fashion before that.'

'So what skills did she bring from the world of fashion to the police force?'

She could tell by the look on Doherty's face that he was enjoying her jealousy.

'She's good at making the tea. And informative about wedding dresses.'

His smile faded when he saw Honey's deadpan expression and knew she had something to say.

'I can do better than that. I was at her wedding.'

CHAPTER EIGHTEEN

She was wearing skinny jeans in a fetching coral colour, a tailored white blouse nipped in at the waist, and a multi-coloured jacket, predominantly jade and coral. The cut screamed quality and fitted provocatively to her figure. Her bag and shoes were of soft suede in three different colours which also matched her jacket. Her earrings were big and bold and her bracelets clinked like a pocketful of money.

Money was what Carolina Sherise was all about; unlike Marietta, she was of an independent disposition, unafraid of enjoying the company of men without actually committing herself to any long-term relationship. She was sporting a tan, sure evidence that she'd recently spent some time in the sun.

Although they were used to some pretty up-market fashion in Bath, heads turned when she entered Manvers Street. They were only coppers, but Bath had certain standards in dress sense. Shell suits and baseball boots it was not, but this was a different league!

'I wish to report a theft,' she said to the duty sergeant.

Once he'd put his eyeballs back in, he cleared his throat and licked the end of his pencil, then realising times had moved on, put it down and turned to his computer screen.

'Right, madam. If you would like to give me the details.'

* * *

Neither Honey nor Doherty had any idea that the woman Marietta had caught in bed with her husband was outside reporting a crime.

The evidence room was a chilly place bound by cupboards, files and fridges — all those places where necessary evidence could be kept safe and sound.

Honey badly wanted to feel the material of the wedding dress, but was aware that doing so would contaminate the evidence.

'Lovely dress,' she mused.

'I dare say it is. Was it the one you saw her get married in?'

Honey shook her head. 'No. Quite frankly this is a bit of a meringue. If memory serves, Marietta had a gorgeous figure and wore a dress that showed it off to best advantage. It was a sheath design, you know, clung in all the right places. And her veil was short, not all like this one.'

Once she signalled she was done, Doherty grunted at Carole to see the dress was returned to where they'd got it out from.

He closed the door to his office. At one time he'd shared it with another officer but someone from Health and Safety had since decreed that it was too small an office for two to share. Quite frankly the 'elf was right. One desk and it was cramped. Two desks and it was skinny people only.

'Has Ahmed been in yet?'

'Tomorrow. First thing. He was pretty upset about his car being nicked on the phone. He'd borrowed money from a family member to buy it on the understanding they would take a percentage of the profits. We can't let him have the car back just yet until it's been fully checked over.'

'That's likely to make a hole in his takings. He said he had bookings.'

'Yep. But not one for your friend Marietta. We showed him her photo, but he didn't recognise her. Not that we'd expected him to. His statement checks out. There are a number of houses overlooking the block of garages where he keeps his car. It was a warm night and the end house was having a barbecue. They waved to him when he left. He told them he'd forgotten his keys and they assured him they'd keep an eye on it. Fat chance. A few burgers and beers and it was all over.'

'Probably in the early hours of the morning?'

'More than likely.'

'Somebody's got an issue here. What was the point of stealing a wedding car and dolling two women up in wedding dresses? There's some meaning to it.'

'Though not to us.'

'Not yet anyway.'

She eyed him thoughtfully.

'Say what you want to say,' he said locking his eyes with hers.

'Don't you think it odd that all this — the dead brides — might be tied up with the nutcase warning us against getting married.'

'You could have a point.'

'Does he?'

'Who? The letter writer?'

She chewed her lips as she carefully considered what it was she wanted to say.

'What I mean is, whoever is warning us off marriage by letter might also be doing the same by deed. You know, there's nothing to put a bride off trotting down the aisle like the prospect of having her head bashed in.'

'I take your point. Oh, and by the way, there was no sign of insulin in the second murder. Just a bash over the head.'

He was considering her feelings referring to Marietta's death as the second murder rather than mentioning her name. It helped. Better still to change the subject.

'Hmm. I think I might not go for a white wedding after all. What do you think?'

Doherty grinned and slid his hand beneath her hair.

'How about we just have the honeymoon?'

'Asking me to marry you requires more commitment than torrid sex for two weeks in the sun.'

'You don't say,' he said, cupping her cheek before bringing his lips down to meet hers. 'We can play let's pretend like I was a kid.'

'Did you ever play doctors and nurses?' she asked.

'My favourite game.'

Her knees were weak by this time. My, but Doherty was one hell of a kisser!

The rat-a-tat-tat of knuckles on bare wood prevented things progressing any further.

The Wizard popped his head round the door. He first smiled and greeted Honey.

'Hello Mrs Driver. As always nice to see you. How's that mother of yours?'

'Absent without leave.'

The Wizard chuckled. 'Well if she can't be off doing 'er own thing at 'er age, then when can she?!'

'How come everyone knows what my mother should be doing better than I do?'

'She's still the adult, you're still the kid — no disrespect intended. It's an age thing you see. The nearer you are in age to the subject of conversation, the more you understand. Um . . .' Realising he was going off on a tangent that had nothing to do with why he was here, the Wizard cleared his throat and fixed his attention on his superior officer.

'There's a woman outside to see you, sir. A Miss Carolina Sherise. And very nice she is too.'

Honey looked at Doherty. A nerve jerked in his cheek. He'd presumed that Carolina Sherise was the woman who'd accompanied Harold Clinker to Spain. He'd guessed wrong.

'Thank you,' said Doherty dismissively. Not that the Wizard took much notice.

'I'm sure I've seen her before,' he said, frowning and scratching his spiky grey hair with one finger.

'I've got it. She's a model!'

'Not that I'm aware of,' murmured Doherty who recalled clearly that Carolina Sherise had introduced herself as an exotic dancer.

'I'm sure she is. Not one of these skinny birds who model clothes at fashion shows and stuff. More the Littlewoods type; you know, mail order catalogues, modelling underwear and stuff.'

Doherty peered at him. 'Right. So we all know which pages of a catalogue you study!'

The Wizard was unfazed.

'Get out, Potter, and bring the young lady in.'

Doherty sat down and gestured for Honey to do likewise. As there were only two chairs and Carolina would want one, she perched on the corner of the desk.

A cloud of perfume accompanied Carolina as she entered the room as though she owned it. If the room was cramped before, it was more than cramped now. Carolina was easily six feet tall and from the top of her head to the tips of her varnished toenails, she was impeccably groomed. The clothes were tight and moulded to her frame because her flesh was tight; this girl worked out. Running, gymnastics, weightlifting; the whole shooting match. It made Honey sick to even think about it.

Carolina's perfect teeth flashed in a winning smile.

Doherty acted as though he were Prince Charming, inviting her to sit down, asking if she would like a drink or anything . . . almost as though he meant it.

Carolina smiled the confident smile of somebody who knows how to tickle a man's fancy — and anything else for that matter.

Doherty acted as though he were smitten; putty in her long-fingered hands.

Honey knew he really could play-pretend. Be disarmingly charming and get the other party on your side.

Carolina's earrings made a tinkling sound when she smiled. Her teeth were as bright and white as a shark. Her bite was likely just as sharp.

'I'm told you wish to report a theft,' said Doherty. Resting his elbows on the desk, he clasped his hands together beneath his chin. It made him look boyish; vulnerable. Easy meat for somebody like the long-limbed exotic dancer sitting opposite him. 'Perhaps you could tell me what it was.'

'A wedding dress. I left it in the back of my car, and when I came to look for it, it was gone.'

'You're getting married?'

Honey received a warning look from Doherty. It wasn't her place to ask questions, but it seemed a bit odd, seeing as Carolina had only recently been to bed with somebody else's husband.

'The wedding dress was for a photo-shoot I did recently. The client gave me the dress once it was over.' She shrugged her toned shoulders. 'You never know. I might meet the right man.'

The smile flashed again. Doherty gave no indication that he'd even noticed.

Honey then realised that Carolina didn't yet know who it was in the car. The veil had been over the victim's face. Before they had chance to go much further, there was another tapping at the door. This time it was Carole, the girl who had fancied the world of fashion then changed course and ended up making tea.

'Excuse me, sir, but there are a load of journalists outside requesting a press conference.'

Doherty looked at her in surprise. 'That was quick. We haven't released any details yet.'

'It's not that, sir,' she said, looking swiftly from Doherty, her eyes settling on the glamorous woman wearing clothes Carole could only dream of. 'It's Miss Sherise. They've been told her wedding dress was stolen and a murder victim was found wearing it. There's also a Manuel Glipp in the reception waiting for Miss Sherise. He's from that reality TV show. You know, celebrities living on a campsite miles from anywhere. Apparently the next one's in Tuscany . . .' Carole threw Carolina a flashing smile. 'I think they're onto you, Miss Sherise.'

Carolina preened like a pedigree cat winning first prize at a championship show. Slowly and purposefully, she crossed one long leg over another, her toothpaste smile firmly fixed on Doherty.

'My agent, I'm afraid. He doesn't believe in letting the grass grow under our feet . . .'

Her long frame unfolded from sitting to half standing.

'Stay right where you are!'

'My dear man,' said Carolina, unaware that her cloying condescension would only make Doherty angrier. 'It was my dress. It was stolen, so I have every right . . .'

'Sit down.'

'But I . . .' It finally got through to her that Doherty was far from pleased. Still smiling she gave in. 'Very well,' she said with a sigh as she sank back onto the chair. 'Have it your way.'

'Where's Harold Clinker?'

She looked at him in total surprise. 'What's he got to do with this? He didn't steal my dress.'

'How do you know that?'

She giggled. 'It wouldn't fit him.'

Doherty's look was frosty enough to freeze her butt to the chair.

'Miss Sherise. A woman has been found murdered in the village.'

'So I heard, but I don't see what that's got to do with . . .'

'Marietta Hopkins!'

Carolina's glossy confidence disappeared. 'Marietta,' she whispered. 'It was Marietta?'

'Mrs Driver here identified the person found dead as Marietta Hopkins, formerly Mary Hopkins, Mr Clinker's wife. As you may recall, we were summoned to Belvedere House as the result of a call you put in to us. Mr Clinker had physically abused his wife. Do you recall that, Miss Sherise?'

Although Carolina had a modestly tanned complexion, she visibly paled. Her eyes opened wide. Honey noticed they were a striking grey colour.

'Why?'

Honey had held her tongue up until now, but the time had come to blab regardless of her civilian status.

'I knew Marietta. Okay, she liked the good things of life, the bling, the bubbly and being on the arm of somebody with a fair-sized bank account. She didn't deserve to die. She was wearing a wedding dress, Miss Sherise. I know it was not the one she got married in. Was it your wedding dress?'

'I don't know . . . I don't . . .' Carolina threw her head from side to side as if she might do the same with the truth; fling it away as though it didn't exist.

Doherty took over. 'Where is Harold Clinker?'

'I don't know . . . he was in hospital . . .'

'So you knew he was in hospital. Was it you who put him there? Was it you who attacked him in the churchyard?'

'No! Of course I didn't. I don't know anything about it.'

'But you knew he was in the hospital. Did Marietta tell you that?'

'Look,' said Carolina, looking less like a TV star and more like a wide-eyed puppet. 'I haven't seen Marietta or Harold since the incident when you were called.'

'You didn't go to Spain with him?' asked Doherty.

'No. Whatever made you think that?'

'We heard a woman went with him and seeing as you two were close, it was an easy presumption to make.'

'Well, it wasn't me!'

'We'll check.'

'Check all you like. I came in here with the best intentions. I heard about this woman being found wearing a wedding dress. I just thought . . .'

'That you would take advantage of it,' said Honey who was feeling sicker by the minute. 'For the sake of your career.'

You not only bedded her husband in her own home, you are a totally self-centred cow!

Doherty insisted she look at the dress before she left. 'Seeing as you think it may be yours.'

She frowned when she saw it.

Honey stood back, watching and listening but not making comment. Doherty had warned her not to.

'Is it your dress?'

Carolina shook her head.

'Are you sure?' asked Doherty.

On seeing Carolina's expression, Honey guessed immediately what was coming next.

A scowl came to the lovely face. 'I wouldn't be seen dead in a dress like that.'

'The boys in the office asked if you've got any autographed photos,' Doherty asked suddenly, taking Honey completely by surprise. He threw her a warning look and she knew instantly that he was up to something.

Her response was instant and dramatic. 'I most certainly do!'

Opening her handbag, she brought out an envelope containing a number of photographs.

'Portrait or full frontal?' She smiled at Doherty meaningfully. To his credit, he managed not to blanch at the prospect that full frontal might be one of her in the nude. As it turned out it wasn't.

'Have you a pen?'

Doherty obliged. Carolina willingly signed a number of photographs.

'Can you leave us a few of each,' Doherty asked her. Carolina was more than pleased to do so.

* * *

'I'll have one portrait and one full frontal,' said Honey once Carolina was gone.

Doherty narrowed his eyes and a grin twitched at the corners of his mouth. 'You're just curious to see whether she's got her clothes on.'

134

Honey tossed her head. 'It makes no difference to me. I just want to know who killed Marietta. That woman isn't exactly weeping is she.'

Doherty leaned forward and tapped her nose. 'You know what happened to the wooden puppet who didn't tell the truth . . .'

'Yes. His nose grew. But I'm not jealous of her. Honest I'm not.'

As expected, Carolina looked good on both photos.

Legs long enough to knit a tennis net, Carolina presented quite a picture especially seeing as she was wearing little more than a few sequins and a feather which looked as though it were sticking out from between the cheeks of her bottom. Honey guessed it was just the camera angle.

'I need more than one of this one. I'll never get it back. Fancy posing like that!'

Doherty smiled. 'Fancy.'

Honey read his look and heard his hopeful tone. She paused by the door.

'Don't even think about it.'

He shrugged whilst wearing his best little-boy-hurt look.

'What have you got against a few sequins and a feather in private?'

'I'm allergic to the glue that sequins are fastened with, and feathers make me sneeze!'

CHAPTER NINETEEN

'What are you doing?'

Lindsey had taken her mother unawares. Honey did her best to look innocent and to hide the catalogue of Italian clothes she'd been referring to. The gorgeous clothes in the catalogue had been modelled by women with lolly stick figures and impeccable manicures.

In a knee jerk response to meeting the gorgeous Carolina, Honey was in the process of trying on clothes.

Carolina had unnerved her with her great height, flashing white teeth and perfect complexion. She was beautiful. No wonder Harold Clinker had shunned the normal rules of his marriage and taken her to bed — the marriage bed that up until then had been sacrosanct to him and his wife.

Honey sighed. Clothes were made for women like Carolina with their long legs and fatless figures. They didn't always seem made for figures with lumpy bits and the need for firm control undergarments.

The clothes in the catalogue were breathtaking, dramatic and beautifully presented in combinations Honey would never have thought of. Mixing jade with flowery jackets, and coral with purple, she'd done her best. Once satisfied she was close to the style of the model in the magazine, she had then surveyed the final effect in the mirror.

Lindsey had taken her unawares.

'Do you think I need liposuction?' Honey asked. She prodded at her hips. 'Here and here.'

Lindsey picked up the magazine and flicked through it. After perusing a page or two, she shook her head. 'No. It's not pounds you need to lose. It's years.'

'Thanks a bundle!'

'So what's brought this on?'

'My wedding,' Honey exclaimed even though it wasn't really the truth. 'I have to look good for my wedding.'

The glamorous photos of Carolina Sherise chose that moment to slide out of the centre of the magazine where she'd been using them as bookmarks and onto the floor. Lindsey picked them up.

'Is this one of the models?'

'No.'

'They fell out of the magazine. You know, like a free gift.'

'No,' Honey replied, more huffily this time because she couldn't evade telling the truth. 'She's involved in the murder case.'

'And she's thin as a stick and gorgeous with it.'

'No comment. Okay, she's a real clothes horse. I'm pretty certain she buys her clothes from this catalogue. Italian clothes. Don't they look drop dead gorgeous?'

'Of course they do. But only if you've got the figure of a bean stick. Oh, and it also helps if you're about sixteen years old. Do you know that some of the models you see on the catwalk and in these magazines are sometimes thirteen and fourteen?'

'So! You're saying I don't need to worry.'

'Not at all. You're fine as you are,' Lindsey responded giving her mother a hug and a kiss on the cheek. 'How does she fit into the case?'

Honey picked up the one showing Carolina smiling at the camera. She'd been smiling this morning too. Even once she knew more details of the murder, a smile had never been that far from her luscious lips.

'She was a friend of the murder victim and an even closer friend of the victim's husband.'

'Is she the prime suspect?'

Honey shook her head. 'No. Not so far anyway. The husband has that position. He's done a runner.'

'Well he would do.'

'They had a fight, him and his wife. They also had an open marriage.'

'Ugh oh! Be celibate or be faithful. That's my view on marriage.'

Mention of celibate brought to Honey's mind her recent interest in becoming a nun.

'You're not really considering it; are you? Becoming a nun, I mean.'

Lindsey curled herself into a comfy chair, the magazine on her lap.

'Think of the money I'd save on buying the latest must-have fashion.'

'Think of the lack of male company.'

Lindsey stopped turning pages. Her eyes appeared to be scrutinising the magazine, but Honey knew she wasn't. The signs were there for the reading; she was biting her bottom lip and the pages were not being turned.

She lifted her heart-shaped face, her eyes gleaming mischievously.

'I need to consider my options.'

'I think you do,' said Honey who had finally settled on wearing yellow trousers and a black and white striped shirt that skirted her thighs. Her Italian court shoes finished the ensemble.

'You're looking good,' she hissed to her reflection. Her eyes glanced at her favourite bag; a big brown one which had room for everything she needed including a pair of loafers to change into when her feet started aching. She'd thought she'd thrown it out after buying the pink bag. The pink bag wouldn't hold a pair of shoes. The brown one would.

'You are looking good,' Lindsey repeated, then added, 'Aren't you going to try and talk me out of it?'

'No.'

She looked surprised. 'Why is that?'

Honey turned, halfway out of the door. 'Because it won't happen. Being celibate isn't in the genes.'

CHAPTER TWENTY

The lock-up garage where Ahmed had kept his Rolls Royce was to the rear of a rank of ex-local authority houses on the edge of Keynsham, a small town sandwiched between Bath and Bristol.

On hearing the garages were up for sale and likely to attract a decent rent, the owner of one of the houses put in a bid and got the lot. His neighbours had been given the chance to buy each garage individually, but most preferred to either park their cars on the road or rip down the front hedge and pour a concrete drive on the front lawn.

Honey parked her car, got out and looked along the back of the houses. There were only three gardens backing directly onto the lane with a good sightline of the garages where Ahmed kept his car. One of them might have seen something. It was planned to put out an appeal on TV detailing the woman having been found dead in the back of a white Rolls Royce and saying where that car had been kept. It was likely it would ring a bell with someone, but it didn't hurt to get ahead. Honey wanted this all to be finished. Her views on getting married were taking a bit of a bashing.

The first man she tackled was using a hedge trimmer to attack a stubby row of conifers that had already been truncated but were now being trimmed.

Seeing as he was wearing a pair of ear defenders, Honey used sign language to attract his attention, apologising for bothering him.

'That's all right, love. I could do with a break.' After shoving his goggles and ear defenders onto the top of his head, he glanced back towards the house. 'This bloody hedge could have been left a week or two longer and I could have sat down and watched the cricket this afternoon. It was an executive decision that the hedge would be trimmed today!' A plug of grey hair surged up over his neckline when he shrugged his shoulders. 'And who am I to argue. Only the dogsbody. That's what I am.'

'You're doing a good job.'

He eyed her suspiciously. 'She ain't paid you to say that, 'as she?'

'No. It just looks very neat and tidy.'

'Bloody conifers. I told 'er indoors not to go for 'em, but she insisted. That was fifteen years ago. And they grew, didn't they, grew and grew until we 'ad moss instead of lawn growing 'ere, and didn't see the sunlight for half the year.'

Honey nodded in agreement. 'That's the trouble with conifers.'

A forest of hair sprouted from beneath his arm when he raised a bottle of water to his thirsty lips. He was wearing an unbuttoned checked shirt over a string vest. His skin glistened with sweat.

'You sound as though you know yer stuff. Are you with a garden centre?'

'No. I'm with the police.'

His eyes opened wide. 'Jesus! 'Ave she in number ten been complaining about me making a noise?'

'No. It's nothing to do with noise. It's about the theft of a motor car from one of the garages. A white Rolls Royce. Do you know anything about it?'

'I heard it got stolen, but by nobody round 'ere, I can guarantee that. If they was goin' to take a car they like something sporty, know what I mean? Something that will outrun the cops' car.'

'You didn't see anyone taking it?'

He shook his head. 'No, though I could 'ave done, now that I've cut these bloody trees down to size.'

Honey began rummaging in her bag for a picture she had of Marietta but instead brought out the head and shoulders portrait of Carolina Sherise. 'Can I ask you if you've ever seen this woman before?'

Marietta's photo must have got caught beneath the naughty photo of Carolina Sherise. Well that can stay where it is, she said to herself. It was the face that people remember. Half-naked wearing sequins and a feather would only serve to cloud a man's recall.

A dirty finger and thumb delved in the pocket of his checked shirt to retrieve a pair of spectacles. A quick flick and he had them on the end of his nose.

Firstly he looked at the photo close up before stretching out his arms and eyeing her from a distance.

'Nice looking girl. A bit like that Naomi Campbell, you know, that supermodel; all teeth and legs that go on forever, though basically a bit too skinny for my liking. I prefer something with a bit more meat on the bones . . .'

'Reginald! What's going on here?'

At the sound of his wife's ear-splitting demand, Reginald handed back the photograph. 'Sorry love. I can't 'elp you. Voluptuous Vera,' he added dourly before his expression changed, a more jovial expression adopted and directed at his wife.

'This lady is with the police, my darling. It's to do with that car that was nicked.'

Vera had arms like legs of ham and a roll to her ample hips similar to that of a hippo about to indulge in a bit of mud rolling.

Her corn-coloured hair looked as though she hadn't long left the stylist and her triple chin quivered with laboured breath until she came to a standstill. She had pink skin. Even her arms. Probably pink all over, Honey decided.

'Doesn't the hedge look nice, dear,' Reginald said to his wife, but Vera wasn't listening. Her expression was focused, intense.

'I just heard that car was involved in a murder,' she breathed, her words expelled in a rush, her eyes bright with interest.

Honey told her she was correct. 'I know you've already been asked if you saw anything, but I wonder if you could take a look at a photograph.'

'Pleased to,' said Vera. 'Anything to help catch whoever killed the poor girl. And in her wedding dress too. How tragic is that? That's one who won't be promising till death us do part.'

'Terrible shame,' said Reginald, shaking his head. Honey wondered whether he was being sincere, or merely agreeing with his wife even though his view of marriage might not match hers.

'If you could take a look?'

Vera took her husband's spectacles and looked at the photograph.

'No,' she said, sending her chins quivering as she shook her head. 'Never see her before. Never seen her before, have we, Reg?'

Reg shook his head too and agreed they'd never seen her before. 'But you don't know all your neighbours these days, do you?'

Honey thanked Reginald and Vera for their time and asked if she might have their surname and telephone number just in case she needed to talk to them again.

'Pludd,' said Vera. 'Mr Reginald Leonard Pludd and Mrs Vera Elizabeth Pludd.'

'Do you think your neighbours might have seen something?' she asked before she headed off down the alley that led from the garage block to the street.

Husband and wife exchanged wry looks.

'That's anybody's guess. Her at number six works nights. At a club. So she says.' Vera's chins folded one upon the other as her eyes flashed in disbelief. 'Still in bed I dare say, though not necessarily alone. Or in 'er own bed for that matter.'

Honey nodded confirmation that she got the picture. It came to her that she didn't know where Carolina Sherise lived. She crossed her fingers, hoping she might have struck lucky.

'Do you know her name?'

'Only her first name,' said Vera. 'Geri. That's what she's called. I presume it's short for Geraldine. I don't know her second name.'

'Evans. It's Evans,' said Reginald.

His wife looked up at him in surprise. 'How do you know that?' She didn't sound best pleased.

'The postman left a parcel here the other week. Something from Amazon I think. It had her address on it.'

'And I suppose you delivered it to her. Once you knew she was home!'

Reginald laughed. 'Now come on, me love. I was only doin' what's right.'

His wife remained po-faced.

Disappointed that the occupant of the house was not named Carolina Sherise, Honey felt obliged to chivvy things along.

'That house there seems to have a good view of the garages.' She pointed to the third house along, another brick-built semi almost identical to that occupied by Reg and his wife. 'Are they likely to be home?'

Vera led the way. 'Oh yes. Him at number eight will be there. He's always there. Not that you'll get much sense out of 'im. He's a bit touched you see. Ain't been the same since his wife went. And I don't mean that he's a widower. She took off with a second-hand car salesman from that place in Temple Street.'

'But I am likely to find him in?'

Reginald pulled a rueful face. 'Oh yes. Nigel Brooks. He'll be very pleased to see you and probably invite you in.' He paused. 'Take my advice. Don't go in. You might never get out again.'

144

CHAPTER TWENTY-ONE

Taking the alley connecting the parking lot to the street front of 1930s red-brick semi-detached houses, Honey smiled at the way Reginald Leonard Pludd had tapped the side of his nose. She took it as a warning that as a woman entering the house of a single man, she might not be safe.

She hadn't been able to deduce much about the two houses she intended visiting from their rear aspect. There was nothing for it but to knock on the front door. Number six and number eight.

She assumed the bachelor pad would be dead scruffy whereas the one occupied by Geraldine Evans would be clean, neat and tidy.

'This is it,' she murmured on pushing open what was left of the front gate. There was no latch, some of the spokes were missing along with one hinge so it creaked when she pushed it open.

The front garden would say it all, she thought, an area of neglect, the windows of the house unwashed, the front door unpainted; the house in which resided a man without a woman.

A jungle of weeds sprouted from what had been a rose bed. Both front door and windows were in need of redecoration, paint peeling like slivers of dried skin.

Not locating a doorbell, Honey rapped at the knocker on the wooden door. The sound reverberated from inside and there was nothing else; no television, no radio, no pinging singing of a play station or computer.

'Come on, Nigel.'

She was getting impatient and this time gave the knocker another almighty rap.

Shoving her hands in her pockets, she stared at the door, willing it to open. Some people had the power to open doors and move immovable objects. Perhaps she could do it. Well you never know until you try. You might have the power and it's called . . .

She searched her brain for the right term. Ah yes. Telekinesis! That was it.

Another minute or two ticked by.

One more minute, one more tap on the knocker and she knew the power of mind over matter simply wasn't hers.

Turning her back on the door she headed back through the scruffy front garden to the rusty gate.

Now for the next house.

The gate was painted mustard and didn't squeak or creak when she opened it. The front lawn was bereft of moss or weed, and bordered with sweet-smelling summer flowers; everything from delphiniums to carnations, cornflowers and Canterbury Bells. All these lesser flowers grew in circles around a multitude of rose bushes.

A pale pink rose climbed neatly up a trellis at the side of the door. The plastic windows and front door looked new, the glass was washed and polished.

The aspect of this house compared with the last one she'd visited couldn't have been more different. It also bore out her belief that a woman, whether she was single or had a man in tow, made all the difference to how a house was looked after.

The doorbell was brass and played the strokes of Big Ben; a little ostentatious perhaps, but better than the lonely sound of a door knocker.

She took another look at the sunny garden, smelled the roses and leaning slightly to one side, admired her reflection in the window. She wasn't kept waiting for long.

The man who answered the door didn't exactly greet her as a long-lost friend, but he was friendly. He was also about six feet tall with blonde hair that might have been natural at one time. He was about fifty and had a deep cleft in his square jaw — like a peach — cleaving it almost in half.

The chin drew Honey's attention so she forgot to check everything else.

'The expected visitor!'

'You've been expecting me?' She couldn't help sounding surprised. How had he known? Then it came to her. Reg and Vera must have phoned him. 'So you know what this is all about.'

He opened the door wide. 'Yes. Nothing's a secret in this neighbourhood. Come on in. I'll make you a cup of tea.'

Taking it as read, she didn't ask that Reg and Vera had alerted their neighbour that she was coming. She also assumed that Geraldine Evans — Geri — was still asleep and had left the man friend to do the honours.

The smell of a clean house came out to greet her. Well, this was more like it. She thanked him and crossed the threshold.

'Take a seat in here,' he said, opening the door into the front room. 'The kettle's boiled. The teapot's warm plus I've made scones. Jam and clotted Cornish cream okay with you?'

Was it? The smell of freshly cooked scones wafted through from the kitchen and up into Honey's nostrils. She told him it would be wonderful whilst trying hard not to salivate.

'I take it Miss Evans is asleep. Understandable seeing as she works nights.'

He looked a little blank for a moment and then said, yes, she did work nights so mostly slept during the day.

She noticed his eyes were blue and although his smile seemed genuine enough, she couldn't keep her own eyes away from that cleft chin. Like a deep dimple or the cleft between a pair of well-rounded buttocks.

Whilst waiting for him to come back with refreshments, she looked around the room and felt blinded by light. Everything in the room was magnolia, ivory or oatmeal with the exception of a series of scatter cushions sporting a rose bouquet design. The latter were placed at regular intervals along the settee and one in each chair. They were so very regular that she wondered if somebody had purposely measured the spaces in between with a ruler. Possibly, she thought. Some people were that sad.

A widescreen television occupied the recess closest to the window. Placed on a small table in front of the window was a bouquet of roses and other flowers tied round with a cream satin bow.

On the wall immediately opposite the window hung a Victorian style painting of a bride signing the register and the attentive bridegroom leaning over her shoulder. The glass covering it reflected the street scene outside the window; privet hedges, red-brick and parked cars.

Her host returned with proper cups and saucers, all in a rose pattern design and balanced on a silver tray.

She tried not to let the smell of the scones cloud her judgement, but on the whole decided that this man — who as yet hadn't given her his name — knew the way to a woman's heart. He was very polite, plus he knew how to make scones.

The tray was placed on a glass topped coffee table.

'It looks lovely,' she said, and meant it. A man who could cook was a definite asset for a woman who worked nights.

She started to sit down.

'Stop!'

Honey stalled, bottom poised above the settee.

'The cushion. Don't lean back on the cushion. You'll disturb it. Sit forward please. I don't want it disturbed.'

So, she thought, the lady of the house was fastidious and he was only following instructions.

She did as required.

'Milk in first,' he said before pouring the tea. 'Sugar?'

Honey shook her head. 'No thank you. I'm sweet enough.'

A trite joke, but he seemed to think it was funny.

'Of course you are. Nobody ever said you were anything else.'

Alarm bells rang. He made it sound as though he knew her well. Had he mixed her up with somebody else?

She wondered what Geraldine — Geri — looked like. There were no photographs anywhere, just bland décor lifted by the bouquet of roses, the cushions, the Victorian painting of the bride and her whiskered bridegroom. Despite those little touches, the room was still too bland, too white, like a near-death experience. Gathering her thoughts and wits into one tidy bunch, she decided the time was ripe to nudge things along a bit.

First she had to try the scones, the jam and the creamily golden Cornish clotted cream. The trouble was that one just wasn't enough. She couldn't resist when he offered her another plus a second cup of tea. She also commented that the jam and cream were excellent.

He relished her approval and seemed set on eliciting more.

'Note the sugar cubes. Cubes. Not that common granulated muck. One lump or two?'

'As I said earlier, I don't take sugar, thank you.'

He looked at her as though she'd said something totally disgusting — like, *How about we settle down for a game of Strip Jack Naked.*

She flashed him her warmest smile. 'I have to watch my figure. I'm getting married. Have to fit into the dress.'

'Of course!' He slapped his palm against his head as though he already knew. 'Sorry, darling. I forgot. You want to look your best. White dress, bouquet of sweet-smelling roses.' His voice was dreamy. His gaze drifted to the floral display of soft pinks, blues and misty white and he began to hum the Wedding March.

Honey tensed, clutched her teacup and wished she hadn't eaten that second scone. Scones slowed you down if you happened to be considering making a sharp exit. And she was!

What was all this about? He was speaking as though he were part of her wedding arrangements — arrangements, she reminded herself, which were far from finalised.

He couldn't know that she was getting married. She'd never met him before.

Neither had she mentioned getting married to the neighbours.

What to do? Handle it. There was nothing else to it.

'Excuse me. What did you say your name was?'

He looked affronted. 'That's very hurtful. You know very well who I am.'

Honey gulped. Humour him, she told herself. Just humour him.

'This is a very lovely room.' Her teacup rattled as she placed it back in its saucer.

'Not as lovely as you.'

He slid forward in his chair so that his knees almost touched hers.

'About the wedding car . . .'

'I think a white Rolls Royce. All brides should have a white Rolls Royce. I won't have any disagreements on that point. It has to be a white Rolls Royce.'

'You saw it, did you? The white Rolls Royce that Mr Clifford used to keep in the garage to the rear of your garden?'

'Oh yes. Do you like it?'

'I've never seen it, and besides, that's what I'm here about. It's been stolen.'

The face of her host set like concrete.

'Who says so?'

Honey thought it an odd thing to say. 'Mr Clifford reported it missing. He left it outside the garage and when he came back to collect it, it was gone. Look,' she said, delving into her bag. 'Do you know this woman?'

This time she'd fetched out the right picture. The man who had fed her the best scones she'd ever tasted, took a long look and shook his head.

'Look, is Miss Evans here?'

He looked at her aghast, drawing his chin in like a pelican retrieving his craw.

'I beg your pardon?'

'Geri Evans. This is her house isn't it?'

'Does this look like her house? That disgusting woman who sleeps all day and keeps all hours?'

'I don't know what her house looks like.'

'Of course you do! Everyone knows she doesn't wash the windows from week to week and certainly doesn't have the place decorated. As for the garden . . . it's a disgrace.'

The truth batted her round the head in one swift strike. She was in the wrong house.

'I'm sorry. You mean this is number eight?'

'Number eight. That indeed the number of this little old house of mine! A nice even figure.'

'So is number six — an even figure I mean.'

Judging by his pained expression, he was about to put her straight on that.

'It is painfully obvious to any sane person that number six is not even in the way that number eight is even. Number six only has one circle. Number eight has one at the top and one at the bottom. That's why the Chinese consider it lucky. Two concentric circles joined together. It means you can never lose.'

Honey stared at him, her jaw hanging slack. Reg and Vera had warned her not to enter number eight on pain of not getting out again — not in a hurry anyway.

She sprang to her feet. 'I need the bathroom.'

The teacup rattled in the saucer and the saucer tottered on the plate as she returned them to the tray.

'Up the stairs, first on the left,' he said. 'Whilst you attend to that, I'll get out the wedding planner and we can decide the final details. Now. Where did I put them?'

Even before he was on his feet and rummaging in a highly polished bureau, Honey was out of the door and up the stairs, leaping them two at a time.

By the time she'd locked the door she was breathless.

Think! Think, she urged herself.

The bathroom was white. More white. The whiteness was blinding her.

Feeling a sense of rising panic, she closed her eyes and tried some deep breathing exercises she'd learned to do at a First Aid class. They were said to keep you calm in an emergency.

This is an emergency, she told herself. Nevertheless, the deep breathing didn't seem to be doing much.

Something here wasn't quite right. In fact something was very wrong. Blinded by her own preconceptions, she'd stumbled into the wrong house. She'd assumed the occupant of the scruffy house to be a man, the neat house to be a woman. She'd been hopelessly wrong. She was in house number eight; the man had said so himself, and it was the man at number eight that Reg and Vera had warned her against.

She could hear Doherty's voice ringing in her ears. 'Sloppy work, Driver.'

She couldn't argue with that. She hadn't asked him and she hadn't checked the number on the front door.

The truth got scarier when she realised she hadn't given him her name. So what was all this stuff about wedding dresses? There was no denying that the house resembled the inside of a bridal shop, all white and pink roses. He also favoured a white Rolls Royce for the bride.

'Shit!' The prospect of reintroducing her cussing jar raised its head, one bad word and in went a pound coin. Amazing how quickly the last jar had filled up.

It was as though somebody had suddenly tipped a bucket of cold water over her. Her time in the bathroom turned out to be worthwhile thanks to drinking two cups of tea.

Before pulling the flush, she gratefully pulled her mobile phone out of her pocket. Normally it resided in her sack of a bag, but today she'd slid it into her pocket — a tight fit, but it was to hand.

Doherty's number was there, but . . . what should she tell him? That she'd been invited in for tea and scones by a man with no name? That she'd failed to ask his name?

She could imagine what he would say. 'Very unprofessional.'

Being in Doherty's good books, at least as far as professional etiquette was concerned, mattered great deal.

She couldn't phone him until she'd done the sensible thing and faced the man who had plied her with refreshments. Nigel Brooks! The name came in a flash. So did the possibility that he was the killer. It wasn't up to her to prove the point. She'd leave that to the police.

Resuming those deep breaths, she tried to be calm.

It seemed a good idea to leave pulling the flush until she'd had a good look round. Leaving the door ajar, she crossed the landing. The carpet was oatmeal coloured — like pale porridge before the sugar is added. The same carpet covered the floor of the master bedroom which was dominated by a brass four poster bed. It had a floral bedspread. The hangings were floral too. Roses. No surprise there.

If he was the murderer she was being stupid hanging around, but Marietta Hopkins had been a personal friend. She had to do something.

She glanced towards the small front bedroom; carpet the colour of clotted cream, walls the same, curtain . . .

And something else.

The door was only slightly ajar; one or two more footsteps — okay, perhaps three — and she could peep inside. That something else, a whitish blob, intrigued her.

If the man downstairs should hear her, the door to the room was right next to the stairs; she'd be down in no time.

One, two, three footsteps. She was there, but somehow at the wrong angle. The door needed to open just that bit more so she could see *exactly* . . .

Using just two fingers, she gently pushed the door open, then blinked and blinked again.

The bridal dress was the biggest meringue of a dress she'd ever seen, unless the room wasn't a room but a broom cupboard, a box room as it was commonly called.

It was definitely a wedding dress. There was also a veil, a great heavy train seeded with pearls.

What was it doing here? Did this man, whoever he was, deal in bridal wear?

No! If that was the case there would be more hanging on a long rail running the length of the room — such as it was. It occurred to her that he might have more wedding dresses elsewhere in the house. Plenty more to fit all ages, sizes and shapes of brides.

Her blood chilled. Doherty had to be told. After that, she was out of here, back downstairs and hot foot it out of the front door as quick as her feet could take her. Luckily she was wearing flat shoes today. Running would have been out of the question if she'd opted for high heels.

First hide your tracks. She nipped swiftly back to the bathroom, pulled the flush and closed the door noisily—just so he knew she was on her way.

The man she now recalled was named Nigel Brooks was waiting for her downstairs standing at the entrance to the milk white front room.

'I'm cooking lamb chops for dinner. Unless you'd like to go out?'

Lamb chops! Was he mad?

Very likely. She only prayed that the front door wasn't locked and she wouldn't end up as his prisoner. Homemade scones and lamb chops were no substitute for the freedom to be a slob whenever you wanted.

It seemed shame to puncture that hopeful expression, but this was a nightmare—like when Alice fell down the well. In Honey's case she'd entered a house she'd been warned not to enter.

'Mr Brooks isn't it?'

154

He looked a trifle confused. 'You know it is.'

'Yes. I know you're Nigel Brooks. Your neighbours told me so. I'm here on behalf of the police to ask whether you saw anything suspicious over the back the night before last. Principally, did you see anyone stealing Mr Clifford's white Rolls Royce.' There was no way she was going to mention the wedding dress upstairs or the fact that both dead women had been wearing wedding dresses. That way led to trouble — and possibly her own death.

The face of the man in front of her suddenly lost the soft pastiness of a man happy to oblige her. The dent in his chin quivered like a peach about to burst open.

'What are you doing in my house?'

It took a lot of courage to remain calm and sound confident. 'I told you, Mr Brooks. I'm asking questions about the Rolls Royce Mr Clifford keeps in the garage at the back there. He didn't put it away the other night because he'd left the garage keys behind. He had to leave it out all night and in the morning it was gone.'

She stopped herself from saying anything about the circumstances of it being found. She didn't want to mention the dead woman in the back and the fact she was wearing a wedding dress.

'Are you accusing *me*?'

His jovial tone was totally absent.

'No, I'm just asking . . .'

'She sent you here, didn't she? That tart next door. That's why you were asking about her. *Geraldine!*' He said her name as though he were chewing on lemons.

'No. I told you, I'm here on behalf of the police . . .'

'I know nothing. Tell the police that. I know ABSOLUTELY NOTHING!'

'Many thanks for the tea.'

Honey made a dash for the front door, fully expecting him to reach out, knock it closed, or grab her shoulder and drag her back in. Then he might make her take her clothes off and put on that wedding dress. A dreadful thought. Big skirts like that giant meringue just didn't suit her!

As with the garden gate, the door hinges were well oiled so one turn of the lock and it flew open and like Meat Loaf's 'Bat Out of Hell', she flew through it.

Breathless she sat in her car, phone pressed to her ear.

Doherty listened. 'Stay there. A car is on its way. Are you parked outside this bloke's house?'

'No. A few doors up. But get here quickly. I'm scared.'

CHAPTER TWENTY-TWO

Nigel Brooks stood at the door, his jaw set and his eyes glittering. Every woman wanted to wear a white wedding dress, didn't she? Even after the wedding ceremony when everything was perfect, the dress perfectly white, the bouquet a mass of beautiful blooms, it didn't mean to say that they could never — or should never — wear that dress again. It didn't even matter if the dress they had worn on that special day had rotted away long ago, or that they had outgrown the actual dress; there was nothing to stop them wearing another white dress.

And that's where he could help them. He had lots of white dresses, not just the one *she* had worn; his wife. He had other dresses up in the attic. Not that he allowed every woman he came across to wear one of his dresses. They had to be special. They had to look like Audrey.

Audrey had been a beautiful bride, but then she'd run away. She'd said that marriage didn't suit her. She said their marriage was a farce and that their wedding was a farce. To him it had been sweet and sacred, but not to her. Never to her. She'd preferred her pet Labrador, a big smelly thing called Roberto, to him.

His head was reeling when he turned away from the door, a cold sweat breaking out on his forehead. His footsteps were soft on the carpet because he wore no shoes. He never wore shoes in the house.

Only once he was back in his beautiful front room, a shrine to his beloved Audrey, the white, creamy softness of it rousing memories of that special day when she'd worn a bridal gown, the fabric seeming to float on air; just like her. And the bouquet! Roses and cornflowers and frothy stuff that he didn't know the name of.

He'd thought it was mostly over, the torture, the anger and the thirst for revenge. Apparently it was not.

The woman asking about the car had upset him. Everything had been going smoothly until she'd arrived. He needed to calm down. He needed to get outside of himself, to become somebody else if only for an hour. So he did what he always did when he wanted to feel happy. He went upstairs and into the box bedroom.

CHAPTER TWENTY-THREE

The Zodiac Club was in full swing, but not everyone was feeling groovy and looking happy. Doherty was pissed off. He was sitting at the bar with his chin resting on his hand staring into space. He shouldn't have been there at all, but he'd had a shit day. For a mind-blowing moment, it had appeared that the case of the murdered brides was solved. Nigel Brooks was up for it. Plain sailing, so it seemed.

The first sign that things might not be quite so simple occurred when Nigel Brooks was arrested dressed as a blushing bride. In fact, his dress had been so huge that they'd had trouble loading him into the back of the police car.

Notwithstanding the bridal gown, it would have brightened his day if Nigel, the man who collected wedding dresses, had not had a cast-iron alibi. On the night stipulated by the pathologist as being the time Marietta was murdered, Nigel had been at a cross-dressing function. Everyone there agreed he'd been the high spot of the evening wearing the meringue of a dress he kept in his box room. One of the witnesses had even gushed that he'd been unforgettable.

Being back to square one with the case in hand was bad enough, but on top of that Lindsey had forwarded him an email.

I've got your mother. Marry that copper and the old lady's for the chop.

Shortly afterwards Honey had phoned him.

'Can you believe this?'

Doherty had groaned. All this business with marriages and brides was giving him a headache. The smooth road to marrying Honey seemed to be climbing up a monkey puzzle tree. He'd received the news with disbelief. Who on earth would want to kidnap Gloria Cross? More to the point, how were they coping now they had her?

Honey's mother was a nuisance. She'd always been a pain in the neck. He found himself almost pitying whoever had kidnapped her.

Honey herself had sounded hesitant on the phone as though she too didn't quite believe it. Kidnappers had a preference for abducting calm, submissive people worth a small fortune. Gloria was comfortably off, though not a millionaire. Besides that she was awkward, interfering and annoying. To say she was likely to be uncooperative was putting it mildly. She had tantrums. Her way was the right way and whoever had been stupid enough to take her was going to have their work cut out for them.

'I don't believe it,' he'd muttered.

On the other end of the phone, Honey was more or less thinking the same thing. Lindsey had suggested her mother was just trying to attract attention. 'What with you and your plans to marry Doherty,' she had mused. 'You know she wasn't pleased when you told her.'

Okay, so he didn't exactly get on with Honey's mother. She was too overbearing, too fond of poking her nose into her daughter's love life. If she had her way Honey would now be comfortably married to somebody with a big car, a big house and a *very* big bank account.

On top of that, Gloria Cross was so active! For goodness' sake, the woman was in her seventies but refused to believe it. She wouldn't even admit to being a grandmother, insisting that her granddaughter, Lindsey, called her by her first name, Gloria.

Whoever kidnapped Gloria Cross had bitten off more than they could chew. If she *had* been kidnapped that is. And if she had, it certainly threw his suspicions about the threatening letters into disarray. He'd had a theory, one he hadn't confided to Honey but writing threatening letters was one thing; kidnapping was quite another.

'We have to be sure,' he'd said to Honey over the phone. 'It could just be one big practical joke.'

'You don't sound as though you're taking this very seriously.' She'd sounded hurt. If he could see her face he knew she would look puzzled.

'Instinct,' he had responded, unwilling to voice the suspicion that had nagged at the back of his mind since the first letter had arrived.

'I'm going round to her flat to check it out. There has to be a clue there somewhere. I'll catch up with you later.'

* * *

That had been on Friday evening. There was hope still for a more smooth-running Saturday. Unfortunately that wasn't the way things turned out. When a day started off on the wrong foot there was a pretty good chance it would stay that way.

First one of the diners had insisted on seeing the box her breakfast eggs had been bought in.

'I only eat free range,' she'd proclaimed in a very loud voice.

Clare, art student and occasional breakfast waitress had assured her that the eggs were indeed laid by free range fowl.

'The eggs come from Mr and Mrs Baker,' she told the guest. 'They keep hens and geese and all sorts of things on their land.'

The guest, a Madam Brussard who came from Rennes, was unconvinced.

'I cannot possibly take the word of a *waitress*. Show me the box.'

161

The woman's head was crowned with a beehive of carefully arranged hair and, as if to balance it, she held her head high. Her voice seeming to exit via her nose rather than her mouth which gave her tone a nasally, throaty burr.

Clare, bless her cotton socks, was aware that although the eggs came from a smallholding on the outskirts of Bath, the box they came in was a recycled grey preformed thing used by every supermarket in the city.

Already flushed because the hotel was full and all the residents had descended on the dining room at around the same time, Clare was at a loss at what to do.

At least one person sitting in that dining room noticed the poor girl was rushed off her feet. Mary Jane had also overheard the Frenchwoman's demands regarding her wish to scrutinise the egg box.

'I'll go get it, honey,' she said, giving Clare a reassuring pat.

Amazingly energetic for her age, Mary Jane marched out of the dining room bumping into Honey before making the kitchen.

'The French broad doesn't believe the eggs are free range. She wants to see the box they came in.'

Honey looked baffled. 'A *box*?'

'The chick has obviously never bought eggs from anywhere other than a supermarket and she wants to a box that confirms they're free range.'

Honey remembered a broken box that had said just that. She rummaged in the bins before finding a suitable free range egg box. On presenting it to her, the French woman almost cradled the shabby grey box to her breast. Honey hadn't the heart to tell her that she'd retrieved it from the same bin that contained wet wipes used on the baby's bottom in room twelve. The box had been sandwiched between that and the baby's discarded disposable, the latter very full and very smelly.

Not long after, the butcher decided to leave his brains behind and delivered a turkey for the Sunday carvery that was below weight. Smudger the hotel chef was not amused.

'Take it back,' he snapped.

Unfortunately the van driver was new, hadn't met many chefs before and didn't seriously believe Smudger's threat to bury the meat cleaver in his head.

Whilst Smudger shot off to collect his weapon of choice, Honey saved the situation, told the driver to take the turkey and deliver them a bigger one. By the time Smudger got back he was gone.

The day calmed down until a trip to the car park of the cash and carry when a woman pushing a large flatbed trolley loaded up with bottles of booze collided with Honey's car. The lady pushing it apologised most profusely on seeing the dent she'd left in the wing of Honey's beloved old Citroen.

'So, so, very sorry. I give you my insurance details.'

On recalling that she had a hefty excess amount before insurance paid out, Honey brushed her offer away. 'I'll cover it myself.'

What the hell. It was only a dent. Minor irritations. That was what they were, she told herself. How about something less irritating?

It was just after agreeing with the woman to forgive and forget that Lindsey sent her the details of the email about her mother being kidnapped. She couldn't tell if it was genuine and Honey was in two minds not to pay anyway. The kidnappers would soon get tired of her and send her back. 'But seriously. What if it is genuine?'

'Can you trace it or something?'

'I'm good, but not that good. But I will try. I do have a friend who works for GCHQ . . .'

'Spare me the details. I've no wish to add an investigation by MI5 to my problems!'

Nobody really believed Gloria had been kidnapped, mainly because they all knew she'd been pretty pissed off at the prospect of Doherty and Honey getting hitched. Getting kidnapped would be a good way of upsetting their plans.

'I'm going round to her flat. If there's no sign of her there, I'll pop round to some of her friends.'

Doherty phoned and told her that he was of the opinion that there was nothing to worry about. 'A few days and they'll bring her back.'

'I knew you'd say that.'

'I just can't help thinking . . . well . . . you know your own mother.'

She didn't like to admit that she'd been thinking the same thing but it did irk her all the same and said, a little irritably. 'I could get Lindsey to reply and say okay, the wedding is off.'

Silence followed before Doherty spoke. 'Is that what you want?'

'No,' she said abruptly. 'Of course it isn't. I'm just thinking it might put an end to this. I did tell you about the frog and stuff didn't I?'

'You're thinking it's all connected.'

'I think so.'

'Don't give up on us, Honey.'

His considered flippancy had turned serious.

Honey was touched.

'What with this and Nigel the Nutcase. You have to see that house to believe it. Everything white and then a wedding dress. I presume it was his wife's.'

Doherty's silence was like a full stop. You had to wait for the next sentence to lay out the bold and bare facts. 'Unfortunately he checks out. Cast-iron alibi; he was wearing one of his dresses at the time. I'll see you later at the Zodiac. Speak to you then.'

* * *

Saturday night and although he was waiting for her at the Zodiac here she was opening the door at her mother's place.

As the door opened the smell of roses and heavy perfume wafted out through the gap.

'Hello! Anybody home?'

Her voice didn't echo off clear surfaces and white walls as it might in a home with minimalist features and furnishings. Her mother didn't do minimalist; she did table lamps with glazed bases in oriental designs, the cone shaped shades big enough to wear as a hat. Bookshelves lined two walls of the sitting room, the television was hidden in a Sheraton style cabinet, the carpets were thick and the upholstered settees and chairs bursting with silk covered cushions.

The curtains were custom-made of pale mustard shantung, a glistening fabric kept in place with silk tasselled tiebacks.

Honey took a good look round. Nothing was out of place, but then, she'd expected it to be that way. Her mother had a woman come in three times a week to make sure everything was picture perfect. If *Home and Style* magazine ever wanted to do a photo-shoot of a discerning older woman's crash pad, Honey was certain that this was the one they would choose.

The bedroom was a place of pink, cream and pale green calm. There was a noticeable similarity between her mother's bedroom and Nutty Nigel's, though at least her mother had added pale green to give it a bit of colour. Also there was no wedding dress standing in the middle of the bedroom; in none of the bedrooms in fact.

All the same, Honey felt herself shudder at the memory.

The bed was made, three favourite teddies from her mother's collection snuggled against the satin edged pillows, their button eyes staring up at the ceiling.

There was no sign of a struggle. No note pinned to the pillow, no sign that anyone had broken in.

Maybe it was a hoax, just as both she and Doherty were thinking. But if that was the case, where was her mother and why hadn't she been in touch?

The key, she decided, would lie with her mother's vast collection of clothes, bags, shoes and other accessories. Everything hung on hangers or was stored in drawers or on shelves in her mother's wardrobe.

Honey flicked the switch that turned on the interior light and stepped inside.

At first glance, everything was neat and tidy. On second glance the gaps were obvious. So was the fact that the set of quality luggage usually kept on the very top shelf at the end of the room was gone. The luggage was new and if she

165

remembered correctly, her mother had told her she'd bought it for a special occasion. Honey had asked what that occasion might be, but didn't get an answer. She assumed a cruise; her mother really liked cruises.

'That's for me to know and you to find out,' her mother had said when curiosity had overcome her and she'd asked the reason. The coy look in her eyes and the blush on her cheeks had not escaped Honey's notice. Something was going on; a new beau? A new business proposition? Please God, no to the last. Her mother had been playing around with online business ventures. So far she hadn't fallen for the digital spiel, with the noted exception of *Snow on the Roof*, an online dating site for seniors. But there were plenty of sharks out there. If her mother wasn't careful she and her considerable income, courtesy of a few marriages that whilst not exactly being made in heaven, had set her up very nicely financially, might be swallowed whole. Honey wouldn't want that to happen. An independent mother could be kept at arm's length. A destitute one might move in with her!

Standing in the middle of the storage space, she surveyed the hanging garments, the dressing table, the shoe bars where feminine pairs of mostly kitten heeled shoes were stored in colour banded order. As with the hanging rails, there were gaps.

And where was her mother's silver handled hairbrush, her toiletries, her make-up, her jewellery box . . . ?

Nowhere!

She opened one of the drawers to the side of the dressing table. No sign of the jewellery box. Very little underwear too. Was it likely that a thief would steal underwear as well as her mother's jewellery? Okay, Gloria Cross favoured silk underwear, but surely a burglar wasn't likely to know the difference. Anyway, it still didn't account for the missing luggage and gaps on rails and in drawers. Judging by the neat gaps in the wardrobe, she was convinced that her mother had not been kidnapped. No, her mother had gone somewhere without telling her, was peeved and wanted to throw a spanner in the works.

She had gone away, but where?

CHAPTER TWENTY-FOUR

By the time Honey had left her mother's flat and arrived at the Zodiac Club, the air was thick with the smell of juicy steaks and garlic-infused prawns, both served on sizzling platters with chips and all the trimmings. Nobody could fail to be moved to hunger pangs when a waiter bearing one of these snake-hipped his way through the clusters of iron framed tables.

She sensed Doherty's welcoming smile was something of an effort. He looked tired and fed up. After giving him a hug, a kiss and commiseration that Nigel Brooks had proved a dead end, she outlined the position as she saw it with her mother.

'I went to her flat. Luggage, clothes, shoes and other things are missing, but everything has been left neat and tidy. No sign of a struggle. That luggage was brand new.'

He managed a sardonic grin. 'It's not usual for a kidnap victim to be given time to pack. Have you checked with her friends?'

Honey nodded and took a sip from the drink he bought her. 'Some. But it's summertime. People go on holidays. Old folk fly to the sun and go on cruises. I blame *Strictly Come Dancing*.'

Doherty nodded and managed a wry smile. 'I'm not sure where this is going, but presume the waltz and the tango have a lot to answer for.'

Honey threw him a wry *don't you know nothing*, kind of look.

'Wrong age group. My mother and her friends are into *Saturday Night Fever*. The old boys on these cruises usually manage to pull a white suit, à la John Travolta, out of the closet.'

'Pax,' he said, raising his hands in abject surrender. 'Pax and goodwill towards men, especially this man. I hereby own up that I kidnapped your mother and presently have her chained up in the cellar.'

'You haven't got a cellar, and anyway, this is still a serious matter. I am now more or less certain that she has not been kidnapped. She's shot off on some last-minute Saga cruise with some hot man who doesn't have one foot in the grave and the other on a bar of soap. That,' she said with an air of finality, 'is my theory.'

A lock of glossy hair fell forward half obscuring Doherty's deep blue eyes. She brushed it back for him with her fingers, smiling as reassuringly as she could. He was bitterly disappointed that the case of the dead brides was not yet tied up. In an odd way her mother had done them a big favour. Doherty needed something else to think about, and although she had adopted a flippant attitude towards her mother's disappearance, it was more to keep Doherty's spirits buoyant than anything else. Although she knew her mother could be very conniving, deep down she was still worried. She wouldn't let Doherty know that. He'd just reassured her that her mother was perfectly capable of looking after herself. A rare moment of affection for her mother had opened up inside her. Poor old mum, she wanted to say, though she knew she was far from that.

'I see where you're coming from,' said Doherty. 'No kidnapper gives his victim time to pack. Throwing a change of clothes into a rucksack is about as far as things are likely to go. It's my experience that top quality leather luggage is never used. Your mother's choosy. I bet everything missing from that wardrobe is colour coordinated.'

That rather dented the affection and concern she'd been cosseting. He was describing her mother as she really was, one who was possessive rather than maternal.

'I think you're right. I know my mother. It wouldn't be the first time she's taken off into the wide blue yonder without telling anyone. However, let's say she has gone on holiday — perfectly understandable. She likes cruises. She also likes intrigue, and the thing still worrying me most is that the sender of the email must know her movements. The email arrived after she had left — to wherever she's gone. How did that person know she was going on holiday, if indeed she has? To start with, I had to believe what the kidnapper said because I couldn't get in touch with my mother. Whoever sent that email must know that. So what now? What are we supposed to do next?'

Doherty's response was interrupted by the urgent ringing of his phone. The moment he began nodding was enough to tell her something important had happened. When he said, 'I'll be right there,' she knew for sure that their Saturday night out was over.

'I'll drop you home,' he said grimly after the call was finished.

'What is it?'

'Let's just say we have another bride to deal with.'

'Give me a break. What is it?' she whispered, purposely leaning into his shoulder so that her breast rested on his arm. 'Another dead bride? Another dead woman in a wedding dress?'

He took his time straightening but she guessed he was happier because his downcast eyes were now fixed on the curve of her breast.

'No. A live man wearing a wedding dress. Your friend Nigel. He's been accused of causing an affray in the village of Wainscote. It was reported by one Janet Audrey Glencannon.'

CHAPTER TWENTY-FIVE

Seeing as the call had ended their Saturday night out, it was only to be expected that Doherty would be a while reporting back to her on his interview with Nigel Brooks. Sunday morning came and went. It was intriguing rather than worrying. Monday was a more likely time for him to get back in touch and tell her what was going on. Still, busy hotelier that she was, her time would be occupied on other things.

She had a dented car to deal with so with that in mind she drove over to see when Ahmed Clifford could book it in and sort it out.

The first question he asked when he saw her was regarding his car.

'Do you know when I can expect it back? Don't the police realise I have a business to run?'

His velvet brown eyes were so full of concern, she half expected him to burst into tears.

'Ahmed, darling, I dare say it won't be too much longer,' she said to him only barely resisting the urge to give him a big comforting cuddle. 'Just a day or so I expect.'

Actually she was only guessing, but she was pretty good at guessing. Guessing was a small part of what it took to be good at what she did — Crime Liaison Officer that is, not hotelier. The hotel game was a minefield, never the same from one day to the next and, on that score she reckoned she was still learning.

Ahmed ran a hand over his plastered back hair. 'I 'ope this don't get 'round. No happy couple are goin' to want to hire my car for their wedding if they hear a dead bride was found in the back of it.'

'I take it they've questioned you about the woman?'

'Steve said I could go into the station and do it tomorrow.' His smile broadened. 'He's a good cop, he is. Got faith in me I reckon.'

Honey couldn't help feeling sorry for him. 'Look, I'm quite happy if you can't repair my dent until after you've dealt with the statement and everything.'

He looked only marginally relieved. 'Okay. I'm not up to speed yet if you know what I mean, what with the business of the car and all that. How about next Wednesday?'

'Let me check my diary.'

Whilst rummaging in the depths of her big brown bag, the photos of Carolina Sherise made their way to the top and fell out.

'Hey!' cried Ahmed as he bent down and picked them up. The full frontal one with the sequins and feather was on top. 'Wow! Sex on legs!'

Honey grabbed it back, letting it fall into the depths of her bag. 'Yes, I'm okay for next Wednesday.'

'That bird. She can wrap her legs around me any day of the week.' Ahmed sniggered. 'Or weekend for that matter. I'm easy. The skirts that chick wears are unbelievable. Nothing left to the imagination. As for her other assets . . .' He cupped his hands in the vicinity of his chest.

Honey was about to make comment that they surely weren't that fantastic, when she suddenly realised exactly what he was saying.

'You've met this woman?'

He nodded. 'Yeah. She wanted to know how much it would cost to hire the Roller. I gave her a price, she wrote it down, and then split.'

'You met Carolina Sherise?'

He nodded again. 'Yeah. I didn't know that was her name though. Come to that, I can't remember her giving me her name.'

Doherty had also given Honey a photo of Harold Clinker. 'What about this man?'

Honey slapped off the mucky thumb he put on the photo. Ahmed again shook his head. 'No. Never seen 'im before.'

'What about the people who live in the houses adjoining where you kept the car, do you know the names of any of them?'

'Oh yeah! A few of them anyway. There's Reg and Vera for a start. They don't miss much and chat plenty over the garden fence. Then there's the Geraldine woman, though you only get to see her at night. Then there's Nigel the Nutcase. I don't think he's really nuts, just a bit lonely since his wife did a runner. Can't understand why he misses her so much. She certainly weren't much to look at. Right dog if you ask me, but then, they reckon that you do get to look like your dog — if you 'ave a dog that is.' His laughter was loud until he saw the disapproving look on Honey's face.

Honey didn't really disapprove; it was just that he'd thrown a spanner into her thoughts. Suspicion was like a satnav; it favoured main roads and tried and tested lines of enquiry.

'Are you telling me that his wife is still alive?'

'Oh yeah. He told me. Talked to me a lot. In fact it was hard to shut him up and I tell you this, if he'd stuffed me with more homemade scones I'd probably burst. If you've met him, you know what he's like. He invites you in for a cup of tea. It's not just difficult to say no, it's difficult to escape. And all he talks about is his wedding day and how wonderful it was. Took a great interest in my wedding car venture. Came round to the garage with me to look it over. Then one day I was there — captured for another cup of tea, and she turned up. Said she wanted him to stop harassing her. Said

172

their marriage was over and she had no intention of coming back. He didn't seem to be listening to her. Kept smiling and looking at her all gooey eyed. Funny smile though. You know all teeth and wide-open mouth. He suggested they could get married all over again, that he had the dress and that he was negotiating with me for the hire of a white Rolls Royce. She went ape!'

It was like a sudden break in a thick mist. She recalled how she'd felt when she'd entered that house. It was putting it mildly to say that Nigel had unnerved her. Who was the ex-wife? Her bet was on Marietta. It wasn't beyond the bounds of possibility that her old friend had married and divorced a first husband before Harold came along with his wedge of cheese torso and superior swing to the backside. Not forgetting oodles of money of course.

Mentally crossing her fingers, she asked the million-dollar question.

'So what's her name, this ex-wife of his?'

Ahmed squeezed his eyes shut, threw back his head and began to click his fingers, mentally perusing a whole list of possible names.

Finally, out it came. 'Janet. She's gone back to her maiden name. Don't know what that is.'

It wasn't the name she'd expected to hear. Janet. Janet who?

It was a wide remit, but never mind; there was still a chance of identification if she had some idea of an address. A long shot, but she went for it.

'Do you happen to know where she lives?'

'Oh yeah. Nigel told me all about it. She runs an animal sanctuary out at Wainscote.'

CHAPTER TWENTY-SIX

Back at the Green River Hotel, a dog was sitting in reception minding its own business, its leash tied to a chair leg. Seeing as it wasn't making any noise and hadn't bitten anyone or cocked its leg, nobody gave it much attention.

'That is a very well-behaved dog,' said Lindsey when she came on duty and went over and tickled beneath its chin. The dog wagged its tail appreciatively.

'The receptionist, Linda, another part timer, agreed with her that it was.

'It's been there most of the morning. Lovely little thing isn't it.'

Lindsey looked at the bundle of white wooliness. It looked similar to a poodle, but her guess was on it being a Bichon Frise — just as fluffy and white but with black button eyes and a shorter snout.

'Did the owner say when they would be back?' she asked.

Linda shook her head as she shrugged into her pale lilac cardigan and prepared to depart. Linda had two jobs: The Green River Hotel from eight to twelve and the afternoon serving in the Edinburgh Wool Shop, hence the lilac cardigan. It was pure wool and she'd bought it cheap in the sale.

'I didn't see who left it there. I don't know who it belongs to.'

Lindsey couldn't bring herself to condemn Linda for not noticing who had left it. Reception had been busy that morning, people coming and going, deliveries from the butcher, the baker and the man who went round checking the burglar alarm system. One thing she did know was that the dog had not been checked in with a resident. He had not been brought in by a guest.

'None of our residents checked a dog into their room?'

Lindsey waited for Linda to answer, but felt apprehensive the moment she saw the fair-haired, pink-cheeked girl chewing her bottom lip at one corner.

'Nobody.'

'Are you *sure* you didn't see who left it there?' She knew that no matter how busy things got, Linda was a sucker for celebrity lifestyle magazines and kept one beneath the reception counter. When she thought herself unobserved, she dipped into it.

She shook her head, face blandly innocent. 'Sorry.'

'Well,' said Lindsey, surlier than she was usually inclined to be. 'I suppose you'd better go and pull a few yarns at the Edinburgh Wool Shop.'

Linda mumbled something that sounded like an apology before taking her leave for her afternoon session selling cardigans and plaid skirts to tourists.

The dog wagged its tail, its black button eyes friendly and full of interest.

Lindsey leaned down to undo its leash. 'Well little chap, we'd better see if we can find out who you belong to.'

She frowned. Poor little thing. It was probably already missing its owner. It didn't deserve to be dumped. It was cute. If she could she would keep it, but she didn't have time to look after dogs. Besides, she had plans for her future and dogs were not included in it.

Just as she was contemplating phoning the RSPCA, Honey came downstairs closely followed by Mary Jane.

Her mother gripped a plunger beneath her arm, rubber protrusion pointing forward like a medieval knight about to take part in a joust. She explained that somebody had blocked the shower in room five again. Par for the course in that particular room where the shower was spacious, big enough for two or even five if you were into that sort of thing. Honey believed that everyone washed their hair in that shower — understandable — and twosomes were the norm. Loose hairs were the problem so hair washing was the number one culprit.

Mary Jane was wittering on about Sir Cedric, the long dead ancestor who she insisted shared her room.

'I'm not always sure he tells me the absolute truth about his life or his conquests. According to the records, he was married twice, but he seems to have had a lot of descendants — too many for two wives to have been responsible.'

Honey pointed out that he was landed gentry and could do as he pleased.

'Well, I'm off to check the parish records. He had an estate in Wainscote, you know. That's the great thing about the Church of England, they kept such meticulous records. I sure am grateful to all them priests and monks noting everything down with nothing more than a quill pen. Beats me how they did it.'

Honey tucked the plunger behind the reception desk. It didn't really belong there, but she had a mountain of paperwork to go through and was also awaiting Doherty's findings regarding Nigel Brooks and the Janet Glencannon woman who ran the animal sanctuary at Bobby's Bottom, formerly Brindley's Bottom.

Mary Jane continued to prattle on about her ancestor and where all his heirs actually came from. She also made mention of what some of them had got up too. Secrets and scandals abounded.

Honey let it all go in one ear and out the other as there was something about Lindsey's stance that drew her attention. It was a look she'd seen before, the kind she had when things were slightly off kilter. It wasn't exactly a frown, but kind of a grimace like when she was small and had had an accident. That was no longer an option, so it had to be something trivial but aggravating. After dipping into the mental filing cabinet, she came out with aggravation number one.

'My mother has married a twenty-four-year-old Tunisian who deals in prayer mats?'

'No. We have a dog.'

'Oh,' said Honey on seeing the pretty little face, the black button nose with matching eyes and the big fluffy ears. 'How cute. What's his name?'

'I've no idea.'

Lindsey was under no illusion that her mother hadn't quite twigged on yet.

'He's been abandoned, tied to the leg of the table and left there.'

'*Oh*,' said Honey again.

Lindsey waited for her to rant and rage or throw her head back, close her eyes, wishing herself lying on a Caribbean beach and not lumbered with a homeless stray — if it was homeless that is. The truth was that the look on Honey Driver's face was calculating, sneaky even. It was the kind of look she always got when she was planning something out of the ordinary, almost as though the dog was an answer to her prayers.

'I know just the place to take it. They cater for abandoned pets. It's not far. Can you cope until I get back?'

Lindsey said that she could.

Honey cooed to the dog as she undid its leash. The dog wagged its tail enthusiastically, placed its paws on her knees and licked her hands.

Aware that she was no longer centre stage, Mary Jane stopped yakking on about her ancestor. Something was going on here that she wasn't part of.

'Is this animal significant in some way?'

In the absence of an immediate response from her mother, Lindsey enlightened Mary Jane, taking it as read that the only course of action was to return the animal to whoever had left him there. 'We need to find his owner. Then he's not our responsibility.'

'We can find somebody to look after him in the meantime,' Honey went on in that same cooing voice the dog seemed to like.

'Look to see if his owner's name and address is attached to his collar,' suggested Lindsey.

Honey picked the dog up, tucking it beneath her arm so she could more easily examine whether it was wearing an address on a little brass bone around its neck. There was none. However, on turning it onto its back, she did discover that this was a fellah. A damned cute little fellah.

'Let's you and me take a little trip pretty doggy,' she cooed against its fluffy ear, though only briefly; it smelled vaguely of candle wax and goose grease.

Lindsey reached for the phone. 'I'll phone the vet. He can check the dog to see if it's been chipped.'

'Oh, I know what that is,' declared Mary Jane who up until this point had only express mild interest in the abandoned hound. 'A microchip carrying the owner's name and address; clever stuff, huh?'

'Very clever,' said Lindsey.

Honey hugged the dog more tightly. 'There's no need of that. I know somebody who would be happy to look after the little guy until we find his rightful owner.'

'But it would be so easy, and . . .'

'No. Leave it to me. Don't ring anyone. I have everything under control.'

Lindsey did as ordered. Something was going down here, but she couldn't figure what it was. What concerned her was that she couldn't always work out what was going on in her mother's mind. Perhaps that was what interested the men in her life, never quite being able to work out what she was thinking or what she would do next. She supposed men found that quite exciting, almost like having a different woman in bed every night.

Her mother's likes and dislikes changed as she got older or circumstances changed. Like now. This dog!

The last dog her mother had been lumbered with had belonged to an elderly lady. That in itself had been fine, except that the dog had never received any toilet training — at least that was the way it seemed. Honey had been desperate to get rid of it, whereas with this one . . .

'If Doherty calls, tell him I've gone to see a woman about a dog. Kind of . . .'

She knew Doherty had been out at Wainscote interviewing Janet Glencannon, the former Mrs Brooks.

Nigel Brooks had been arrested on Saturday night for causing an affray and taken to Manvers Street Police Station. He should have been released by now.

Going out to Wainscote to ask Janet Glencannon about wedding dresses was blatantly nosy, but she owed it to Marietta. The dog, whatever the circumstances of his abandonment, provided a suitable excuse for her to visit Janet Glencannon and maybe ask a few questions. After all, Ms Glencannon, formerly Mrs Brooks, ran an animal sanctuary. It was her vocation in life to look after waifs and strays. She found herself wondering whether Nigel Brooks had once fitted into that category.

CHAPTER TWENTY-SEVEN

With the late afternoon sunlight warming her back, shining as it was into the nave of St Michael and All Angels, the Reverend Constance Paxton thanked the ladies in charge of the flower arranging for their steadfast resolve in producing such splendid floral displays despite recent difficulties. She had only just returned from jogging hence being attired in grey jogging pants, pink trainers and a long line matching grey top with '*In Training for Truth*' emblazoned in pink across the front.

'The church looks wonderful. Absolutely wonderful and very summery. Lots of lovely roses I notice. And the smell is fabulous. I'm really grateful that you've soldiered on despite everything. I really don't know how you do it but thank you again.'

'Mrs Flynn would have done the same if one of us had been . . . taken.' The speaker was Hermione Thompson, her shoulder length hair listed by the sunlight steaming through the windows from mouse to faintly gold; her floral dress gently skimming her slender calves. Her dress was duck egg blue, a colour she often favoured.

She looked quite satisfied as she said it, and indeed she was. The three women with her, Mrs Granger, a forthright soul of sixty-seven years with work-worn hands and clear blue eyes, and Ursula Pitt, a retired and unwed woman of nearly sixty, had no affection for the dead woman either, but were not the sort to speak ill of the dead. The third woman was Janet Glencannon, the only woman Mrs Flynn had stayed well clear of.

Constance Paxton nodded and said that yes, Mrs Flynn would have carried on. She did not remark that the old bitch would have carried on regardless even if every single one of them had dropped dead, though she firmly believed it was so. Mrs Flynn had enjoyed being in control. The flower arranging committee had been her life as had the church and its surrounding precincts. So had the village. In such a close-knit community, secrets were shared. Mrs Flynn had collected peoples' secrets like some people collect fossil shells or postage stamps. She'd thrived on gossip as nobody else thrived. She'd told the vicar that she kept a record of what people got up to.

Constance had been appalled and told her it was not a very neighbourly thing to do. Mrs Flynn had laughed at her. 'What are you worried about, Vicar. Frightened that I might have jotted something about you in my notebook?'

'When was the last time you saw Mrs Flynn to speak to, Vicar?' That's what the police had asked her. She had said that night when she'd shared sherry and cake with Mrs Flynn. They'd asked if she was sure. She'd told them she was, having been invited that afternoon when she'd come across Mrs Flynn sitting in front of a computer in the central library in Bath. She'd told them how she'd complimented Mrs Flynn on being able to use a computer at her age. She didn't tell them what Mrs Flynn had said besides inviting her over. Neither did she mention what she'd seen on the computer screen, but then, they hadn't asked.

'I'm so glad you approve,' gushed Hermione Thompson, her face still pink in response to the praise she'd received.

Mrs Granger and Miss Pitt voiced their thanks. Janet Glencannon said nothing, but gave a little nod. The other women smiled tight smiles. Out of all of them, Janet had been the only one Mrs Flynn did not pick on. In fact it often seemed as though she went out of her way to avoid her. That wasn't to say that Mrs Flynn hadn't tried to intimidate her. She'd told the police that. She'd also told them that she'd taken the wrong pill from her medicine cabinet, a sleeping pill instead of an arthritis pill and that she'd. nodded off and woke up to the sound of somebody threatening somebody else. Janet had Mrs Flynn by the throat. She heard Janet say something like, 'Don't think I don't know about you. I know everything about you, *Mrs Flynn!*' Hermione shivered at the thought of it. Interacting with the flower arranging committee was much more calming and, dare she say it, much more in keeping with what she expected from a village community. They were so very civilised.

One half of the stout arched church door creaked open. 'I'm sorry. Am I interrupting anything?'

Bright sunshine entered along with a woman wearing figure-hugging jeans and a dark cotton top. A twisted strip of blue and green scarf complemented a mop of dark hair, keeping it from outright disarray. It needed restyling, but Honey had been holding on. She was getting married at some point. She would fit it in then. For now she was pretending that she had only just entered the church, hence making sure the door creaked when it opened. It hadn't at first so nobody had heard her come in.

On recognising Honey, the vicar smiled broadly and held out her hand, her eyes twinkling with welcome.

'Ah. Mrs Driver. I thought we said next Thursday evening at seven? That's if you've come on personal business. Or is this professional?'

Her expression wavered between happiness and serious concern.

Honey shivered at the difference in temperature between the day outside and the coolness of the church.

An arched window of predominantly blue glass depicting St Michael and his Angels overlooked the altar, the crucifix and a pair of handsome candlesticks.

'Actually I was looking for Ms Glencannon. I have a problem. Somebody left a dog tethered to a chair leg at the Green River Hotel. I'm trying to find the owner, but in the meantime I thought Ms Glencannon could help me out?' Honey looked pointedly at Janet. 'I went to Bobby's Bottom, and your kennel maid said I would find you here.'

At the mention of a hound in need, Janet Glencannon dropped her surly expression, her face instantly wreathed in smiles.

'Bloody people. Shouldn't have animals,' she said. 'Ought to be horse whipped. Ought to have collars put around their necks and drag them around. You could have taken him to vet to see if he's micro-chipped. You do know that, don't you?'

'So I understand, but . . . well . . . you were the first person I thought of. I mean, I do have an hotel to run. Though he's a lovely little chap, I can't keep a dog on the premises. The Environmental Health Department would have a fit.'

'More fool them! Where is this poor creature? Lead on.'

Honey apologised to the vicar and the other ladies before following Janet Glencannon outside.

'There he is,' exclaimed Honey on opening the back door of her car.

To her amazement, the dog immediately leapt out of the back door and into the arms of an extremely amazed Janet Glencannon.

'He seems to like you,' exclaimed Honey encouragingly as the dog whined and howled and wagged with pleasure, pink tongue licking Ms Glencannon's pink face.

Honey was surprised when her comment failed to elicit a reasonable response, such as, '*dogs know who like them and who don't.*'

Janet then turned to Honey, her black eyes glittering with anger. Her stormy white hair, as curly and fluffy as the dog she held in her arms, seemed to stand on end.

'Is this some kind of joke?'

At first Honey didn't have a clue what she was referring to. And then it came to her. The white hair — both Janet's and the dog. The black eyes. Was it Ahmed who had said something that in turn had reminded her of the phrase about people looking like their dogs?

'I'm sorry. I don't know what you mean? I found him . . .'

'You stole him! Or someone did.'

'Are you saying this is your dog?'

'Of course he is! Can't you tell?'

It was plain to see all right. The dog was going ballistic with joy. Janet Glencannon had to be its owner.

Honey stepped back. This was such a surprise. She had brought the dog out here purely as an excuse to speak to Ms Glencannon about her ex-husband, Nigel Brooks.

'I can assure you . . . and I have witnesses to prove it. Look, Ms Glencannon. I think we need to have a talk about this,' she said at the same time indicating by her stance and tone that she wouldn't take no for an answer.

'I have nothing to say,' Janet snapped.

Honey hardened her stance. There was no way she was retreating now. What *was* the connection between wedding dresses and this village? And how were those wedding dresses connected to Nigel, Janet, Marietta and Mrs Flynn?

'Oh, but I think we do need to talk, Ms Glencannon — or should that be Mrs Brooks? Mrs Nigel Brooks?' she said, making it sound as though she really was somebody official, somebody who had a right to ask questions.

The dog still licking at Janet Glencannon's neck and whining with pleasure, the woman who had once been married to Nigel Brooks stopped glowering and instead eyed her suspiciously.

'Nigel!' she scoffed. 'He should be locked up. That's what should happen to him. I should never have married him. I should have known he wasn't all there.'

Her voice sounded hollow. The little dog seemed to sense her change of tone and her sudden tension, curling up in the crook of her arm.

The other two women on the flower arranging committee chose that moment to exit the church, glancing their way

184

before disappearing off down the lane that led back into the High Street.

The vicar was the next to exit the church, closing the door behind her and locking it before jogging off around through the tall grass where Mr Clinker had been found naked, bound and gagged just days before.

'You must know that Mrs Clinker, Marietta Hopkins, was found dead in the back of a stolen car. The owner kept it in a garage in a parking lot at the back of the row of houses where your husband lives.'

At first it looked to Honey as though Janet was about to deny having any idea it was kept there. No way. She wasn't going to let her get away with it. A little nudge was in order.

'The guy who owns the Rolls Royce was there having tea with your husband one day and saw you.'

She didn't add that Ahmed hadn't formally identified her as being Nigel's ex-wife, but that no longer mattered. Nigel had broadcast the fact in Wainscote village for everyone to hear.

Janet's face registered defeat. Shoulders that had been square with tension suddenly turned sloping and relaxed. Honey knew she had broken through.

'Okay. I admit it. I did see the car there when I went round to tell him to stop hassling me. The stupid prat even introduced me to the man. Ahmed, I think he was called. But so what? I didn't steal the bloody car.'

'And you didn't kill Marietta?'

'Hmph! I had no reason to. A murderer has to have a motive to murder, don't they? And I didn't have one. I didn't have one then, and I don't have one now.'

'How about Mrs Flynn,' growled Honey, warming to the task. 'Did you like Mrs Flynn?'

'No!'

'Did you have a motive for murdering her?'

There was a slight hesitation, barely perceptible, but she was sure she had seen something.

'That bitch deserved to be put down. If she was still alive, I might have said Marietta had killed her. She liked to cause

185

trouble did that one. It was her, no doubt, who told Marietta that her husband was *"entertaining"* another woman. She had something on him too. That was why he let her into his garden to pick bunches of flowers for the church. She used to sit with him on the back porch drinking tea with him. Gin too if I know Mrs Flynn. They cackled together like witches, them two.'

'Mr Clinker and Mrs Flynn?'

'Yes. Thick as thieves.'

'So Mrs Flynn was not very popular?'

Janet laughed. 'About as popular as snow in summertime. Nobody liked her, and with good reason. She was a gossip and a bully. Ask Hermione Thompson.'

Honey recalled the slender woman with mousey brown hair and wearing the silk dress who had just left the church.

'She bullied her?'

'Ask her.'

'Can I ask you something first?'

'Go ahead.'

'Do you think Nigel took your dog . . . ?'

'Pascal . . . His name's Pascal.'

Honey misunderstood, presuming she was referring to a human being named Pascal who had taken the dog until, before making a faux pas, it came to her that Pascal was the name of the furry canine.

'Had he visited you lately? Nigel, I mean.'

'He doesn't visit. He sneaks in and sneaks out again. I don't know how he does it, but he does. I have complained to the police, but nothing has been done. It's a cross I have to bear. A far bigger and heavier one than her in there,' she added, nodding at the church. 'Though you'd think the Reverend Hermione been through hell if you listen to her praying and sobbing in front of that altar. Mysterious past and all that; according to Mrs Flynn that is. Always something to say about everybody,' she said with a cruel twist of her mouth. 'That was our Mrs Flynn.'

It did occur to Honey to ask more about the vicar crying at the altar, but she was here to ask questions about Nigel

Brooks and the more she found out about him, the more it worried her. He might not have committed the murders, but he did behave strangely.

'Why would he steal the dog and leave it tied up beneath a hotel table?'

'Nigel is not a predictable man. He has behavioural problems. I take it from our conversation that you have met him.'

'Briefly.'

'That's enough.'

It was on the tip of her tongue to ask out loud why the hell she'd married him, but on recalling her own choice of husband, who was she to talk? How was she to know that Carl Driver's sailing hobby would take him away from home so much, leading the jet set lifestyle, flying and sailing all around the world — complete with an all-female crew.

Janet answered the unasked question. 'Nobody knows anyone, not properly, until they actually live together.'

Honey had to agree that what she said was true, but on the other hand they hardly looked the ideal couple. They just didn't match.

Bearing Janet's comment about the vicar in mind, Honey wondered what else she knew about her neighbours. Had Mrs Flynn been the only gossip in the village?

Janet informed her she'd lived in the village for seven years and in that time had learned plenty.

Just what I was hoping for, thought Honey.

'What about you? Did Mrs Flynn bully you?'

'She wouldn't dare,' Janet growled. Funny how her doggy expression now looked less like a bichon frise and more like a Pitbull.

'You stood up to her?' She pretended to be greatly impressed. In a way she was, but only to the extent that it was necessary in order to gain Janet's trust.

'You bet I did.' Janet lifted her chin proudly.

'So what did you have on her that she left you alone but had a go at everyone else?'

There was something about Janet's expression that gave the game away. 'I told her I had something on her, so not to mess me around.'

'Did you have something on her?'

For a moment Janet's pale eyes held hers. 'I'm not sure.'

Honey held her ground, convinced there was more. 'I think you are.'

Janet looked away, burying her face in the dog's silky body as she considered whether to say anything more. She didn't have to of course, but Honey was counting on Janet presuming she worked with the police professionally and was not just an amateur. Fingers crossed it would work.

'It's nothing much. Not by today's standards. She called herself Mrs Flynn, but she wasn't married. I only discovered this after I was perusing the old parish register for an article I was doing for the parish magazine. Although she told everyone she got married in St Michael's, her name wasn't mentioned. It wasn't until I found some old newspapers in the loft of my house that I discovered what had happened. Mrs Flynn was jilted at the altar, stood there in her wedding gown. Brian Flynn had joined the army, but come back after doing active service specifically to marry her. Only he changed his mind. There was even a letter with the newspaper from him to her. Mrs Flynn, Gladys, went away shortly after. Everyone knew the reason why. She was pregnant of course and back then being a single parent wasn't what it is today. A bastard was a bastard. If you weren't married you were a fallen woman. Even after all these years, her generation can't cope with that.'

It was said that all is fair in love and war and as far as Honey was concerned, the same rule applied to asking sneaky questions. The end justified the means and all that. With this in mind, she adopted a fixed smile and said, 'Look. Is there anywhere we can have a coffee? Perhaps we could put our heads together and work out what's going on here.'

It hurt to smile in such a fixed, false manner, but Honey was determined.

Janet's slack lips shifted from side to side as she debated the suggestion. The dog chose that moment to snuffle up under her chin, pink tongue flicking all the while. It then looked across at Honey and wagged.

Janet nodded. 'Okay.'

'That place looks nice,' said Honey, nodding to the pretty frontage of a small cafe across the way, called the Bath Bun according to the embellished sage green sign.

'They don't let dogs in. Uncivilised out of towners! The Angel does though.'

Janet had a gruff way of speaking, though Honey had noticed a passable improvement since their first meeting thanks to Pascal the dog.

'Am I right in thinking he's a bichon frise?' Honey asked her as they made their way to the pub.

Janet turned her head sharply, her expression brighter, her manner less defensive. 'You know about dogs?'

'Not really. I just happen to know the difference between a poodle and a bichon frise.'

* * *

The clatter of crockery being collected and the smell of warm meals greeted them at the Angel Inn. The barman took one look at Janet and her dog and nodded at a spot over in the corner.

Honey went up to the bar to order coffee.

'And biscuits,' Janet called after her. 'Chocolate digestives.'

The barman, a thin man with round glasses and thinning hair glared in Janet's direction. 'Only if you don't leave crumbs all over the place.'

Janet tossed her head.

Honey paid for the coffees and took them and the biscuits back to the table.

'Look, Pascal. We have biscuits,' Janet cooed to the perfectly behaved canine who seemed to be totally at home in the pub. She broke one in half then in half again. The dog wolfed down the first piece.

Janet handed him another piece then dipped a piece of her own biscuit into her coffee.

'Plain chocolate. Yummy,' she said as she sucked off the chocolate before swallowing the biscuit. 'He prefers milk biscuits. I prefer chocolate.'

Honey declined a biscuit. Normally she might have mentioned a need to lose weight but she reckoned Janet wasn't the sort to be interested in a trim figure or fashion. That's how people got once dogs or cats ruled their world.

'So!' said Honey when enough time had gone by without Janet opening her mouth except to gobble down another shared biscuit. 'Why would Nigel leave a dog tied under a table at the Green River Hotel.'

Janet frowned as though she were chewing it over — in reality she was chewing another biscuit.

'Where is this hotel?'

'In Bath.'

'Strikes me he wouldn't go there unless he knew someone staying or working there. Do we know who the manager is or the owner, anything like that?'

She sounded very offhand as though she didn't really care, but Honey didn't want to tell her that she was the owner. Up until now she had only visited this village with Doherty. People presumed she was police and it didn't hurt for the belief to continue.

'I spend a lot of time at the Green River.'

'Ah!' said Janet, her eyes as round as that of her dog. 'That explains it. You went along to ask him questions. That in itself might not have been enough to get him going, mind you. Not Nigel. One certain subject. That's all he thinks of. So there you are. It must have been something you said.'

Clear as mud. Now it was Honey with the deep frown. 'What kind of thing?'

Janet was now holding a biscuit between her teeth and offering it to Pascal who neatly bit off the end. 'Mention anything about weddings, did you?' Janet asked after wiping excess crumbs from her lips.

This cannot be happening, Honey thought to herself. Weddings. The man was obsessed with weddings and I mentioned I was getting married.

She couldn't bring herself to admit it. 'I don't recall.' It was a necessary lie if she was going to get Janet to admit talk about the village.

Janet shrugged her substantial shoulders. 'No matter. You obviously inspired his interest in brides in some way.'

The more Janet mentioned her ex-husband and his chilling interest in brides, the more Honey wanted to pick up her phone and tell Doherty to go and arrest him.

'Have you found Harold Clinker yet?'

The question was sudden and for a moment Honey couldn't quite recall what had happened on that front.

'No. I don't think so. We are making further enquiries.'

'I see. They do say it's always the husband, don't they? That's what I gather from some of these crime novels I read. The husband is always the prime suspect.'

Honey had to agree verbally whilst mentally swapping Harold Clinker for Nigel Brooks, Janet's ex-husband.

'Was Nigel ever violent towards you?'

Wrong thing to say. Bichon frise lookalike face turned rapidly to Pitbull.

'I would have made a purse out of his assets if he'd ever done anything like that.'

Honey winced. 'Okay. I'm with you on that one. How long has he known where you lived?'

'Not long after we parted. He was a problem at first, the telephone calls, the visits, the hanging about at the end of the lane. Then it fell off and I heard nothing from him.' She shrugged. 'No idea why he suddenly began plaguing me again, reappearing as though there'd been no gap at all.'

Honey frowned. 'You don't know where he was during that time? When he didn't bother you?'

'No. Our home was sold, the money divided and we both went our own way. I heard he had a flat in Bristol for a while before he bought the ex-council house in Keynsham. Don't know what brought that on, I'm sure. Why would a single man want to buy a family house?'

'No. I see your point.' Unless he had a family, thought Honey. Perhaps he had for a time. Or perhaps he wanted a family. It was worth looking into.

'He didn't make the acquaintance of Marietta or Mrs Flynn?'

'Not that I know of, but there, who knows where Mrs Flynn's claws were hooked? Though I do understand where you're coming from, what with my husband's obsession with weddings and all that. Bloody idiot.'

Honey nodded in agreement. 'Odd both of them being found wearing a wedding dress. One elderly woman and one much younger; two very different women.'

'Odd indeed. Odd how they were found both dead and odd that they ever got close in the first place.'

'Close?' Honey's ears pricked up at the prospect of the two dead women having anything in common besides being found dead and wearing a wedding dress.

'As I've already told you, Mr Clinker allowed Mrs Flynn to pick flowers for the church. I was called to Belvedere House to take away a nest of hedgehogs. Mrs Flynn was sitting in the kitchen having a cup of tea with Marietta. I mentioned it to Mrs Flynn when we were changing the flowers. She asked me if there was any law against it. I said that no, of course there wasn't. Anyway, she took umbrage and told us to clear off. She could finish changing the flowers herself. Hermione was ordered to stay. The rest of us cleared off and left them to it. Hermione was a dogsbody and did everything Gladys told her to do. I told her to sod off.'

So Mrs Flynn and Marietta had shared morning cups of tea. Honey asked herself what they might have had in common. There was nothing she could think of, unless it had something to do with the wedding dresses, but what?

'Well thanks for your help.'

'Not a problem. Now if you don't mind I've kennels to muck out.'

She turned her back. Honey got the message. The woman cared more for her dogs than helping anyone.

CHAPTER TWENTY-EIGHT

'Will you please note that my client is here of his own voli-tion. He was dealing with business interests on the Costa Del Sol when the news of his wife's death came to him.'

Doherty agreed that he would. Harold Clinker coming into Manvers Street of his own volition had come as a com-plete surprise. It had also disappointed him. Sure as eggs were eggs, this man had an iron-clad alibi. A white linen jacket and open necked shirt accentuated his tan. He was also wear-ing dark pink trousers and white loafers on tanned feet. No socks. Doherty tried not to let his gaze fall to Clinker's chest where he guessed he would see a gold sovereign medallion glinting among a thatch of grey chest hairs.

They piled along to the interview room, Clinker and his lawyer, Mrs Hamilton-Jones, a slim woman in her late thirties with black hair and glossy red lips. She was wearing a red suit with a white blouse, a black tie loosely tied, and the top two buttons were undone.

She glows, thought Doherty reflecting that most law-yers wore sombre dress and their skirts were never as tightly moulded to their bodies as hers was. Few of them wore such high heels either or smelled of expensive perfume.

The Wizard accompanied them. It would most likely have been a younger officer, but somebody had messed up the holiday rota so they were a bit short-staffed.

'Are you going to tape this?' Clinker snapped.

Doherty told him he was not. 'You're not charged with anything. Just tell me the details of your alibi. Once it's checked and I'm satisfied, then we will require you to make a statement.'

'Before my client left Marbella, he had the hotel manager swear a statement in front of the Spanish police stating my client's time of arrival and length of stay. My client also swore a statement. I have both here.'

Long fingers tipped with bright red nail varnish passed a sheath of paperwork across the desk to Doherty who glanced through it, noting the stamp and the signature — all in Spanish.

'We also have the boarding pass receipts. My client would like to get this over and done with. He would also like to know when his wife's body will be released so he can make the necessary arrangements.'

Doherty wasn't exactly gutted that Harold Clinker had a cast-iron alibi, but he was put out. The husband was always the prime suspect. It would have been so much easier for him if it was so in this case. Unfortunately it was not. The odds were in Clinker's favour.

'So where were you on the night of Mrs Gladys Flynn's death?'

A flush of anger lit up the cheeks of the lawyer. Both her and her client exchanged surprised looks before Mrs Hamilton-Jones bounced back.

'As it was pointed out on our arrival, my client came here of his own volition purely regarding the death of his wife and not in connection to the earlier death.'

'If you would recall, I was indisposed that night, Inspector,' Clinker cut in. 'Attacked, bound and gagged. And in the buff! Wonder I didn't bloody freeze to death. I was in no fit state to murder Mrs Flynn and I had no reason to bump her off. There's plenty in the village ready and willing to do that. I could give you a list,' he added, narrowing his eyes with what could only be described as malicious intent. 'If I had a mind to.'

'I do recall. You accused your wife of doing it.'

'I smelled her perfume.'

'Did she admit doing it?'

'Not as such. We just agreed to forgive and forget.'

'And that included you dropping charges against her and your wife dropping charges against you of violence against her person.'

Clinker tugged at his trousers before crossing one leg over the other. 'That's about the size of it.'

It was a warm day and the room was getting warmer.

Doherty lay back in his chair, hands in pockets, muscles flexing fit to burst the sleeves of his T-shirt. He disliked men who wore gold medallions.

Putting that particular prejudice aside, he continued his line of enquiry.

'Setting your comment about writing us a list aside, do you have any thoughts on who might have killed Mrs Flynn?'

'Humph!' Clinker exclaimed. 'Damned near everyone I should think. She liked to stir things up in the village.'

'Really?' Doherty raised his eyebrows. 'Did she say anything to stir you up Mr Clinker? Anything that might have stirred you to murdering her . . .'

Mrs Hamilton-Jones jumped in. 'Now just a minute . . . ! My client does not need to answer that.'

Clinker raised a restraining hand. 'It's all right, Ruth. I don't mind answering. I've got nothing to hide. As commander in chief of the flower arranging fraternity, she was grateful I invited her to pick flowers from our garden. She liked to use fresh flowers for the church displays and told me she couldn't provide much from her own garden, and they were expensive to buy. So I let her in to pick some of ours. We've got plenty.' His mouth curled in a triumphant sneer.

At the same time his eyes seemed to recede further into their pits, chips of bitter blue glittering like molten silver.

'So there you are, Inspector,' exclaimed Ruth Hamilton-Jones, her smile as triumphant as her client's sneer. 'My client has been cooperative over his wife's death and is being so over that of Mrs Flynn, a woman he allowed to pick flowers from his garden.'

There was the sound of the stocking of one leg making a rasping sound as it crossed over the other.

Talk about the cat who got the cream, thought Doherty. Feline woman. Provocative with it.

But he wasn't finished yet.

'Did you ever talk to Mrs Flynn?'

'Sometimes. Nothing much more than passing the time of day.'

'Did she ever confide in you?'

Clinker laughed; a deep throaty laugh that made his chest heave.

'That depends what you mean by confide, Inspector. Mrs Flynn asked questions.' He tapped the side of his nose. 'She liked to poke her nose into other peoples' business. I was not having any of that, I can tell you. One hint of scandal and it would be all around the village.'

'You mean with regard to your open marriage?'

Clinker half rose from his chair, only restrained by the exquisitely manicured hand of his lawyer. 'There's no law against it,' he said through gritted teeth. 'Not that I let on to Mrs Flynn. It was none of her business. None of yours either.'

'No need to shout, Mr Clinker. I'm just trying to get some background on Mrs Flynn. I thought you could help.'

Unruffled by her client's outburst, Ruth Hamilton-Jones attempted to calm him down.

'Now, now. Harold. It doesn't hurt to be helpful. We all want to catch the perpetrator, don't we? Are we cool with that, Harold?'

Harold was hardly the type of man the word cool applied to with his quick temper and arrogant attitude. His clothes didn't help either. He only *thought* he was cool. He was too old and too fat for that look, thought Doherty whilst running his own palm over his own firm stomach muscles.

The soothing words of his fetching legal companion seemed to do the trick.

'So the only interaction you had with Mrs Flynn was when she came to pick flowers.'

'Interaction! What sort of word is that? Bloody hell, you make it sound like I was sleeping with the old bat. No thank you!'

Again Mrs Hamilton-Jones interrupted. 'Harold! Please.'

'OK,' Clinker growled in response. 'We didn't have any *in-ter-act-shun* then,' he said, emphasising each syllable as though Doherty had never heard of the word. 'I told you. All she did was come in and pick flowers.'

'Did you see anything of Mrs Flynn that night?'

'No.'

'Did your wife know Mrs Flynn very well?'

'Hardly,' Clinker responded sneeringly. 'Let's be fair, Inspector, they had bugger all in common.'

'Did Miss Sherise ever meet Mrs Flynn?' Doherty asked.

'Not that I know of.'

'Do you know a man named Nigel Brooks?'

Clinker blinked. 'No. Should I have?'

'He lives close to the garage where the Rolls Royce was kept. In a lock-up garage in Keynsham.'

'Don't know the man and I don't frequent Keynsham. Wrong side of town for my tastes.' He said it as though he were a cultured pearl. Doherty doubted he could even spell the word!

'But you do know your wife was found dead in the back of a Rolls Royce. A white Rolls Royce used for weddings. That's where it was kept.'

'Nothing to do with me.'

'You don't know the owner of the Rolls Royce?'

'Should I?'

'Ahmed Clifford. He's got a repair workshop down along the railway arches. Ever taken your car there?'

'Are you kidding? Do I look like the sort of man who takes a top of the range Mercedes along to an Asian bloke working out of a dump beneath the arches?'

'Who said he was Asian?'

'His name. Didn't you say his name was Ahmed? Hardly an English name now, is it?'

Clinker's voice was getting louder despite his lawyer's constant warning.

Sensing this was going to become a sparring match, Doherty closed the interview.

'Thank you for coming in, Mr Clinker. It was much appreciated.'

Clinker shifted the chair away from him with a backward movement of his leg.

'Is that it?'

'That's it.'

'Then I'm out of here, but bear this in mind, Mr Copper. I came in here in all good faith to straighten things out. I didn't want you lot blaming me for something I didn't do. Strange as it may seem, I loved my wife, Inspector.'

'Yep,' said Doherty, firmly shutting his mouth against referring back to Mrs Clinker's bruised face. 'I'm sure you did.'

Clinker left first, Mrs Ruth Hamilton-Jones followed. She paused at the door, the fingernails of one hand blinking like jewels, the other hand firmly clasped around the handle of her briefcase. The smile on her glossy lips was full of sexual promise and that was definitely a glint of triumph he could see in her eyes.

'Should you need any further clarification of my client's movements, or his further assistance, you can contact me.'

She handed him her card, the tip of her fingers touching his as she passed it to him.

Doherty knew a come-on when he saw it, but didn't want to know.

'I see no reason not to go direct to your client if I need to,' he replied coldly.

She flinched at that, but wasn't quite down and out.

'I see no particular reason why you should need to speak to him again at all, Inspector. His alibi is quite firm. The firmest thing about him in fact.' A smile twitched at her lips.

Doherty knew what was implied. 'And you would know?'

'On hearing of his wife's death and bearing in mind past disturbances between them, he phoned me right away. It was me who advised him to have a witness swear a statement and to swear one himself. So my client is definitely off of your radar. He could not have killed his wife.'

Eyelashes too thick to be anything but false fluttered over her violet eyes. Yes, she was enticing him, but in a mocking, emasculating way.

She's taking the piss, he thought. Taunting and enticing all at the same time.

'You're quite right,' he said to her, his smile sardonic.

'So glad you agree.'

'Unless he paid somebody to do it.'

The smile vanished, her eyes flashed and Doherty-sex was no longer on the menu.

Her finely chiselled features turned to stone. 'You have no proof even if it were true.'

Doherty closed in until his face was only inches from hers, their eyes in direct line.

'Not yet. I'll be in touch with you when I have.'

CHAPTER TWENTY-NINE

Honey was in the kitchen helping Smudger. A new toy had arrived; a neat device for making fruit shaped marzipan petit fours. The great thing about it was that there were bits left over once the shapes were squeezed out of the plastic mould. Honey ate them as she went. If there was one thing she truly loved it was marzipan. Chocolate didn't come anywhere near it.

Finally there were no little bits left. Lemon, apple, plum, orange and banana shaped petit fours lay gleaming up at her. They looked good, too enticing. Her fingers hovered over the rows counting to see if there were equal numbers of each. If there did happen to be thirteen on one row instead of twelve, it wouldn't be missed.

There were fourteen bananas! Fourteen! How brilliant was that.

Then Smudger, her head chef spotted what she was doing. His voice rang out loud and clear.

'No! Don't eat.'

'Just one!' She popped it into her mouth. Smudger dived in to rescue the rest grumbling that people should control their urges which was damned nerve coming from him, a man who brandished a meat cleaver when diners dared criticise his food.

Her mobile phone rang scuppering any chance of grabbing another banana marzipan before Smudger shut them away.

'Mum,' came her daughter's voice. 'I think you need to see this.'

The phone went dead.

'Remind me to have a word with my daughter about ringing me on the mobile when I'm only yards away,' she grumbled as she left the kitchen and headed for reception.

Members of staff, plus the hotel's one and only long-time resident, Mary Jane, were gathered around Lindsey who was seated at the computer. Comments were muffled though sounded complimentary.

Honey just about managed to break though the group. The scene on the computer screen made her jaw drop.

The normal screen display was all to do with the hotel reservations system, emails or pictures on the website.

This was nothing to do with Bath or the Green River Hotel. The sky was blue, the sea turquoise and two people were smiling out at her from the deck of a Saga cruise ship. One of them was her mother. The other was a man she did not recognise. Underneath the picture it said, 'Just Married.'

Honey was stunned. Lindsey was stunned. Mary Jane remarked on how happy they looked, and hey, what was the big deal about getting married for the fifth time in later life. Life was for living, right?

Honey had difficulty finding her voice. Her mother had gone on a cruise without telling her. Her mother had got married without telling her. It was downright thoughtless! If the intention had been to divert interest from Honey's own wedding, then her mother had certainly done that.

'My God!' she finally managed. 'She's got married. She didn't tell me. She never even mentioned she was going on a cruise! Did any of you know about this?'

Everybody shrugged or shook their heads.

'He is quite a dish,' Lindsey remarked.

Both Mary Jane and Honey closed in on the screen again.

Honey narrowed her eyes so she could focus better. Mary Jane had a gold cord hanging around her neck attached to her spectacles. She felt for them, found them and put them onto her nose. Gloria, Honey's mother, had bought it for her.

The light from the computer screen was reflected in Mary Jane's spectacles.

'Wow,' said Mary Jane once she'd had a good look. 'She's got herself a younger man.'

Honey pushed her way up front and central. Mary Jane was right. The man snuggled up to her mother's side had fair hair, an open face and a broad waistline. Not young, but definitely younger than her mother. Honey put him at around fifty-five.

The email accompanying the photograph stated that his name was Stewart White and he was a bookie from Whitechapel, London.

Her mother went on to say that she hadn't mentioned him because Honey and Lindsey had strong objections to gambling. 'He's made a fortune from gambling. He owns a chain of betting shops. Will celebrate and take questions when I get back. In the meantime we have the bridal suite and are having fun.'

'I bet they are,' muttered Honey. Everything had been arranged in secret and nobody had guessed what they'd been up to.

She caught Lindsey eyeing her curiously.

'What? What? What? What????'

Lindsey turned her head slightly away whilst eyeing her sidelong and trying not to grin.

'You did tell me it was in the genes. What a turn up! Gran getting married before you. What will you say to them when they get back?'

'Hello, Dad?' Honey offered.

The shock wore off as the day wore on. As Doherty remarked when he came in to see her, 'Look on the bright side. She'll spend more time with him and less giving you grief.'

'Stop looking so pleased about it.'

He shrugged but the grin stayed in place. She had to admit it to herself, he had the most tantalising grin.

'Okay, Okay. It could be that I'm being short-sighted here. There are advantages to having a stepdad. Could be we might have similar music tastes. That's besides the fact that my mother will be indulged by him.'

'How do you know that?'

'My mother favours men that indulge her. She wouldn't have it any other way. So. I give in. Lunch on the house. Let's celebrate.'

Anna was around to run reception so Lindsey joined them. So did Mary Jane, dressed up to the nines in a pink satin party dress and elbow length gloves; a bit over the top for a lunchtime, but Gloria Cross would have appreciated the gesture.

Dish of the day was meatballs, made to Smudger's own recipe of beef mince, sultanas and basil, cooked in a tomato and onion sauce, dotted with mozzarella cheese, washed down with an Italian Syrah.

Once the meal was over, Honey and Doherty were left with a second cup of coffee they talked about Harold Clinker coming into the station with his brief.

'He's got a watertight alibi; he was in Spain at the time his wife was murdered and has a witness to prove it. The maid who said Carolina had gone with him got it wrong, so Carolina couldn't vouch for him. He also made a statement to Spanish police confirming where he was and they, of course, had to agree he was indeed in Spain. Slippery bastard though, getting it in writing then knocking on the door at Manvers Street.'

'So no easy wrap.'

He shook his head. 'No.'

'And Nigel Brooks?'

Doherty sighed in frustration. 'What did he have to do with Marietta or Mrs Flynn? Okay, his ex-wife lived in the village, but what's that got to do with anything?'

Honey eyed him as he said all this, thinking that perhaps he wasn't really being entirely up front.

'Are you thinking both killings might be random? Both carried out by a serial killer with a penchant for wedding dresses?'

'Penchant? That's a long word to use just after lunch.'

She grinned. 'I'm celebrating remember.'

'You've got over the fact that you've acquired a stepdad?'

'Just about.' Honey poured the last of the wine into her glass. 'Cheers.'

They clinked glasses.

She eyed him over the rim of her glass. 'That's what you think though isn't it? You think you may be dealing with a serial killer. You didn't take those letters you received seriously and now you're having second thoughts. And getting more concerned.'

He had been watching the stream of pedestrians trooping past the window, the cars trailing round looking for a place to park. With an air of reluctance, he stopped looking out the window and turned back to face her.

'I have to consider it, though . . .' That evasive look again.

'You had other thoughts.'

She paused, recalling that she'd considered her mother the sender of the letters seeing as she'd never approved of Doherty. She wondered whether she should voice her new suspicions. Nobody liked to think that a member of one's own family would do such a thing. She took the plunge.

'Did you think your daughter sent them?'

Doherty was slow to look at her. That in itself was enough to tell her she'd hit the nail on the head.

'I wasn't sure. She's off travelling again, so I phoned her mother. Apparently Karen is on a course in Scotland . . . but my daughter hates anyone knowing where she is. Far from being a routine-loving child I'm afraid. She might just as well have been here in Bath – or anywhere else for that matter.'

Although Honey had the urge to berate him for not telling her earlier, she held back. 'How would she know my mother was away?'

He shrugged. 'That, I suspect, was a shot in the dark. I can't see how she *would* know. Anyway, she was never that good at English, always getting her tenses wrong. From what I can gather from her mother, she'd meant to threaten kidnap not imply it had already taken place.'

'Well, that's two reasons for being relieved. My mother has remarried and I am not under threat from a serial killer. Which brings us back to the case in hand.'

Honey wasn't sure how to process the fact that her future stepdaughter had been threatening her. Kids were jealous of parents living their own lives — there was a kind of ownership thing. It had happened, but she guessed that in time things would mellow, at least she hoped so.

Resting his lower arms on the table, Doherty leaned forwards. Honey matched his stance. Their faces ended up about six inches apart. Doherty kept his voice low.

'Somebody killed Mrs Flynn with a lethal injection. We don't know who. A second person, finding the old girl supposedly at prayer, head resting on the pew in front of her, took advantage of the situation and bashed her over the head not realising she was already dead. We haven't found the weapon as yet.'

Honey looked down into her coffee, twirling the liquid round and round in the cup as she worked it through based on the information he'd given her. Her mind was clear of worrying about her mother's kidnap or a serial killer so there seemed more room to manoeuvre.

Gradually things slipped into place.

'The second murder. Marietta. It wasn't the same person who bashed Mrs Flynn. We're now sure of that, right?'

He registered his pleasure at her deduction with a brief kiss on her nose.

'Clever girl. A smokescreen carried out to put us off the scent. Whoever injected Mrs Flynn thought they'd committed the perfect murder. David Chan informs me that an injection under the tongue is not discernible like it is if done into the skin. It also means the insulin enters directly into the bloodstream bypassing the gut which tends to lessen its properties. Mrs Flynn was given a large dose. The other fact is that after twelve hours, the insulin itself is absorbed into the bloodstream and destroyed. Undetectable.'

'She wasn't discovered until the next morning, sitting there in her wedding dress.'

'That's right. Chan jumped through hoops in the days following the death. There were no obvious injection sites and only a tiny amount of insulin found in her bloodstream. But he'd read somewhere about injections under the tongue, that and the fact that her dress was soaked in sweat. He was a bit bashful about admitting where he'd read about insulin injected under the tongue,' Doherty added with a wry grin. 'A murder novel. Apparently our Mr Chan reads them by the bucketful. He told me he was lucky to find the tiny amount he did. It should have all been destroyed by that time. He also assured me that healthy adults are likely to recover from insulin overdoses, but babies and the elderly are more at risk.'

Honey frowned. 'That couldn't have been her I saw running to the church then, even though she was wearing a wedding dress. A very old one. It had to belong to her.'

'No. Instead, I think you saw Nigel looking for his wife. At her interview, Janet Glencannon told me he's always doing stupid things like that.'

'Not a pretty sight. He's hardly a dainty man.'

'I promise that at our wedding you can be the one wearing the dress.'

It was her turn to kiss his nose.

'So where did Mrs Flynn get her wedding dress? And what was she doing sitting in the church at that time of night?'

Doherty took both her hands in his. 'The vicar had only just left. The vicar had also been hit on the head and we took her home. The church was left open, not that it being left open is neither here nor there. As gang leader of the flower arranging committee, she had a key. The vicar assured me she did.'

'I take it the person who injected Mrs Flynn has to be a professional — like an ex-nurse.'

'Possibly. Whoever it was also needed access to a supply.'

Doherty nodded. 'Such as a hospital, clinic or medical practice.'

'Or a diabetic friend or relative.'

'Hmm. It's possible. My thoughts are that whoever gave Mrs Flynn the injection panicked when somebody hit the old girl over the head. It complicated matters. Mrs Flynn saw her doctor regularly on account of her age. In those circumstances an old lady found dead would not have attracted the intervention of a pathologist. A visible injury from a blow on the back of the head was a different matter. The real murderer attempted to divert attention away from any forensic findings, so he or she orchestrated a second murder. Marietta fitted the bill.'

'So who did it?'

'The same person who hit the vicar over the head.'

'Why the vicar?'

'The murderer was disturbed.'

Honey frowned. 'The vicar had only just come from Mrs Flynn's house. Bearing in mind the time difference between when we discovered the vicar and when Mrs Flynn was murdered, the murderer hung around.'

Doherty's eyes met hers. 'The murderer remained there after we left. Damn!' His fist hit the table. 'I should have had a good look round.'

'Our first thought was the vicar and anyway, it didn't seem as though anything was disturbed and nothing was reported taken.'

'Right. Just an opportunist. It usually is in church thefts.' Doherty's expression had turned deadly serious. 'Harold Clinker told me Mrs Flynn kept records of everyone in the village.'

'How did he know that?'

'He might have meant it in a general kind of way, but what if he didn't. What if Mrs Flynn kept written records. If so, where did she keep them? We didn't find any notebooks or diaries at Mrs Flynn's house. Only one fresh notebook if I remember rightly. Nothing written in it.'

'Yet?'

He nodded in agreement. 'Yet. So what if there was one already current. If she didn't keep it in the house, where did she keep it?'

'In the place she frequented more often than anywhere else. The church. Let's ask the vicar about her frequenting the church and that wedding dress. I'll give her a phone call.'

Honey kept her eyes on him as he spoke to the vicar. At first the conversation seemed hesitant, but finally the call was finished and disconnected.

'The vicar said that Mrs Flynn kept the wedding dress in an old coffer in the church. She found her one night sitting there wearing it, but didn't disturb her. I asked her why. She said she didn't know but felt sorry for her.'

'Miss Haversham,' said Honey.

'Who?'

'The jilted bride from Dickens who wore her wedding dress and never altered anything in the house.'

'Never read it. I prefer Mickey Spillane myself.'

CHAPTER THIRTY

When Honey phoned her, the vicar promised to meet them at the church as soon as she could and that she would bring her diary with her so Honey and Doherty could set a date.

They drove down the narrow alley to the parking area in front of the church.

'Harold's home,' said Doherty and nodded to the black Mercedes saloon glimpsed through the gaps in the gates of Belvedere House. Next to it was a deep blue Porsche. 'I wonder who that belongs to.'

'I expect it's one of his lady friends. He's not one to let his bed get cold.'

The day was surprising bright, sunlight streaming through the open door of the church, brightening the old stonework so it shone like honey.

The slight figure of Hermione Thompson was gliding between flower displays topping up the water for the thirsty blooms. She smiled when she saw them.

'Can I help you?'

'We're here to see the vicar,' said Doherty and flashed his ID.

'Oh yes,' she said, her voice hushed and respectful. 'You're the policeman aren't you.'

'We're also hoping to get married here,' Honey added. 'The flowers look lovely.'

'We do our best,' said Hermione, sounding and looking more like a little girl than a fully grown woman, though judging by her face she was on the plus side of forty.

The sound of Doherty's mobile echoed around the church.

'Sorry,' he said apologetically after seeing who was calling. 'I'll take this outside.'

Honey shook her head. 'Sometimes I think we won't ever get to the altar.'

'Oh I dare say you will. If you really want to,' said Hermione.

Hermione Thompson struck Honey as one of those people who can't speak unless somebody else leads the conversation. With that in mind she plunged straight in and asked her about the murder.

'I suppose it must have come as quite a shock to the village?'

'Yes,' Hermione murmured. 'It did.'

'I heard Mrs Flynn wasn't exactly that popular.'

'She told the truth about people; saw beneath the surface,' Hermione retorted hotly.

This was not the response Honey had expected. Hadn't Janet Glencannon said that Mrs Flynn had picked on Hermione?

'Oh go on!' she said conspiratorially. 'There's no need to be frightened. She's not around to bully you anymore. You speak your mind.'

The pale face reddened.

'It wasn't like that!'

'You mean she didn't bully you?'

'Her attitude towards me was misunderstood.' A sudden change came over her face. 'It was her, wasn't it? Janet Glencannon. It would be her, having a dig at us because she had to compensate us for Quincy's problems that she should have told us when we bought him from her.'

'Quincy is your dog?'

'A Labrador. He had fits. She said it was because he was a puppy, but that was a lie. Quincy is epileptic. It costs us a fortune to keep him topped up with barbiturates. She said he would grow out of it, but he didn't. And before you suggest we should have put him down, we couldn't do that once we'd grown fond of him.'

'Oh, of course you couldn't,' Honey said sympathetically. So even though Janet Glencannon had told her that Hermione had been bullied unmercifully by Mrs Flynn, Hermione didn't see things quite that way. However she wasn't here to pass judgement, only to ask questions.

Hermione rubbed tears away from her eyes. 'I'm sorry. I shouldn't let things get to me, but there you are. I'm not a hard-boiled type like some around here.'

'Some? Do you have anyone in particular in mind?'

Hermione blinked at her as though trying to make up her mind whether to spill the beans or not.

'I'm not a gossip but I wasn't surprised when Marietta was found dead. I suspect her husband. He had good reason too, you know, though it's not for me to condemn — not really, but . . .'

Sensing there might be something to be learned here and notwithstanding the fact that Harold and Marietta had an open marriage, Honey urged her on.

'It wouldn't be condemning if it helps apprehend the killer, Mrs Thompson.'

Head inclined over the vase of flowers, Hermione began deadheading the flowers that weren't likely to last the week.

Judging by the fact that she was sucking in her lips, she was yet again considering exactly what to say and how to say it. Honey suddenly entertained the view that Hermione was not quite the innocent little woman she made herself out to be.

'Well. Let's put it this way,' she said eventually. 'She was always home on the days the gardener was there. He's a big burly fellow is Dave Lee and despite English summer weather, was often to be seen mowing the lawn or pulling weeds without his shirt on. Perhaps it was a prerequisite for the job,' she added.

Honey perceived a sudden spitefulness in Hermione Thompson's smile, one corner of her pale pink lips curled up making her plain face more animated, more interesting even. It was as though her outward show of pliable innocence had turned brittle and cracked in the corners.

Although she already guessed the answer, she followed Hermione to where a vase of flowers with drooping heads were dropping dead petals all over the floor. She asked the obvious question. 'Do you think they were having an affair?'

'Excuse me. I have to take these outside to the compost heap.'

'Fine,' said Honey. 'I could do with a bit of fresh air myself.'

She followed her outside. Doherty was nowhere to be seen. She wondered where he'd got to, but wouldn't go looking for him just yet, not whilst she had Hermione in her grasp.

Flies were buzzing around the compost heap and bees around the rose hedge bobbing against the wall. The compost heap was just before the long grass and the place where Harold Clinker had been discovered.

'So what do you think?'

'About?'

Was this woman seriously obtuse or just evasive? The urge to give her a good shake was exceedingly strong. Patience, said one of Honey's inner voices. Another one said plough on. She wasn't sure whether that second voice meant with regard to asking more questions or to giving the limp looking girl a good shake.

Patience won out. 'I said do you think Marietta and this Dave Lee were having an affair?'

A breeze suddenly sprang up from nowhere blowing her fine fair hair across her face. Hermione brushed it back. Honey noticed her fingernails were painted black which seemed at odds with the rest of her outfit.

'I'm not sure it's right to describe it as an affair. I can think of a more lewd phrase,' she replied, her lips quite thin and taut, her eyes hidden by spoon shaped lids. The malice was tangible.

Wow, thought Honey. She'd put Hermione down as soft hearted and sweet but the woman in front her was hard, cold and, now she thought of it, potentially dangerous.

'This is a very pleasant church,' Honey persisted as she watched Hermione tip the dead flowers into the bin before pouring the stagnant water into the long grass. 'It's very pretty, the church and its gardens.'

'It's a *churchyard*,' said Hermione. 'Not gardens. It's a churchyard and it's full of stone angels and empty urns.'

'I stand corrected.'

'It's hallowed ground. Those who hadn't been christened or were too poor to pay for their own plot were buried over there,' she said, jerking her chin towards the area where the long grass whispered in the breeze. 'Smothered in grass and weeds.'

Honey could see that the grass seemed longer there, the ground and the wall falling away down a steep incline behind the church.

'That's where Harold Clinker was found bound, gagged and naked. I suppose the village was shocked at that too.'

'A disgusting man!' Hermione spat.

'Do you know him?'

'He took advantage of peoples' good nature. Once he got the lay of the land, so to speak, he used everything he learned to his own ends.'

As she digested what Hermione was saying, Honey let her gaze wander. Sunlight dappled the grass. The smell and sound of summer was in the air, cornflowers and poppies growing in the oldest part of the churchyard, the place where the grass was longest. If she recalled rightly, it was also the place the vicar had wanted cleared and was opposed in that pursuit by Mrs Flynn.

'So only poor people were buried over there,' said Honey, nodding towards the place Hermione had indicated.

'That's correct.'

'Nobody in recent years?'

Hermione frowned. 'Why, should there be?'

Honey shrugged. 'Just a notion.'

The more modern graves were all set out in neat orderly lines, the grass around them cut short, flowers sprouting from marble and pewter urns.

'It's a lovely church,' Honey persisted. 'No wonder so many people want to get married here. Did you get married here?'

'No!'

Her tone was abrupt and when she turned her back to the breeze and bent down to turn on the cold water tap to refill the vase, her flyaway hair hid her expression.

Honey thought carefully about what to do next. There was one question she was burning to ask but wasn't at all sure she would get an answer.

'I know you say it was nonsense, but do you think it might have appeared to other people that Mrs Flynn tended to pick on you? More than one person thought so,' Honey put in quickly before Janet Glencannon was again accused.

Hermione Thompson straightened up sharply, both hands around the cut glass vase. Eyes that were usually pale and impassive were now as hard and sharp as the cut glass vase she held to her breast.

'It was mmmmmy own . . . mmmmmy own . . . fault. I made mmmmistakes sometimes.'

Honey felt her blood turning to water. Hermione's sudden stuttering and her overall reaction was that of a person who was typically abused, yet it wasn't with reference to her husband. Honey didn't think it was a man at all. Hermione was referring to an elderly woman. Mrs Flynn.

Suddenly she saw Doherty waving at her from the side of his car. Before joining him, she walked into the long grass, almost as though just being there might give her that bit more insight into what had gone on here. As it turned out there were a few nettles amongst the grass and she got stung.

'Ouch!'

She looked for Hermione Thompson meaning to thank her for her assistance, but she'd already gone back into the church, the door slamming behind her.

Doherty was looking pleased with himself. 'We've found Alice Flynn.'

'In Scotland?'

'No. She was staying with a friend in Keynsham.'

'A friend? Anyone we know?' Somehow she had already guessed the answer.

'Geraldine Evans.'

* * *

There was a lot to do at the Green River, so Honey wasn't that put out when she wasn't invited to attend Doherty's interview of a woman they knew slept most of the day and worked most of the night.

It wasn't just that she had paperwork to sort out and emails to send to people who had enquired about rooms, there was also her mother to contend with.

It turned out that she could send an email to her mother aboard the cruise liner.

'They have satellite phones and other sophisticated communications equipment,' Lindsey told her.

'Are you going to tell me how it works?' Honey asked her daughter.

'Same as it always works,' Lindsey responded. 'Don't worry, Mum, you're not suddenly going to hear something like ground control to Major Tom. It's pain free.'

Lindsey gathered up her things from behind the reception desk.

'You're going?' Honey asked her, slightly alarmed at having to deal with new technology and her mother herself.

'Yes. I've got a special meeting to attend.'

Her attitude was uncharacteristically brisk as though she had no wish to be asked where she was going.

215

'Mrs Gloria has big energy,' Anna, Lindsey's replacement, said when peering over Honey's shoulder at Gloria's wedding picture. 'I have big energy too,' she added. 'We are very alike where men are concerned. We both have big energy.'

Honey blanched initially at the thought that her mother could have anything in common with Anna. But on reflection she realised that Anna was right. They both liked men, Anna's taste resulting in a number of children by different men, and Gloria having had substantial pay outs following each of her four divorces. Both of them had made fruitful marriages, though not bearing the same fruit.

So what about this one?

Anna jabbed a finger at the screen. 'Oh! It is him!'

Honey stared at the screen.

'Him? Who?'

'The man who did tricks.'

Honey's eyebrows shot up to her hairline. 'Tricks? What sort of tricks?'

Tricks was a bad word in Honey's books rating alongside tricksters, scams, scammers, crooks and crooked. Dishonest was only a mild description to add to the list, but still worth considering.

'He did card tricks when he stayed here. You must remember him, Mrs Driver. They called him the Prince of Cards.'

'Anna, I don't understand what you're talking . . .' Then it came to her. 'The Conjurors Convention?'

'Yes. The men who do tricks with cards and swords and pull rabbits out of hats. They were all very good, but the Prince of Cards was the best.'

'Ah!' Honey let the recollection flood over her. The Green River had played host to a convention for conjurors, stage acts mostly who came together to exchange ideas or show off their latest trick. So her mother had married a conjuror, a stage magician.

'You do not look very happy about it, Mrs Driver. He was a very nice man. I liked him.'

That did it. Honey sat back in her chair puffed cheeks gradually diminishing as she expelled a deep breath.

It was true. Anna and her mother had the same taste in men. Following the failure of their respective relationships, both had been left to their own devices. In Anna's case it was coping with the resulting children of her unions. With Gloria Cross it was a prenuptial agreed account limit with American Express.

Honey took a deep breath as she thought about what to say in the message. She'd already sent one of congratulations via an email greeting card website, but that was before she'd learned that Stewart White was more — or was it less? — than a bookie, an owner of a chain of betting shops.

Lindsey had promised to do some research, but that could take time. In the meantime Honey couldn't really accuse her mother of being duped. This email would be of the common type asking her mother on what date she expected to return and where the newlyweds would live.

She sent it off as per normal then proceeded to stare at the screen as if the reply would appear by return of post. Anna reminded her that it was email.

'You'll get it when you get it.'

'She'll have her phone with her. I'll give it a try.'

Anna shook her head and muttered, 'You'll be lucky.'

She had turned out to be right. Honey found herself listening to a recorded message saying, 'I'm on my honeymoon. I'll be in touch when I get back.'

Comfort! Honey told herself she needed comfort and that meant comfort food. Her recent denial in the hope of being a slim-line version of herself gliding down the aisle had disappeared over the horizon along with her mother and a stage magician who might also own a chain of betting shops.

She told Anna she would check back in later, then balancing a cup of coffee and a cream bun in one hand, she closed her office door behind her giving instructions that she was not to be disturbed.

The coffee went quickly enough, though not as fast as the cream bun. She needed it.

In an effort to take her mind off whether or not her mother had married in haste and might very well repent at leisure — if she lived long enough — she forced herself to think of other things.

Number one was Mrs Flynn. It now seemed certain that it wasn't her who had been running through the village in a wedding dress. Nigel Brooks made a habit of that.

Number two, they also knew that Mrs Flynn had been jilted at the altar and still had her wedding dress. Had the vicar known that she kept it in the old coffer and came in regularly to try it on and sit there as though she were still waiting for her long-lost husband?

And what had happened to the husband? Had he ever come back as Alan Price, one of the villagers had suggested?

The more she thought about Mrs Flynn sitting there in her wedding dress, the sadder she became. Being jilted had ruined the woman's life. Luckily she had had open access to the church so it was logical to suppose she could sit there in that dress whenever she liked. But surely somebody would have known. Somebody would have seen her.

The vicar. The vicar must have seen her.

Doherty's phone was off.

Her own car being at the garage in the tender hands of Ahmed Clifford, she put her life on the line and asked Mary Jane if she could oblige her with a lift to Wainscote.

'I'd love to. Just give me a minute whilst I get all my notes together. I need to have a word with that vicar one more time and take a look at some of the old papers she keeps in that vicarage.'

Mary Jane was still tracing her family tree. It seemed to Honey that the amount of stuff Mary Jane had gathered was enough to a forest let alone a single tree!

'Here we go,' cried Mary Jane as she nudged her way into the traffic and floored the pedal on the first piece of straight road they encountered.

CHAPTER THIRTY-ONE

'Alice Flynn. I'm looking for Alice Flynn.'

It was four o'clock in the afternoon, the blue sky had turned a disgruntled grey and the woman who answered the door at number six, Rochester Gardens looked disgruntled too.

'She ain't 'ere.'

Geraldine Evans went to shut the door but Doherty jammed his foot into the gap and flashed his warrant card.

'Then I'll wait.'

The door was partially reopened.

'Got a car to wait in?'

'No. I'd prefer to while away my happy visit by asking you some questions.'

'Look, I've only just got up. I've got to work tonight.'

'Where do you work?'

'Bristol. Red Cross Street.'

'On the street?'

Her scowl matched the bags under her eyes; deep and black. 'Do I look like a tart?'

Doherty thought she did, but knew if he said so she'd be even surlier than she was now.

'I'd take a guess you work at the Lemon Tree. Am I right?'

The Lemon Tree was a nightclub housed in a red-brick building sandwiched between the old Central Commercial School and the back of the buildings that fronted Old Market. In years gone by Old Market had been just that; a market. Now it was given over to a traffic system that did nothing for the quality of life round there and precious little for traffic efficiency.

The Lemon Tree opened at around nine at night and didn't close until four in the morning. Doherty surmised the money must be good, though by the looks of the outside of Geraldine's house, she certainly didn't spend it on property maintenance.

Doherty nodded at somebody taking out their wheelie bin a few doors down. As far as he was aware it was not rubbish collection day tomorrow. The operation was being done slowly. The woman pushing the bin was looking in his direction, curious no doubt as to what might be going on.

Doherty voiced what he was thinking. 'I expect your neighbour there is wondering what's going on,' he said to the pale faced woman keeping him at bay. Judging by the panda eyes, she hadn't bothered to take her make-up off last night.

She blinked which caused specks of dried mascara to transfer from her lashes onto her cheeks. Her jaw slackened.

'Nosy cow!' she shouted, and did a two fingered salute to her neighbour before letting him in.

The room she showed him into might have been a shrine to IKEA; cheap, square furnishings, if it hadn't been so untidy. Minimalist it was not!

Clothes that might have been dirty though could just as easily have been clean and waiting to be ironed, sat on a dark blue sofa. Newspapers, magazines and handbags cluttered up most of the available surfaces. The room smelled and looked grubby. The carpet looked as though it hadn't seen a vacuum cleaner for months.

A TV guide lay open on the coffee table alongside dirty plates and wine glasses; two of each.

She saw him look.

'I had a guest last night.' She snatched up the plates and glasses, holding them against her body, standing there in the middle of the room between him and the sideboard that was groaning with handbags.

He beamed at her as though he understood that she was a busy woman with too much to do.

'Do you want to take them out to the kitchen? I don't mind waiting.'

She looked in two minds about doing so.

'I wouldn't mind a cup of tea,' he added. 'If you're making one. Then we can sit down and talk about Alice. That's all I want,' he said.

Despite his reassuring tone, she still seemed in two minds.

'That's the trouble with takeaways. Having somebody cook it for you is all well and good. Trouble is that once it's all tucked away you need somebody to wash up the debris. That's what I always find.'

A flick of dried lashes and she did what he was hoping she'd do.

Left alone for what he knew would only be minutes, he zeroed in on the handbags. They were of all shapes and sizes; all different colours too.

He was pushing his luck, but he had to have a look inside one or two. A bright yellow one lay on its side. He pulled one side of it up and looked in. Nothing.

He did the same to a smart tan one that looked as though it was designer label — not that he could tell one designer from another. There was nothing in that bag either.

Working on a hunch, he got out his phone, daring to take as many pictures as he could before Geraldine came back.

The sound of running water came from the kitchen plus the clatter of crockery. At a guess she was washing out a mug or cup. Judging by the debris left on the coffee table and the general air of laziness, whatever his tea might come in had probably been piled in the sink for days.

If Alice Flynn was staying here, why hadn't she washed up? Not that he had any intention of drinking anything. Geraldine Evans was the sort to spit in a copper's tea. Hopefully they would chat long enough for it to go cold — a good enough excuse.

'Here. You can have the piggy one.' She smirked as she handed him a mug decorated with a pink pig. 'Don't mind about me. I've just had one,' she said before he could ask.

She didn't ask him to sit down but looked tellingly at her wristwatch.

'Can we make this quick?'

'You do know that Alice's mother was murdered.'

'Alice told me. That's why she's here. There's arrangements to be made.'

'Ah yes. The funeral. I take it she'll be buried in the local churchyard.'

Geraldine snorted. 'I doubt that! It's full, and anyway, burying is expensive. Gladys is being cremated. As soon as the body is released of course.'

Doherty nodded. A murder victim was not released until the pathologist was fully satisfied, and even then held on to a bit longer if the body was to be cremated. A buried body could be disinterred whereas ashes could not.

Doherty put his mug down on the table and just as tellingly looked at his own watch.

'What time did you say she'd be back?'

'When it suits her.'

Typical nightclub woman, thought Doherty. No matter whether she was a dancer or hostess, or even whether she was only a hat check girl, the plastic smile broke with the dawn.

His tea remained untouched as he reached into his pocket and pulled out his card.

'Can you give her this and tell her I'd like to speak to her?'

Geraldine's face remained impassive. The card was allowed to flutter down onto the coffee table.

He knew it was more than likely that Alice Flynn wouldn't get the card. He promised himself he would give it two days before he called again.

* * *

He was just about to get into his car when he saw Reg and Vera walking towards him. Following Honey's visit and the arrest of Nigel Brooks, they had come into the station to give a statement which was how they'd met.

Reg and his wife were loaded down with shopping, one bag in each hand.

'Thought it was you,' Reg called out.

Vera's face was red and as she walked she waddled from side to side.

'Would you like a cup of tea?' offered Vera.

Doherty thought of the cup of tea he'd left on Geraldine's coffee table and decided he was thirsty.

'Don't mind if I do.'

Reg and Vera's place was best described as a family gathering spot, their front room cluttered with family photographs and white china rabbits. Doherty surmised that they had plenty of family get-togethers.

Vera saw him looking at the ornaments.

'I bought one, told the family I liked them, and they've been buying them for me ever since,' chortled Vera.

'Very nice,' said Doherty.

He was pretty sure that rabbits carrying tennis rackets, playing golf or dressed in ball gowns were collectible, but they were not something he'd indulge in.

However, the room was clean and bright and the only smell he detected was pleasant and seemed to be coming from the shopping they'd lumbered through into the kitchen.

Leaving Vera in the kitchen making the tea, Reg half closed the door, glancing through the gap as though to check that Vera wasn't listening.

'We've been keeping an eye on things,' said Reg, leaning so close Doherty could see the black hairs up his nose and smell the toothpaste on his breath. 'Vera feels a bit embarrassed about admitting it, but we've been jotting down times and descriptions of visitors to number six and number eight — the two houses you visited.'

Doherty eyed Reg wondering what had given them the impression that there was anything particularly suspicious about either of those houses.

'What made you decide to do that?'

Reg's bright expression soured. 'It ain't illegal, is it?'

'No, but I bet your neighbours wouldn't like it if they knew.'

'They don't speak to us anyways—well not numbers six and eight anyways. Funny buggers both of them—begging yer pardon for the language.'

Doherty frowned.

'If I was a copper,' Reg continued hastily, 'I'd be suspicious of Mr Brooks. Let's face it, he's one sandwich short of a picnic is that one, the lift don't quite go to the top floor if you know what I mean.' He gave Doherty a knowing look.

'I haven't given you any reason to be suspicious of Mr Brooks.'

'That you haven't, but there's been a stranger staying there and there's been visitors; people calling there who we ain't seen before.'

Sceptical at first, Doherty now expressed interest.

'Can I see your notes?'

Reg got up just as Vera was coming in with a tray of tea and digestives.

Doherty's curiosity overruled his thirst. He flicked through the notes getting more and more surprised the further he flicked. There were dates and times — not many because they hadn't long begun their quest — all the same, they made interesting reading.

'And we took these,' said Vera, passing them her tablet. 'Got some lovely pictures.'

Doherty put down the written notes and took the tablet, swiping one picture after another.

Some of them he didn't know. Nigel Brooks was there, knocking on the door of number six but obviously receiving no response. He had a face like thunder.

Reg enlightened him. 'He's always complaining to her about her scruffy house.'

He swiped as far as the penultimate picture, swiped over it then went back. Amazed at who he was seeing, he zoomed in just to make sure. There was no doubt.

He asked Reg and Vera if they had ever seen this person over there before.

Both of them shook their heads.

'A suspect, you reckon?' asked Reg, his eyes bright with interest.

Doherty stared at the picture. It showed a woman wearing a pale blue dress, her hair kept back with the use of a matching pale blue Alice band.

He apologised for not being able to stay for tea. 'Just a sip,' he said, grabbing the cup and drinking as much as he needed to stop his mouth from getting too dry. He needed his voice. He had a few more questions for Geraldine Evans.

CHAPTER THIRTY-TWO

Before leaving, Honey phoned the vicar on the hotel landline phone to let her know she was coming. Voicemail kicked in so she left a message, trusting that the vicar checked her messages on a regular basis.

Halfway to where she was going, she pulled her phone out of her bag meaning to let Doherty know her whereabouts, to report in all the stuff relevant to the case that she'd found out, and also to tell him she'd decided she'd quite like a white wedding and was off to see the Reverend Constance Paxton to arrange things. That would be after she'd had another look around the church.

'This phone isn't working,' she said to Mary Jane whilst giving her phone a thorough shake. 'I think the battery's dead.' She blew the blasted thing a big raspberry, and threw it over her shoulder onto the back seat.

On the drive Mary Jane told her all that she'd found out about her family. 'They owned a lot of land around here. There were a lot of descendants.'

Honey only half listened. She still needed to phone Doherty. Perhaps the vicar would let her phone from the vicarage — if she could remember Doherty's mobile phone number that is. There was no question of it, remembering numbers was not her strong suit.

Mary Jane drove carefully along the narrow alley leading to the apron of parking in front of the lychgate. The sun had travelled with them as far as here but the weather was changing. There was a blue sky behind her back in the High Street. In front of her a cloud the colour of severe bruising hung over the church roof.

Apart from weddings on Saturdays, the church was best attended on Sundays. Today was Tuesday so there was nobody around.

She toyed with the idea that the ladies of the flower arranging committee might be inside.

Mary Jane dropped her off and turned the car round. The vicarage was at the other end of the village, a semi-detached that somebody thought more efficient than the original stone-built Gothic place with its grand rooms and many bedrooms.

Honey decided she would try the church first then drive up to the vicarage. She might have walked up, but the blue sky was swiftly being swallowed up by the dark grey bruise.

Those areas of the churchyard that had been bright faded into shadow. Light rain began to fall and a sudden breeze shifted the long grass and sent late-flowering apple blossom drifting directly into the church porch.

Using her foot to move the blossom to one side, she stepped onto stone and reached for the cast-iron handle. To her surprise it was not locked.

The flower committee were probably responsible for that.

The smell of old dust, old polish and perhaps even old prayers, came out to greet her. So did the sweet smell of summer roses and lilies. The flower arranging ladies had already done their stuff.

The floral decorations were the brightest spots in the church, though not enough to lift the gloom.

'Is anyone here?'

Nobody answered. She wished for a sound, any sound, with the notable exception of the scurrying of a mouse. Or a bat. Bats were lovely creatures at a distance, but not up close and personal. Especially if they got tangled in your hair.

Wishing she'd brought a hat or maybe an umbrella, Honey tucked her hair behind her ears.

'Reverend Paxton?'

She waited, listening for the slightest sound.

This whole thing, hunting a murderer, arranging a wedding and worrying about her mother, was very tiring. That was besides running a hotel.

'Thank God for Lindsey,' she whispered into the silence. If God was going to be listening, this was the place to voice exactly what was on your mind.

The rain beat against the window. No point in going yet. She yawned. Yes, things were certainly catching up with her. Might as well get comfortable, she thought, leaning her head against an adjacent pillar. The pillar stood between where she was sat and the aisle. Whoever happened to take this seat during a service couldn't see a bloody thing! On the other hand, the vicar in the pulpit or anyone else in the church, couldn't see them either, handy during a boring sermon especially if you'd been out on the tiles the night before.

Just until the rain stops, she thought, wrapping her arms around herself. Her eyes began to close.

Whilst she dozed she thought about Marietta when she'd been younger. There had been something different about the woman married to Harold Clinker from the schoolgirl she remembered. Her hair for a start used to be mousy, dead easy to change to blonde. She also used to squint because she was short-sighted, but that was nothing that contact lenses couldn't sort out. But what else was it? What else had changed?

CHAPTER THIRTY-THREE

Before retracing his steps up the garden path of number six, Doherty contacted the Wizard at Manvers Street.

'Any joy on the handbags?'

'All stolen. Do you know, guv, some of those bags are worth a couple of thousand? You wouldn't credit it would you. Looks just like handbags to me.'

There had recently been a spate of muggings where handbags had been snatched. Most of them were late at night and in some pretty up-market areas. The fact that the handbags had been bundled on Geraldine's sideboard with nothing in them had been a good indication that she was fencing them. Muggers took the contents; Geraldine took the handbags and sold them, either to personal contacts or on eBay.

Geraldine looked surprised to see him. 'Now what?'

'Another word.'

'I ain't got time!'

She tried to close the door but Doherty's foot was too far inside, the door ramming his leg.

'I need to talk to you about Alice Flynn again. I also need to talk to you about Hermione Thompson.'

'I don't know them.'

'You already told me you knew Alice and that she was staying with you. Didn't tell me about Hermione though, did you?'

'Look. I've got a job to go to. Come back tomorrow.'

Doherty hissed through pursed lips and shook his head. 'No, Geraldine. If I leave things until tomorrow all those bags piled up there on your sideboard will be gone. I couldn't possibly allow that. Now, in view of the handbags and your involvement in this murder, I think you can spare me some time. Right?'

The hard-edged woman, with her heavily made-up eyes and figure going to seed, looked totally deflated, her complexion turning pale despite the tan make-up.

She opened the door wider so he could go in and stand in the middle of the scruffy front room just as he had before.

'Well,' she said, folding her arms protectively across her chest. 'What is it you want to know?'

Before he had chance to answer, he heard the sound of heels tip tapping up the garden path and the sound of a key in the front door.

'Oh. Sorry. Am I interrupting anything?'

The woman was about forty-five and might have looked pretty good if it hadn't been for her dress sense. She was wearing tight jeans and an equally tight top, both in black. A studded belt hung low around her hips and her hair was dyed black. Her face was very white.

Doherty addressed her. 'Are you Alice Flynn?'

'Yeah.' She looked from him to Geraldine and back again. 'Are you a copper?'

Doherty nodded. 'Yes.'

'Have you found my nan's killer yet?'

'Your nan?'

Alice smiled. 'Yeah. She told everyone she was my mother, but she was really my nan — my grandmother. That's what comes of having a mother who died of a drug overdose. Nan brought us up.'

'Us?'

'Me and my sister.'

'. . . Hermione Thompson.'

'Yeah. Done all right for herself, she 'as. Don't want anyone to know though. Nan kept an eye on her just to make sure nobody put on her. That's what she told me. Nan was a bit of a card, though I suppose you already know that.'

Although not invited, Doherty sat down on the settee. It seemed that unlike Geraldine Evans, Alice Flynn liked to talk.

'So how do you two know each other,' Doherty asked, indicating the two women in turn.

It was obviously Alice who answered. 'Used to work the same nightclubs, that was before I got hitched and had the kids. Worst day's work I ever did marrying that git. My nan told me he was no good before I married 'im, but there, I thought I was in love. I love the kids though. Must say that.'

'Are you still married?'

'Never married 'im, did I. My nan told me not to, so I didn't.'

'I thought you said you got hitched.'

Alice laughed. 'Not in the accepted sense. We took the modern approach. My nan's advice again. She reckoned that marriage should be approached like a business, and she certainly knew about all that, though . . .' She paused and eyed him speculatively. 'You probably know all that already.'

Doherty was intrigued. 'A little. Would you like to elaborate?'

Quite frankly he didn't have a clue what she was talking about. It might be something. It might just as easily be nothing at all.

Alice Flynn struck him as an open and honest person. The moment she began relating facts about her grandmother, the more he liked her.

'She used to be a marriage broker, finding brides for foreigners in need of a British passport. It wasn't such a crowded marketplace back when she was doing it around fifteen years ago. Not like now. Nan said she could see the writing on the

231

wall so got out of it, told her partner that she wanted to spend more time with me and the kids. She was speaking the truth there. The kids were young back then and I needed the help. Made a load of money and bought that cottage of hers. Loved that cottage she did.' Alice paused to wipe a tear from her eye. Doherty was in no doubt that it was genuine.

'So she gave up the business about fifteen years ago.'

Alice nodded. 'Yep. She'd made her pile and nobody came after her. But then, knowing my nan she was careful. A bit of an old dragon, but not stupid.'

'Did she marry any of these men herself?'

Alice smiled sadly. 'No. She got divorced and never got over it. What with that and me mum ruined by drugs. She blamed my granddad for that, for not honouring his promise and all that. I didn't think it mattered that much, but as she said to me, it did back then.'

'So he never came back?'

Alice frowned. 'I don't think so, but sometimes I wondered whether he did. Sometimes she seemed to get the timeline a bit muddled, especially as she got older.'

'How about Hermione. Does she know all this?'

'Oh yes, but you won't tell her husband, will you? Nan made sure that nobody knew they were related. She went out of her way to make people think that. Hermione moved there to keep an eye on her but they kept it a secret. Even Hermione's husband didn't know. Hermione got him to put in for a job in the area and chose where they were going to live. He didn't mind that. He loves her. Besotted with her he is, not like my old man. Right bugger he was.'

Doherty laughed with her. He could understand her being popular with the men in a nightclub. Never mind the sex, she made them feel at ease and she was so incredibly open.

'So these marriages were arranged in order for people to get a British passport.'

'That's right, but only men. She had a partner you see. It was the partner who played the part of the bride. They had heaps of names they used on the marriage certificate and for the upfront paperwork. Don't ask me how it worked, but Nan told me. I promised not to tell until she was dead and gone, and I wouldn't now except that it might help capture her murderer. You see Nan did a runner with the lion's share of the money they earned. They used to dib out what they called 'running money', by way of a weekly wage really, but the bulk of it was stashed away in a bank account in my nan's name.'

'Do you know the name of this partner?'

Alice shook her head. 'No. She never told us. She said that they never revealed their true names to each other. The only thing she did say was that her partner sometimes wore glasses and sometimes had a black mole on her cheek. The mole changed shape and so did the glasses. It was all part of the business, adapting disguises and never revealing their true selves. So there you are.'

Her head drooped and she looked sad again before raising her head and looking him straight in the eyes.

'I know my nan wasn't the most perfect person in the world, but you will find her murderer, won't you? You will find whoever did it?'

* * *

What was that?

Honey's eyes flicked open. The storm outside was still raging, the rain lashing the arched windows and an angry draught blowing around her ankles.

She moved slowly. The hospitality trade had served her well. Don't let on that you're there, not if you wish to avoid hotel guests that you didn't like, especially serial complainers. People who went out of their way to find something to complain about were rife in the hotel and catering industry. From experience it was the home-grown customers who did the most complaining. Honey blamed the consumer programmes on national television and some wretched presenter who stated

233

the British didn't complain enough. Obviously said presenter had never run a hotel. If they had they wouldn't have said it.

Anyway, she knew instinctively when to keep her head down.

The voices were hushed but intense, one slightly colder than the other.

'I've brought you a wedding dress.'

'Don't be ridiculous.'

'Why don't you put it on?'

'I haven't come here to try on a wedding dress. I've come here with fresh blooms.'

'Fresh blooms!' The tone was mocking. Honey tried to remember where she'd heard that tone before.

'I know you, don't I?' The voice was that of Janet Glencannon. 'I've seen you before . . . I know! You were with your father that day . . .'

'HE WAS NOT MY FATHER! Let me enlighten you, lady. That man was my husband. I was thirteen years old. He married me so he could get the passport he wanted. I hated him but was tied to him in marriage. He told me that if I complained to the authorities, I would be put in prison because he had the proper passport and I did not! I was scared. I believed him. I was *thirteen*! Thirteen! Can you imagine what he put me through?'

She heard Janet's intake of breath. 'I didn't know. How could I have done? He told us you were his daughter.'

'I tried to tell you. I thought you might have surmised by the expression on my face that I was terrified. He'd bought me from my family. Bought me! Do you understand that? Now. Put this on.'

Honey heard the rustling of many layers of net and silk, the sound only a wedding dress or a ball gown could make.

'Get out of my way!'

'Put this dress on.'

'No!'

There was a strangulated sound. Honey dared to peer out from behind the stone pillar.

The other voice she recognised belonged to a tall figure who moved like a gymnast, was much taller than Janet Glencannon, and had a firm, finely muscled body. She was holding Janet in a head lock. Janet was resisting, but no amount of tugging could pull Carolina Sherise's strong brown arms from around her neck.

'I read it all,' Carolina was saying, her voice alternating between emotional trembling and vengeful anger. 'You and Mrs Flynn were involved in wedding arrangements for foreigners wanting to acquire a British passport. Mrs Flynn made the arrangements. You were the bride, always with a different name and sporting a slightly different look. Including that scar. I will always remember that scar,' she said somewhat melancholy. 'I didn't realise it wasn't real, but then I wouldn't. I was only a kid and I'd never got to play at dressing up. I was a child bride. I suffered badly for it, sharing his bed, cooking his food, giving him his injections. He was a diabetic you know. That's how I learned how to administer injections.

'It would have been the perfect crime; she wouldn't have been discovered until the following day and by then the insulin would have been absorbed into the blood stream. Just an old woman who had lived her time. But you had to come along and hit her on the back of the head. Why did you do that?'

Janet was struggling to answer, choking against the tightness of Carolina's arms against her throat. Honey stepped out from behind the pillar. 'Yes. I'd like to know that too.'

Carolina's slate grey eyes widened, but she held on. Janet Glencannon was going nowhere.

'Do you think you might loosen your grip just enough so she can tell us why she and Mrs Flynn had fallen out?'

Carolina, her piercing eyes shining with violent intent, shook her head.

'No. I don't really need to hear it. I already know. They fell out over money. That was all they cared about. Money.'

'Well if you know, then what's the point of choking her? You've got your answer so you might as well let her go.'

'No.'

'I think you should. I've already phoned the police. They're on their way.'

Carolina threw back her head and laughed. It struck Honey that it was a high, lonely laugh, full of bitterness and regret for a childhood that had ended too early.

'I don't care,' said Carolina in a high-pitched voice, her eyes looking upwards to the towering rafters overhead. 'I really don't care.'

'So what next?' Honey asked, trying to keep her voice calm.

Carolina's eyes seemed to glow from the shadows that lengthened and shortened by virtue of the storm still whirling outside. 'I might kill you,' she hissed, her lush lips stretching over ultra-white teeth.

'I don't think so.'

Honey began heading for the door, striding quickly and showing no sign of fear. Inside she was wobbling like a jelly.

'Stop right there! If you don't stop she dies!'

Honey didn't stop until the door was within arm's length.

She turned round adopting a defiant stance that bore no resemblance to how she was feeling inside.

'I don't believe you.'

Carolina's eyes glittered. Janet's bulged.

Honey was horrified. One swift flick and Janet's neck would be broken.

Some foolhardy streak kicked in propelling Honey down the aisle at a speed she'd never thought herself capable of.

Janet Glencannon was thrown aside like a broken doll. Honey ducked low, her head colliding with Carolina's ribs.

Any normal woman would have been bowled over, but Carolina was strong and evidently worked out. Honey realised this the moment those arms were around her own ribs, squeezing her tightly until she thought her lungs would pop up out of her mouth. It was the first time she wished she'd done the same, but hey, she led a full life, and anyway, she had Doherty; her kind of exercise.

Honey didn't know quite how she did it, but using her weight as a lever, she ended up almost standing on her head, her legs kicking upright into the face of the taller woman.

In a skirmish use your weight.

She hadn't a clue where she'd got that little saying from; probably a self-defence article in a weekend magazine, the sort included with Sunday newspapers.

Using all her strength she kicked and kicked again. One more kick knocked Carolina off balance. First she tottered, and then she fell.

CHAPTER THIRTY-FOUR

There was no way Doherty could let Geraldine Evans off the hook and she must have known that. She hung around in the background whilst Alice Flynn had given the account of her grandmother's life. By the time Alice had poured out everything about her grandmother, Geraldine was gone.

Doherty wasn't overly perturbed. Like a bad penny she would most likely turn up. In the meantime he had a few things to check.

Back at Manvers Street he got his team in motion, ordering them to contact the immigration authorities with regard to one Gladys Flynn and a wedding racket.

'I want to know if they have anything about her on record — my instinct tells me they will have — and also any record of the identity of her partner. Let's say a woman in her thirties, although I'm flexible on that score.'

He tried ringing Honey from the landline in his office but got no answer. On seeing the Wizard passing his office door he asked if there was any chance of a cup of tea.

'Sorry guv. Can't stop. I'm off to a wedding,' he said, his body seemingly jammed in the doorway.

'Oh sorry. I forgot. Hope all goes well.'

'So do I. Oh, before I forget. You know I said about seeing that leggy piece in an underwear catalogue?'

Doherty gave him a look. 'You'll get a reputation, you know.'

'I was wrong. It wasn't underwear. It was in a wedding magazine, one of those full of dresses. She was modelling the dresses. I think there were other models of course, but she was the one that stood out, I suppose because of the contrast between a pearl studded veil and the colour of her skin.'

Doherty's head jerked up. 'Bride's dresses?'

'Yeah.'

'You mean the dark girl, Carolina Sherise?'

'That's the one.'

* * *

A quick phone call to Lindsey, Honey's daughter, and Doherty knew where she'd gone.

'Her car is in the garage. She's gone in Mary Jane's car. I think she wanted to look in at the church, then see the vicar.' She paused. 'Are you two really going to get married?'

'Yes. Why not?'

'You both take your time getting round to it.'

Doherty was ready to leave his office, when he got way-laid by Agnes Mackenzie.

'Sir. I've been doing some research on some of the people involved in the wedding dress murders. Two people, one of them the first victim, are recorded by the immigration authorities as being suspected of arranging passport marriages. I've listed the details. Another woman is also of interest. Her real name is Anesha Pukir. We believe her to be of Somalian origin and to have been brought into this country illegally as the bride of an older man. It also appears that the name on her passport is that of an infant who died before her first birthday. One, Anne Steadman. This is her photograph.'

Doherty took the details, read them through. He recognised Anne Steadman as Carolina Sherise.

'Her husband died, presumably of natural causes. He was a diabetic.'

* * *

They had a warrant. They knew who they wanted. The sirens screamed all the way there.

The vicar looked stunned when she answered the door, before almost pouncing on him with what sounded like an excuse. 'I remembered something about that night,' she said excitedly. 'There was a chisel sticking up from between the flagstones, as though there was something buried under there. Mary Jane here helped me to remember it. She put me under.'

Doherty looked at Mary Jane who had appeared behind the vicar, his expression puzzled. 'Under?'

'I hypnotised her. Remembered as easy as that.' Mary Jane clicked her fingers.

'I was very upset that night. You see I'd had a glass of sherry with Mrs Flynn and something she said upset me. She said she kept tabs on everyone in the village. She said she knew secrets about everyone and kept the notebook hidden in the church. I told her it was wrong, but she only laughed and said, I've found out about you, vicar. I found out about your husband. The woman was a witch. Wicked. My husband died in a car crash. I was driving. I was drunk you see. I think that was why she kept plying me with that awful sherry. She was playing with me. She played with everybody.'

'Where's Honey?' Doherty asked, distracted. 'I thought she'd be here.'

'Down at the church. She wanted to think about flower displays, where to put them.'

He swore under his breath when his phone began to ring.

'Must take these,' he exclaimed.

The vicar nodded.

Phone messages came through to say that the woman whose professional name was Carolina Sherise was not at her known address and neither was she in the company of Harold Clinker. There was another message regarding the serial bride, Janet Glencannon. She too was not at home.

'Her assistant said she'd gone to the church to check the flower arrangements.'

'Everything leads to the church,' muttered Doherty.

It was a short drive, but on the way he calculated what had happened and put it into some kind of cohesive order. Like pieces in a puzzle they gradually began to make sense.

It was Mrs Flynn who had arranged the passport marriage between Carolina's husband and Janet Brooks — formerly and latterly Glencannon. He guessed that it was also Mrs Flynn who had provided Harold Clinker with the old deeds relating to the disputed land in front of the church. She spent a lot of time in that church, sitting there by herself in her wedding dress. And her notebook, he guessed that had been there too. She really like to stir things.

Carolina was athletic and strong. On finding Mrs Flynn in the church, she overpowered her, administered the injection and left her there, slouched forward onto the pew in front.

The vicar had arrived later and disturbed whatever else she'd been doing, possibly looking for Mrs Flynn's notebook even though she hadn't been in the village that long and wasn't well known. Unfortunately Harold was just getting out of his car so she knocked him out too. The evidence suggested that she'd already drugged Marietta and some of Marietta's perfume had rubbed off in the course of getting close to her. Gossip had it that Marietta liked a drink so a little extra drop of something wouldn't have been noticed.

Carolina had then panicked. The only way to avert suspicion as far as she could see was to fabricate a second killing pointing to death by a severe blow to the head. She didn't realise the true cause had already been discovered.

Getting a wedding dress was no problem; she had carved out a career modelling wedding dresses for catalogues and specialist bridal magazines. Sometimes she was offered the dresses she'd modelled. Most of them she sold on, but one or two she still had hanging around.

Ahmed gave her all the details about the car which she thought would be a nice touch. She'd seen the car whilst delivering a dress to a client who lived in a house overlooking where Ahmed kept it. She had been going to hire it, but instead decided to steal it. Ahmed had struck her as the sort who was sometimes unfocused. Her guess proved correct: he had left the key in the ignition. With a drugged Marietta dressed as a bride in the back, she'd purposely crashed the car. It didn't occur to her that it was hardly a perfect murder. It merely fed the bitterness she felt inside.

Mrs Flynn was gone. Marietta had merely been an inconvenience. Janet, the woman who had played the 'bride' was next. Unfortunately Carolina had not allowed for Janet recognising her and had dashed out of the village store when she saw Carolina there. Somehow Carolina had to get Janet alone. She'd prefer it to be in church. She would also prefer if Janet was wearing a wedding dress. It would be so perfect, so fitting that the woman who had caused her so much suffering with her sham marriage, should be wearing a wedding dress when she killed her.

* * *

The car tyres of three police cars screeched to a halt outside the church.

Followed by a whole flock of uniformed police, Doherty ran into the church. He feared what he might find, but also had a sneaking suspicion that Honey, whose unorthodox methods he sometimes despaired of, would have come out on top.

He hadn't expected to literally find her on top of Carolina Sherise who looked to have been knocked unconscious.

They were both lying on top of a mass of broken bits of wood and what looked like pieces of parchment.

The vicar, having hitched a lift in Mary Jane's car, came rushing in but was held back at the church door by one of the uniformed constables.

'Oh my goodness.'

Her eyes were out on stalks.

'We've called for an ambulance,' said one of the constables.

Honey was helped to her feet. So was Carolina Sherise, her lips tightly shut, her eyes dark with hatred. Only Janet Glencannon remained lying flat on the floor — out cold.

Doherty gave the nod for the vicar to come forward.

'Sorry about the mess. Still, I suppose the insurance will pay out for a new one.'

'It's a thousand years old. What happened?'

Doherty looked at Honey. Honey looked right back.

'I landed on it. Still, look on the bright side, there's a whole lot of old parchments for you to add to the archives. Lots of plans and deeds and things you didn't even know were there.'

The vicar's face brightened. 'Yes,' she said with sudden and inspired interest. 'You could be right.'

* * *

'So there is such a thing as coincidence.'

The air hostess interrupted them. 'Champagne. I believe you're on honeymoon?'

Honey and Doherty exchanged smiles. 'Why not?'

The champagne was cold and crisp.

'Amazing how they do it on board an aircraft,' said Doherty as he poured his second glass.

Once her glass was refilled, Honey expressed her opinion on the smaller problems she'd had to deal with of late, all of them alluding to the Green River Hotel.

'Coincidences. There are such things. It was Doris who did it.'

'Doctored the punch?' Doherty looked surprised. Doris was addicted to food not drugs of any description — not even alcohol.

'No, not the punch. The worm. My, but was she embarrassed. The worm turned out to be an elastic band she'd wound around her little finger to remind her to buy carrots on the way home. It slipped off into the porridge. So no malice aforethought there! On reflection I came to the conclusion that one of the wedding guests had doctored the punch. You know how it is somebody sneaks it in just for a laugh — or an act of revenge. I'm sure it's already reported in one of the tabloid newspapers that the marriage is already over. The bride was courting fame; the bridegroom was just another step up the ladder. On to pastures new and all that.

'Anyway,' she went on, warming to her subject, which had a lot to do with the champagne she was knocking back, 'My number two conclusion was that the frog was left in the Scotsman's bed by his wife. They'd had a row and she'd stormed off. Goodness knows where she got the frog, but does it really matter! The Scotsman had drunk himself stupid and wouldn't have noticed it.'

'Coincidences, so not malicious.'

'No. The dog was a different matter. Nigel was not so daft. The dog was his little message to me. He wouldn't actually betray his wife, but found out where I was based and guessed I would use the dog as an excuse to speak to his wife. If she was in enough trouble, she might come back to him.'

'He went out to the kennels . . .'

'Animal Sanctuary . . .'

'OK. Animal Sanctuary, and stole the dog.'

'Janet said he was always harassing her.'

Doherty refrained from mentioning the supposed kidnapping of her mother because that would mean bringing up the subject of his daughter. But still, he could go some way to consigning it to history.

'Sorry about my girl. She's calmed down a bit now. She did muddy the waters a bit. My fault to some extent.'

Honey touched his hand affectionately.

'Water under the bridge. All coincidences, though they hadn't seemed that way at the time.'

* * *

244

Hawaii. Palm trees, sand, sea and pina colada. Doherty swirled his glass just for the pleasure of hearing the ice cubes clink together.

He sighed, took a sip then shook his head. 'Shame we didn't get around to getting married.'

Honey sighed too, stretched her legs and pushed her sunglasses up onto the bridge of her nose. 'We can always do that again.'

'I suppose so. I think the vicar was disappointed she couldn't fit us in.'

'Never mind,' she said, stroking his arm affectionately. 'At least the wedding cars can park outside now the church has reached an agreement with Harold Clinker.'

Doherty pulled an ice cube out of his drink and popped it into his mouth, crunching it thoughtfully as he considered all that had happened.

'Good job Mary Jane found the rest of the old documents.'

Honey looked embarrassed. 'It would have been better if I hadn't landed on top of it, though I have to say, the woodworm did a lot of damage before I did.'

Doherty tucked his bare arm behind his head. 'All's well that ends well, as old Bill Shakespeare once said.'

'I am especially grateful to the travel company allowing us to bring our honeymoon booking forward — even though we aren't on honeymoon. Not really. Honeymoons are supposed to follow weddings, strictly speaking.'

'Strictly speaking it doesn't matter a hoot to me whether we're married or not.'

Suddenly realising what he'd said, Doherty eyed her nervously. 'I don't mean that I don't want us to get married. I just mean . . .'

Honey laughed and patted his hand. 'I know what you mean. We're a pair well met, as my old grandmother would say. And your daughter is getting used to the idea.'

'She seems more comfortable with us just living together.' Suddenly aware of what he'd said, he turned to her. 'You're okay with that, are you?'

'Of course I am.'

Relieved with her response, Doherty adjusted his sun bed so he was lying flat.

Honey eyed his torso. He was already tanning nicely and he looked so relaxed. However, that comment . . . mustn't let him off too easily.

'Agh!'

Ice cubes on his belly, ice cubes down his bathing trunks and a loud splash as Honey hit the ice blue water of the swimming pool.

THE END

THE JOFFE BOOKS STORY

We began in 2014 when Jasper agreed to publish his mum's much-rejected romance novel and it became a bestseller.

Since then we've grown into the largest independent publisher in the UK. We're extremely proud to publish some of the very best writers in the world, including Joy Ellis, Faith Martin, Caro Ramsay, Helen Forrester, Simon Brett and Robert Goddard. Everyone at Joffe Books loves reading and we never forget that it all begins with the magic of an author telling a story.

We are proud to publish talented first-time authors, as well as established writers whose books we love introducing to a new generation of readers.

We have been shortlisted for Independent Publisher of the Year at the British Book Awards three times, in 2020, 2021 and 2022, and for the Diversity and Inclusivity Award at the Independent Publishing Awards in 2022.

We built this company with your help, and we love to hear from you, so please email us about absolutely anything bookish at feedback@joffebooks.com

If you want to receive free books every Friday and hear about all our new releases, join our mailing list: www.joffebooks.com/contact

And when you tell your friends about us, just remember: it's pronounced Joffe as in coffee or toffee!